TUESDAY JOCKS

AND OTHER STORIES

Fin J Ross

Clan Destine
PRESS

First published by Clan Destine Press in 2024

PO Box 121,
Bittern Victoria 3918
Australia

National Library of Australia Cataloguing-In-Publication data:

TUESDAY JOCKS AND OTHER STORIES

ISBNs: 9781922904843 (paperback)
9781922904850 (eBook)

Cover design by Willsin Rowe
Cover photo by Liz Olle

Design & Typesetting by Clan Destine Press

Clan Destine
PRESS

www.clandestinepress.net

CONTENTS

TUESDAY JOCKS

THE MISSING TUESDAY JOCKS BUGGED ME. ACCORDING TO HIS wife, Brian Sheridan was anally retentive about his wardrobe; so much so that he compelled her to place his day-labelled jocks in order in his bedside drawer – Monday to Sunday. He'd been missing since Monday night, yet Tuesday's jocks weren't in the drawer. Julie Sheridan was as perplexed as I was when Sergeant Dave Dryden and I had searched the couple's bedroom two days earlier. I'd noticed the neatly layered undies and wondered why anyone needed prompting to change them every day. Or were the Kmart bestsellers designed to remind men what day it was every time they peed? Julie could only speculate that Brian had planned ahead by taking clean jocks to change into after soccer practice. He hadn't been seen since he'd been left to lock up the Kershaw Soccer Club around 9.30pm.

Why was I pondering about a man's smalls while wading thigh-deep in a muddy dam? The mud oozed between my toes and sucked up my legs, immobilising me. And I'd thought quicksand was the stuff of B-grade movies or long-forgotten Tarzan episodes.

Dryden stood on the bank, arms akimbo, face supercilious. Obviously he was relishing the fact that I'd drawn the short straw to wade in and retrieve the bloated, floating body. Two weeks into my posting here and I was acutely aware of the gender bias of Kershaw Police.

Even Joe Green, who'd reported the floater in his dam an hour earlier, sat in his Ranger, 20 metres away, reluctant to assist. But then, he was pushing 80.

Where were the search and rescue heavies when you needed them? 'Don't s'pose you'd care to help?'

Dryden shrugged. 'Nah. You're doing fine. You're nearly there, Cunst.'

'Easy for you to say. And don't call me Cunst.'

Sheridan, face down and clad in a striped polo shirt and jeans, was still three or four metres away, but the effort to get to him sapped every muscle. So, he *had* showered and changed after practice. With Amazonian effort, I finally reached out and wedged my fingers under Sheridan's super-tight waistband and pulled him towards me. The thud as his body bumped into me would have knocked me over had I not been stuck fast. My first objective was to peel his waistband down to reveal the elastic band of his jocks. *Huh?* Thursday. Not Monday, or Tuesday. *Thursday.* Now I was truly perplexed. This wasn't the fastidious man his wife had described. Where were his Monday and Tuesday undies? In his missing sports bag?

We'd searched his car, still parked at the soccer ground, along with the clubhouse, on Tuesday morning and found no sports bag. Where was it? 'Oh,' I groaned. Probably at the bottom of the damn dam. This was one of many questions swimming in my head. Like how did he end up in a dam seven kilometres from the clubhouse? Was he suicidal? What didn't his wife know about him? Was he in financial strife? Was he having an affair? We'd asked Julie and all his teammates these questions on Tuesday, but had unearthed nothing untoward. On the surface, Sheridan was an honest, likeable, stand-up guy. A real team player. A respected club captain.

And did Joe Green know more than he was saying? Or was it, as he'd said, mere coincidence that he'd inspected his dam this morning?

I started the sludgy haul back to the bank, thankful that a floating body doesn't weigh much. Then, as my left foot sank into the mud, it met resistance an inch or two down. Something hard and smooth. A tree root? The sports bag? No avoiding getting completely sodden now. I locked one end of my handcuffs around Sheridan's hand and the other around my belt to stop him floating away. Then I plunged my arm into the opaque brown water and felt around my foot. I clutched the object, about the diameter of my closed hand, and levered it up and down to break the suction of the mud. I pulled hard and when my hand emerged with it, I gasped. A femur. A distinctly human-looking femur.

I brandished the bone at Dryden. 'Well, looky what I found.'

He looked unimpressed. 'Probably a cow.'

'Looks human to me.' I looked across to Green, who appeared to be contemplating his navel. Or asleep. 'Think we might have some questions for old Joe.'

'Think we should wait for the Homicide guys to arrive.'

'Have you called them?'

'Not yet.'

'Well, hello. Isn't that your responsibility?'

'Don't need you to tell me how to suck eggs, *Cunst.*'

Arrgh. 'Chances are there's a whole lot more bones down here. I mean, somebody would surely miss their femur, don't you think?'

Dryden pulled out his phone and dialled while I continued to tow Sheridan to the edge.

'They reckon it'll be six to eight hours until they can get anyone here, possibly longer for the coroner. Double shooting in Melbourne.'

'Guess that's more important than a probable murder and equally probable cold case in Hicksville,' I said as I hauled Sheridan up the bank. I undid the handcuff and plopped onto my bum beside him to recover. I drummed the 40-centimetre bone on my hand momentarily before placing it carefully aside. With a few good breaths on board, I asked Dryden to help me flip the body over. That was when I saw the deep gash in his forehead; so deep it appeared his skull was fractured.

'Well, I'm not thinking suicide,' Dryden observed.

'I didn't from the start. If he were going to come here to drown himself, surely he'd have driven, not walked.'

'True.'

I put my socks and shoes back on. 'I'm going to ask Joe if he heard anything Monday night.'

'Good luck. He's deaf as a post.'

I was halfway across to Joe's car when the glint of sun off the windscreen of a vehicle approaching across the paddock almost blinded me. Finchley Crime Scene Investigation unit. Hallelujah to that. I jogged to steer them clear of the unexamined tyre marks over to the right; no doubt the vehicle in which Sheridan was transported, dead or alive, to his watery grave.

'Hi, I'm Jordan Mulcahy. You guys might have your work cut out for you,' I said as the van pulled up.

They introduced themselves as Matt and Shannon, no formalities. I explained that, aside from the floater, we had another suspicious find on our hands. I pointed to the bone. 'I'm just going to ask the property owner if he has a pump. We'll have to drain the dam. Dryden'll give you the heads-up.'

I knocked on Joe's window and motioned for him to wind it down. As he did, country music blared from his car radio, drowning out any prospect of discussion.

'Could you turn that down please?'

'What?'

'The radio,' I yelled, 'turn it down please.'

'Oh, didn't know it was on.'

'Do you have a pump? We need to drain the dam.'

'Why?'

'We need to investigate further.'

'Yeah. Pump's up at the house.'

Not being a forensic expert, I had no idea how old the femur might be, but I suspected it had been there a very long time. 'How long have you lived here Mr Green?'

'Twenty years. Yeah, 2002 we bought the place.'

'We? That's you and your wife?'

'Yeah.'

'What's your wife's name? Is she at home?'

'Sheila. Nah. Gone to bingo. Thursday's bingo arvo. And Saturday, and Tuesday night.'

'Who owned the property before you?'

'The Helliers. John and Denise.'

'Are they still around?'

'Well, John is. Lives in town, but he'd know that,' Joe said, pointing towards Dryden. 'And you should know. I mean, their son's your boss. Never met her. They were separated or divorced or whatever.'

I'd heard the name Sean Hellier mentioned around the station, but evidently Joe didn't know he'd retired a year earlier. 'Thank you. Now, if you wouldn't mind getting the pump.'

I headed back to the dam and found Matt examining Sheridan's body and Shannon snapping off pictures.

'Where's Joe gone?' Dryden asked.

'To get a pump so we can drain the water.'

'Oh, good thought.'

'You didn't tell me this place was originally Hellier's folks.'

'Didn't think it was important.'

'Think it is now. I guess one of us needs to notify Julie Sheridan.'

'You go. We can sort this. Might pay to clean yourself up first. I can get a ride back with these guys.'

'Or if I'm not too long, I'll come back.'

'Whatever.'

As I exited the driveway, I sniggered at the sign, *Shady Grove,* a complete misnomer for a treeless, Weetbix-coloured acreage. I dashed home, showered, dumped my muddy clothes in the washing machine and donned a fresh uniform before driving the three blocks to Julie Sheridan's home.

She was distraught at the news, though I suspected she'd expected a fatal outcome. I made her a cuppa and waited for her to collect herself enough to speak. It wasn't just that Brian was dead – he'd been murdered.

'God, how am I going to tell the kids?'

I couldn't offer much advice there, aside from saying I could be on hand when they arrived home from school if she wanted.

'How the hell did he end up in a dam seven kays away?'

'We're still trying to figure that out. Can you think of anyone who might have done this? I'm doubtful it was a random attack.'

Julie shook her head. 'Everyone loved Brian. He was really popular.'

'You're sure he wasn't having an affair, or perhaps owed money to somebody?'

'I can't see how he could have had an affair. He always came straight home from work, he was only out on Monday nights for soccer, and aside from his Saturday morning matches, he'd be here all weekend.'

'What time did he usually get home from soccer training?'

'Around 10.30, sometimes 11.'

'The other players said they all usually left by 9.30. Why was Brian always later?'

'He'd stay back to do paperwork, you know, team selections and stuff.'

'You're only, what, half a block from the soccer ground. Why would he drive?'

'He usually goes straight from work.'

'Did he usually shower and change before he came home?'

'Sometimes. Not always.'

'It appears he did on Monday. He was wearing casual clothes, but there's one mystery.'

'What?'

'He was wearing Thursday jocks.'

Julie shook her head. 'No. Not likely. Really weird, at least.'

'That's what I thought. Can we check his drawer again?'

Julie led me to the bedroom. We looked at each other quizzically upon discovering Brian's Thursday jocks in the drawer.

'Did he only have the one set?'

'Yes.'

'Tell me, do you know the Helliers? They originally owned the property where we found Brian.'

'Actually, John lives just down the street, number 43 I think, but I don't really know him. I think he must be old or sick because I occasionally see the district nurse's car there. I never met Denise. I gather she left him about 25 years ago. Word was she took off to Queensland with another bloke.'

'What about their son?'

'You mean Sergeant Hellier?'

I nodded.

'Only time I ever met him was when he pulled me over for speeding in Main Road a few years ago. He seemed like a reasonable guy.'

'I'm new here; haven't actually met him.'

'Have you found Brian's sports bag?'

'Not yet. We're about to drain the dam. Now, is there someone you can ring for support?'

Julie said she'd get her neighbour to come in, so I told her I'd be back in touch if we needed more information.

What was it with men? It seemed the older they got, the grumpier and more recalcitrant they became, and John Hellier was no exception. I was greeted – no, harrumphed – at the door by a weedy, wheezy man with what I suspected was a perpetual scowl.

'Whaddya want?' No courtesy to my uniform.

'I have some questions. May I come in?'

He rolled his eyes, backed away and gestured into a dark, musty living room.

'What's this all about?'

'You may, or may not, be aware that a man went missing on Monday. His body has been found in the dam of your former property this morning.'

'What's it got to do with me? Haven't lived there for nigh on 20 years.'

I nodded. 'Yes, I realise that. Can I ask why you sold the farm?'

'Had a heart turn. Couldn't manage the place on my own after that. Those bloody Greens screwed me on the price, then switched from cattle to sheep, which was bloody daft. You'd wanna talk to Joe and that bitch of a wife.'

'What about *your* wife. Did she help on the farm?'

'Yeah, up to a point. Till she had the bloody accident. After that, she was friggin' useless.'

'The accident?'

'Yeah. Got squashed against a fence by a bull. Lost her leg.'

'Oh. That's terrible. Where is she now?'

'Blowed if I know. Bitch took off with someone. Haven't heard boo from her since.'

'When was that?'

'Geez. You want to know the ins and outs of a duck's bum, don't you? Around 24 years ago.'

'And you've no idea where she went?'

'Nope. Why are you asking about her anyway? She's ancient history.'

I'd decided not to mention my find yet. Setting a trap was sometimes more productive. 'What about your son? Has he had any contact with her?'

'Nope.'

'He never tried to find her? Why? He'd have had the means. As a police officer, I mean.'

'Dunno. Ask him.'

'I will. What's his address please? Oh, and is he married?'

'Not anymore. Murray Street, number 19, but he won't be home. He'll be at bloody golf.'

'Thank you for your time.' I was about to leave when I had a thought. 'Sorry, one more thing, does Sean play soccer?'

'Not anymore.'

I bet my bottom dollar that Hellier Senior was on the phone to Hellier Junior before I'd even crossed the threshold to let him know that some *bitch* of a policewoman was on his path. Though something about dad's tone gave me the impression he and his son weren't best buds. Why? I was itching to get back to *Shady Grove* to see what was transpiring. After stopping at a milk bar to grab some Cokes and a salad sandwich (minus beetroot because I didn't want to risk messing another shirt), I headed back out to Willow Road. I'd thought that today was going to be one of those *nothing happened* days. Now I was confronted with two dead bodies. Were they connected? *How?* Was the *Shady Grove* waterhole the local dumping place for inconvenient corpses? Were there more bodies? Sure, this was all the domain of the Homicide squad, but given they were conspicuous in their absence, I figured I could demonstrate my detective skills. Detective training with a later view to Homicide were both on my forward agenda.

Despite knowing that Sheila Green wouldn't be there, something prompted me to drive up to the house instead of turning into the paddock. At least one of the Greens was obviously a keen gardener, judging by the neatly trimmed roses, flowering shrubs and well maintained pots in the house yard. I parked and got out to survey the place. A beeping drew me onto the back veranda. I peered into the first window; a green light flashed on a washing machine indicating the cycle was finished. In the garden flanking the porch below the potted geraniums and hanging baskets of fuchsias and vivid zygos, a string of hearts spilled from an unusual planter – a deep, pink plastic cup-shaped thingy attached to a metal post. I'd seen something like this before; the stainless steel button on the shaft a dead giveaway. *Interesting.*

Must be one hell of a water pump, I thought, as I parked by what was now a mud bowl.

Matt and Shannon were knee-deep in the quagmire, while Dryden stood, barefoot, at the edge, laying more bones onto a tarp as they were handed to him. A skull, a seemingly entire, though broken, ribcage, two scapulas, a pelvic bone, several spinal knuckles, almost enough arm bones, and a jumbled collection of phalanges formed an almost entire skeleton. Beside that, a tarp-covered Brian Sheridan was baking in the sun.

Dryden grunted at me. 'You're back then.'

'Any sign of the sports bag?'

'No.'

Matt was moving his forearm back and forth in the mud, evidently trying to locate something particular.

'If you're looking for another leg, I suspect you won't find it,' I called out to him.

He looked up at me. 'Why?'

'Because I suspect that's Denise Hellier, and she only had one leg.'

'Oh. That explains a lot.'

'I thought you'd have figured that out, Dryden. You must have known about Denise.'

'Jesus, *Cunst,* I was what, seven, when she took off. Far as I know, she was never reported as missing, so why would I suspect...anything? Who have you been talking to, anyway?'

'John Hellier.'

'Yeah? What'd he say?'

'Told me Denise left him for another man 24 years ago.'

'That's as much as I knew.'

'Well, I've just found her prosthetic leg in the Greens' garden. You'd think she might have needed that if she were going away for the rest of her life.'

I held up the Cokes. 'You guys want a break?'

Matt and Shannon slogged out of the dam and sat, grateful for the respite and refreshment.

I walked further along the dam bank and spotted two parallel scores in the dirt running from the rim to the waterline. 'Hey Shannon, you might want to photograph these. Might be where Brian was dragged in.'

She came over and snapped some pictures. 'Still have to take casts of those tyre prints.'

I headed back to the others. 'Tell me Dryden, what was Sean Hellier like as a boss?'

'Okay. Why?'

'Just wondered. His dad's a grumpy sort, I thought Sean might have followed suit.'

'Had his moments, but he did everything by the book.'

'Any idea what he's doing with himself now?'

'Keeps himself busy. You know, Rotary, golf, fishing, the Men's Shed I think. Why?'

'Hello, we're going to need to talk to him.' I pointed to Denise Hellier's remains.

'Yeah. Nah. I'd leave that to the Homicide guys.'

'That mightn't be until tomorrow. He'll have got a whiff of this from his father by then.'

'Are you suggesting–'

'That's exactly what I'm suggesting. I also want to find out what he knows about Brian here.'

'Doubt there's any connection.'

'I don't know, but it's highly sus to me.'

'Leave it. You're not on overtime, you know. Time to call it.' An order, not a suggestion.

I said bye to the others and headed home. What would I do with the rest of the day? Sit at home twiddling my thumbs? No. I detoured to the soccer ground. Parked a few metres from where Brian's car had been parked. We'd scoured the whole car park for evidence on Tuesday and had found nothing. No blood, no churned gravel. Nothing at all to suggest that a murder might have happened there. But something told me Brian hadn't left there alive. If he had, who did he go with? Dryden had started Brian's car; nothing wrong with it. I checked my notepad, found Nathan Foster's number and dialled. Apart from Brian, he'd been the last player to leave the club on Monday night.

When he answered, I asked whether he could recall if Brian had showered.

'Don't think he does, usually. Pretty sure he was still in his soccer gear when I left.'

I'd just figured there wasn't anything more to be gleaned here when I heard footsteps in the gravel. I turned to see a woman, led by a beefy black Labrador, emerge from the trees. I waved to her and she walked over.

'Something I can help you with?' she said.

I introduced myself, asked her name and whether she walked the dog here often.

'I'm Simone Blake. Oh, and this is Rufus. Every day, if I can. I live across there.' She pointed across the soccer ground.

'At the same time?'

'No, depends on my shift. I'm a nurse at the hospital. Why?'

'You haven't heard that a man went missing from here on Monday night?'

'No. All I seem to do these days is work, eat, walk the dog and sleep. Don't even watch TV.'

'What time did you walk Rufus on Monday?'

Simone thought for a moment. 'Would have been around 10.30 maybe.'

'In the morning?'

'No. Night.'

'Do you recall seeing any cars here then?'

'Yes. There was a ute, like a tradies' ute, parked there. Couldn't tell you what colour it was, because that car park light wasn't on.'

'Did you see anyone?'

'No.'

'Were the clubhouse lights on?'

'No, I don't think so.'

'Any other cars?'

'Yes, but not in this car park. It was round the other side of the clubhouse.'

'Can you describe it?'

'Pale colour, maybe white. Think it was one of those old Toyota things with a fiberglass canopy over the tray, but I really didn't pay much attention to it. Didn't see the number plate. I can show you where it was though.'

I followed Simone around the back of the clubhouse to a grassy area we hadn't searched.

'It was parked about here,' she said.

'Nose in or nose out?'

'It was backed in.'

'Thanks for your help.' I noted Simone's phone number in case I needed to speak to her again and patted Rufus on the head. When they'd gone, I trod carefully through the grass looking for any clues. It took a while to spot it. A spray of dried blood stuck to a capeweed leaf. I stuck my pen into the ground beside it and called Dryden.

'When you're done there, might pay to take Matt and Shannon back to the soccer club. Check out the grass around the back. I've stuck a pen in the ground to mark the spot.'

'What are you doing there? I thought you'd gone home.'

'I just spoke to a woman who saw another car here late Monday night.'

'Oh. Okay. Now, go home woman.'

I didn't go home. I didn't know when Sean Hellier would arrive home from golf, but I intended to be there when he did. Nobody else was doing much actual questioning, so why not me? I sat in the divvy van outside Hellier's 70s-era brick veneer house drumming my fingers on the steering wheel. I hoped he wasn't one of those golfers who spent hours after the game at the 19th hole.

Something didn't make sense. More than one thing actually. I was pretty sure that either Sean or his dad, or both, knew that Denise was in the dam – *and* how she got there. But did Sean have some connection with Brian Sheridan? Was it his Toyota? I'd checked his details and he did have a Hilux registered. Nobody mentioned him being at the soccer club. Did he come later? *What for?* Did he murder Brian? *Why?* Did Brian know something about Denise? And if Sean killed Brian, why would he toss him in the dam and risk his mother being found? Maybe he *didn't* know she was there. Nothing made sense. What the hell happened? Simone said two cars were there at 10.30, yet no lights were on. *Strange.* So many questions.

Then I remembered. Not so strange. The blackout. Power went out 20 minutes into *The Closer.* Yeah, I like it because I reckon I can learn from Brenda Leigh Johnson's interviewing technique – minus the twangy accent. But I didn't see the rest of it. Power was off for a good 40 minutes, so I gave up and went to bed around 10.40. How could Sean have been doing paperwork in the dark? Why didn't he leave? Was he in the shower? Was he alone?

Oh.

I'd no sooner thought that thought when I looked up to see a white Toyota ute indicating to turn into the driveway. That answered one question. I had no way of knowing whether his father had warned him about my likely appearance.

I got out of the van and followed him into the short driveway. I could see his golf clubs and buggy in the trayback through the canopy window, along with something lumpy under a chequered blanket. A swarthy, sweatless, impeccably dressed Sean Hellier got out and spoke before I had a chance to. 'Guess you're the new girl. To what do I owe the pleasure?'

He seemed affable. Or was it deflection? 'Yes, Sergeant, ah *Mister* Hellier. Constable Jordan Mulcahy.'

'Everyone still calls me Sarge.'

'Good game?'

'Yeah. Good day for it.'

Enough small talk. 'I have some questions, if that's okay.'

'Sure. What about?' Was his calmness rehearsed, or was I barking up the wrong tree? 'Do you want to come in?'

'Here's fine, for the time being. Do you know Brian Sheridan?'

'Of course. I was his soccer coach. Have you found him yet?'

'We have.' I divulged no more than that. Hellier remained disconcertingly deadpan. 'When did you last see him?'

'Pfft. I don't know. Maybe a month ago at the hardware store. I was stunned when I heard he was missing.'

'Yes, I'm sure you were. So, you weren't at the soccer club on Monday night?'

'No. Hardly go there anymore.'

'This is your vehicle, yes?'

'Sure is.'

'It was seen parked behind the soccer clubrooms on Monday night.'

'Not likely. I was home all night.'

'Can anyone verify that?'

'Really don't think my neighbours keep tabs on me.'

The bombshell question to catch him off guard. 'Are you homosexual?'

'Huh? You've no right to ask me that, you little upstart.'

Good. I was rattling him. 'I believe I do. I believe that you and Brian had a regular little Monday-night tryst. Perhaps you liked to shower together. A bit of rumpy pumpy.'

'Rubbish. You know, you ought to not overstep your rank with foolish suppositions. What are you, straight out of the academy?'

Yeah, be condescending. That'll shut me up. 'I *suppose* then, that if I inspected your underwear drawer or clothes basket I wouldn't therefore find two pairs of Monday jocks and no Thursday jocks.'

'What the hell are you on about?'

'I'll tell you. Sometime during your shower, the power went off, which would explain why you were wearing each other's jocks. You couldn't see whose were whose in the dark. I'm guessing you're not as fussy as Brian about which day you wear which undies. But what happened then? Did you argue about something? Something serious enough to kill him for? Or...or did you *rape* him and then murder him?'

Hellier rolled his eyes. 'Oh, do go on. This little scenario of yours is just fascinating.'

I hoped to God I was right about my next suppositions. 'So, I *suppose* that if I checked under the blanket in the ute I wouldn't find Brian Sheridan's sports bag, or that if I checked your phone, I wouldn't find a call or message from your father earlier. A warning message?'

'You got a warrant? Bet you don't.'

'You could make my job easier if you just agreed to let me look. You know, give a girl a break.'

I pulled out my phone and texted Dryden. *Get a warrant to search Sean Hellier's car for sports bag, and house for evidence, including undies, and meet me there.*

He replied instantly. *You're kidding. What gives?*

Not kidding.

Hellier handed me his phone. I checked it. No messages from dad. That surprised me.

'I suspect you already know that we found Brian's body in the *Shady Grove* dam.'

Hellier feigned surprise. 'How could I know that? I'm out of the loop now, you know.'

'And I suspect you put it there.' Hellier opened his mouth to speak, but I cut him off. 'What I can't figure out is why you chose there. Was it to be certain your mother would also be found after all these years? Did you murder your mother too?'

'No, I didn't bloody murder my mother and nor did I murder Brian.'

'But you knew about your mother, didn't you? Do you get along with your father?'

Hellier shrugged. Then it dawned on me. Senior hadn't warned Junior, ergo, they weren't on friendly terms. What was their secret?

'Your father killed your mother, then. And you *knew*. Either you covered his tracks, or...you suspected she was in the dam. Which was it? Either way, you're an accomplice.'

I expected Hellier to chuck a wobbly. He didn't. He denied nothing, but nor did he admit anything. Yet his shoulders sagged in defeat.

'Look, I get that you'd cover for your dad. But I don't get Brian. Why did you kill him?'

'I didn't kill him, *all right*. I *loved* Brian. Loved those precious moments we had together.' Hellier wiped his eyes. No charade. 'Dad killed him. He'd found out about me and Brian and, well, he's an absolute homophobe. We didn't know he was waiting outside the clubhouse with a crowbar. Didn't see him in the dark. Also wouldn't have thought he'd have the strength to clobber anyone so violently. I could've killed him, but–'

'But he's your dad.'

'That, and I'm no murderer.'

'So, let me guess. You put Brian in the dam so we'd be sure to find your mother.'

'Yes. Only way I could think to get back at the bastard. I'm sick of covering for him. He bludgeoned Mum to death and now he's killed Brian. But I didn't want to dob him in directly and...shit, I wasn't thinking straight, you know. Besides, I wanted to spend more time with Brian without risking being sprung. I sat out there by the dam for a good hour, just holding him in my arms before I, you know, floated him. Might sound stupid, but I thought it appropriate that he and Mum would be found together.'

I couldn't help feeling for the man. Shit, I even had a lump in my throat.

Hellier wiped away a tear, collected himself. 'And you're right. Until you mentioned it, I could *not* figure out how I ended up with two pairs of Monday jocks. You're very astute, you know. Ever thought of detective training?'

'I have, actually. We'll have to charge you, you know.'

Hellier nodded resignedly.

I rang Dryden. 'Charge John Hellier with the murders of Denise Hellier and Brian Sheridan.'

THE MURDER BUTTON

HE'S PUSHED MY MURDER BUTTON ONE TOO MANY TIMES.

The previous hundred times, I'd collected myself, bitten my tongue, run into the middle of the back paddock and screamed the F-word until my reset button clicked. Very cathartic. It also gave me the bravado to return inside, a calmer version of myself. Unfortunately, it also meant our neighbours were probably privy to another of our "episodes". Episodes is how I describe these increasingly frequent occasions when he just doesn't get it.

But then narcissists never do "get it".

I only ever get the dishes done mid-argument. Washing up his beer glasses and sauce-imbued dinner plates, as aggressively as possible, is merely a means to prevent myself throwing them at him. He can't fathom my frustration. It's *my* job, after all, along with mowing the lawns, taking the garbage out, washing, ironing, cleaning, feeding the horses, feeding him whatever he wants – whenever he wants. Oh, and earning our sole income.

What does he do? Nine-tenths of bugger all.

I long ago learned not to complain, but sometimes my boiling frustration erupts to the surface in a blast to rival Mount Vesuvius. I hate that he's turned me into a tantrum-throwing child, stamping the floor and screaming vitriol until I'm hoarse. This isn't me. It's only me when I'm with him. Despite calmly explaining that ten minutes of his help wouldn't go astray; that he'd be more of a man if he deigned to do something useful, he still doesn't get it. Instead of doing it, he prefaces his response with, 'all you have to do is...'

He's picked the wrong time to stand behind me and say, patronisingly, 'if you'd rinsed that, you wouldn't now have to scrub it.' What the fuck would he know? So, I employ my signature double-handed backhand, and slam the frypan in his face. If I'd been on the tennis court, the ball would have cleared the fence. Instead, his head sags on his neck, and he staggers backwards, arms flailing. He thwacks the back of his head on the stone bench in a slow-motion avalanche to the floor.

Good. He's out cold. I rewash the frypan, dry it and stow it in the drawer. Wipe the blood off the edge of the bench. Pull off my rubber gloves and survey the damage. He'll come to any moment. I kick him in the ribs. No reaction. Any second now, he'll come to life, like a bad guy in the movies who you think is dead three times before he *actually* dies. You know, the ones who still try to kill you when they can't possibly have any blood left in their veins. He always has to have the last word.

It can't be this easy.

I put the kettle on and watch him for signs of life while it boils. Nothing. I kick him again and stare at his chest. It's not moving. His mouth is open; contorting like the mask in *Scream*. It *can't* have been this easy. Can it? Shit, if I'd known that, I'd have done it years ago.

I pour a coffee and sit at the bench. I'm unfathomably calm. I *should* be distraught. My phone buzzes. Cheryl. I switch the camera on. Don't even get to say hello before she's ranting. 'Fucking Mike, he's taken off with that bitch. For good this time, he reckons. Told me I whinge too much. Can you believe it? Me, whinge? Like, when do I ever whinge?'

Like, all the time. 'Bastard,' I say. 'But honestly Cheryl, you'd be better off without him. You're always going on about what a prick he is.'

'Yeah, but *I* wanted to leave *him*. But he's fucking left *me*.'

'Don't complain. At least you'll get to keep the house.'

'Didn't think of that. Anyway, thought I might come over with a bottle.'

Shit. 'Can you wait until about eight? Shithead's in one of his moods, but he'll be gone about seven.'

'Whatever.'

I finish my coffee. Drum my fingers on the bench. Look at the body that was once my husband. Typical. Never did clean up after himself.

I don the rubber gloves, pull a bin liner from the drawer, kneel down and lift his head – trying to avoid the bloody bits – place the bag over it and tie it off around his neck. I swing him around so that no part of him is touching the pool of blood on the floor. I clean the tiles with disinfectant and pile baking soda onto the grout lines. I chuck the blood-soaked sponge in the bin, tie off the bag and take it through to the wheelie-bin in the garage. Good thing it's bin night. I come back in, grab his feet and drag him into the garage, making sure his head doesn't bang on the step. Don't want the bag to tear.

Getting him into his car will be the hard part. I prop him against the Hilux and open the back door. I climb in, turn around and grab him under the armpits. I haul him onto the seat, backing up as I go. I get out the other door and close both back doors. I dash back inside, put on one of his checked flannel shirts, grab his phone and snatch his Ferrari baseball cap and car keys off the hallstand beside the garage door.

I tuck my hair up into the cap, place his phone in the console. Fortunately, it's almost dark as I drive out of the garage and head down the drive. I've timed it well. Should arrive at the footy ground after everyone is already inside sucking on tinnies.

I jog up the driveway, keeping to the middle strip of grass so there's no crunching of gravel. Don't want Jill and Ross next door hearing me come in. Didn't see a soul on the 2k cross-country sprint home.

I whack Tom's shirt back in the wardrobe and head back to the kitchen. I clean up the baking soda, ensuring there's no skerrick of blood remaining, put the sludge in a bag and chuck it out in the bin and trail it behind me down to the gate, as loudly as possible. I'm half up the drive, waving the torch ahead of me, when Jill calls out.

'You putting the bin out again? You'd think Tom'd do it once in a while.'

'About as likely as him mowing the lawn,' I yell. I speed up, as it's starting to rain.

Back inside, I crack a bottle of Sav Blanc, pour two glasses, turn on the back light and wait for the knock on the door. Ah, there she is. She's already talking before she clears the laundry. She's dripping wet. 'Fucking rain. I'm drenched. Can you believe that bastard just rang and said he's coming to clear out the shed tomorrow?'

'Guys can't live without their shit, you know.' I throw her a hand towel.

'I could fucking kill him.'

'At least you *know* who he's been fucking around with.'

'Huh? What, you mean Tom?'

'Gotta be. The club doesn't have social nights *every* night.'

'Bastards.'

'I'll drink to that.'

I set the alarm for six – have to be on set at seven – and fall into bed, wishing I hadn't had the third glass of wine. I re-read the three pages of script and lock it in.

The doorbell jolts me awake. It's just past 12. Uh-oh. Here goes. I'm still fastening my robe as I open the front door. The two cops standing there – one he, one she – look suitably sombre.

I draw on my arsenal of expressions; first, bleary-eyed, then astonished, then worried. 'What's happened?'

They introduce themselves; Senior-Constable Wright – him, and Constable Day – her. 'Can we come in please, Mrs Hickey?' she says.

'Sure, but what–?'

'Might be best if you sit down,' she says. She shepherds me into the living room.

'Oh God. What's happened? Is it Tom? Has he had an accident or something?' I plonk into a chair, convincingly distressed.

They both sit. 'We are sorry to inform you,' he says, 'that your husband's body has been found at the football ground.'

'Oh my God,' I put my hand on my mouth. Too soon for tears yet. 'You mean he's dead?' *Enter stunned expression.*

She nods sympathetically.

'How? What happened?' *Just enough quaver in my voice.*

He clears his throat. 'He was found beside his vehicle by a couple of his teammates. It appears he has sustained fatal head injuries.'

Turn on the shock, horror. 'God. How?'

'It appears deliberate. Homicide and the coroner are on their way from Melbourne.'

'You mean he was murdered?' *Really quavering voice.*

'It looks most probable,' he says. 'Mrs Hickey, do you know of anyone who might have wanted to kill your husband?'

I shake my head wildly. 'No. *Nobody*. He's really popular. Everybody loves him.' I invoke Jemma Caldwell's tears, like I did in the episode when her husband was burnt to a crisp in a fiery smash. Easy. Think of the closing scene of *Schindler's List.* Works every time.

They ask me a bunch of questions: How is our marriage? Do we argue? Financial problems? Does he owe money? Does he gamble? Is he having an affair? My answers? Fine, no, no, no, no, maybe and not to my knowledge. All the time, she's giving me queer looks. Then they drop the bombshell. Do I know someone named Cheryl Holborn?

'Huh?' My surprised look is genuine. 'Yes. She's our neighbour; over the back. She was here tonight. Why? What's she got to do with anything?'

'Drinking wine, I see,' she says, eyeing the empty glasses still on the table.

'Yeah. She's upset because her husband's taken off with another woman.'

'Aha,' he says. 'Can you explain why your husband has made 32 phone calls, and exchanged dozens of text messages with Cheryl in the past two months?'

My mouth falls open. No acting. 'You're kidding. I didn't think he even *liked* her.'

'Their messages would indicate otherwise.'

That duplicitous bitch. Fucking bastard. I throw in a sob. 'I don't believe it. You don't think she...? No, she couldn't have. She got here after he left and stayed until about 11.'

'Initial observation was that he might have been dead for four or five hours and there's some doubt about whether he was killed there or elsewhere.'

Shit. 'Why?'

'Not enough blood at the scene.'

Double shit. 'Oh. But how could they tell that?'

He's nodding. 'Yes, most likely it's been washed away, given it's been raining for four hours. That will be for the forensic pathologist to determine. What time did he leave here?'

'Just before seven. That's usual.'

She's still looking at me queerly. The light bulb comes on. 'It's just dawned on me. You're Jemma Caldwell.'

'Yep. Well, I *play* Jemma Caldwell.'

He looks at her. 'Huh?'

'Jemma Caldwell, you know, from *Whitby Street.* I didn't recognise you with your hair like that.'

I flick my hair over my shoulder. 'This is me – without the bob wig.'

He still looks vague. 'Sorry. I don't watch it. And you say Cheryl arrived here just before eight.'

'Yes. I'm guessing you should be over there talking to her.'

'Our colleagues are there. And detectives are interviewing everyone at the club.'

'Oh.'

'Is there anyone who could verify the time your husband left?'

'Probably Jill next door. She'd have seen him leave. She spends half her life smoking on her front porch.'

After more condolences, they leave, taking Tom's laptop and telling me detectives will come tomorrow to check out Tom's stuff. So much for the 7am shoot. But it'll be all over the news in the morning – 'Husband of soapie star murdered' – so the guys will understand my no-show.

I'm still half asleep. Any wonder since they arrived at 7.30. I'm wearing long sleeves to ensure they don't see the bruises on my arms. They might see it as grounds for motive.

The older detective looks solemn. 'Pretty sure we can rule you out as a suspect. And Cheryl Holborn.'

Phew. 'Did she confess to an affair?'

'Yes. Three months, she said.'

Bitch was welcome to him. 'I guess there's no law against that, though.'

'No. You'll have to decide how to deal with that. Now, were you aware of your husband's connections to the Martino brothers?'

What? Like, no. 'You're kidding. Aren't they in jail for some murder or another?'

'They are, yes. But their network is vast. Any number of thugs willing to do their dirty work. It appears your husband owed them thousands. His murder has their trademark all over it. That's the direction our investigation is heading, though finding the culprit to pin it on will be the hard part.'

'I don't believe it.' *I really don't, but how neat is that?*

His offsider, who until now has sat there mute, says, 'Just one thing we can't fathom. There was no sign, at the crime scene, of his cap; the one all his mates said is never off his head.'

Fuck. His frigging Ferrari cap. Should have left it there. I shake my head. 'No idea. Pretty sure he was wearing it when he left.' *Jesus, don't look in the laundry.*

'It's possible the murderer souvenired it,' the other detective says.

I hear the back door click. *Fucking Cheryl. What a nerve.* Before I can move, she's standing in the doorway sobbing into the red cap. *I could kill her.* Her face is pressed into it. 'Tom, Tom,' she wails. She lifts her head long enough to see me approaching. Erupts into tears. 'Sorry Jo. I'm *so* sorry.'

I snatch the cap from her. 'Sorry doesn't cut it Cheryl, you back-stabbing bitch.'

She's a mess. Blubbering like a...whatever blubbers. I have not one iota of sympathy. 'What am I going to do? First Mike leaves me then Tom's... all in one fucking day.'

Diddums. 'Hey. Do you want to stop a minute and remember it's *my* husband who's been killed?' I have my back to the detectives long enough to pluck a long blonde hair from inside the cap. 'Where'd you get this, anyway?' I ask her.

'Mind if we see that?' Detective One's half out of his chair. I walk across and hand it to him.

Cheryl's still sobbing like a baby. 'It was on the washing machine. Tom was going to give it to me. Said he was getting a new one.'

The detective inspects the cap. 'Might've been a good idea, since this one has bird crap on it.'

'Ew. Yuck,' Cheryl says, 'I had my face in it.'

'He must have chucked it there for me to wash before he left,' I say innocently. 'And you can leave now Cheryl.' My tone entertains no comeback.

The detectives get up to leave. Tell me they'll keep me posted on the investigation.

God, I'm good. Should be up for a Logie Award. Just wait until they see my performance at the funeral.

DEADLY ERNESTINE

It was another one of those Monday mornings that conspired against me. I had to be on campus for a ten o'clock tutorial but Zeus himself seemed determined to throw every possible obstacle at me. My kettle had had a conniption so I was coffee-less, Fudge had vomited green bile all over my tutorial papers and then I'd broken a heel on the front steps, requiring a total wardrobe change as no other shoes matched my outfit. The first two trams on St Kilda Road were chockers and then it started to rain. What else could go wrong?

Everything, as it turned out.

The tram stopped in Swanston Street to allow an ambulance and a convoy of police cars to turn east into Collins Street. An accident? A terrorist attack? I sent a message to the senior lecturer to explain my tardiness. ETA 10.30am. Whoever dreamed up Monday morning tutorials should be clobbered with a dictionary – a big one. Hell, half the students were usually still asleep, or hungover, or both.

Three hours later, I was sitting in my office, eating a limp egg sandwich from the Uni cafeteria, when someone knocked on the door. God, couldn't I get a minute's peace from my students? I opened the door to be confronted by two policemen, a sergeant and a senior constable. Surely this was overkill for an unpaid parking fine.

'You are Alison Jordan?' the sergeant asked.

'Yes.' I eyed them both warily. 'What's this about?'

'You are acquainted with Ernestine Grey?'

'Ernestine? Yes. Why, what's the matter?'

'I am sorry to inform you that she has been found dead.'

'Oh my God. How? Where?'

'A staff member found her body in the library this morning.'

'At the Athenaeum?' That explained the emergency up Collins Street.

The sergeant nodded. 'Perhaps you should sit down.'

I plonked into my chair, shell-shocked and fighting back tears. Ernestine Grey was an institution at the Athenaeum Library; as much a part of its fabric as the stucco on its three-storey façade. Since retiring as Associate Professor in Applied Linguistics at Melbourne University 22 years ago, she had become a stalwart at the library. Not as a paid employee; more as the go-to person for patrons with language-related enquiries. 'Was it... natural causes?'

'No. We are still investigating, but there was,' he paused, 'a suicide note.'

'No. No way. There's no way Ernestine would commit suicide.'

'You knew her well, then?'

'We have been good friends for maybe ten years. I met her at the library. Mutual interests, you know. She was a professor in linguistics here, though long before my time. But she was like a grandmother to me, and mentor, I guess.'

'When did you see her last?'

'Last Thursday night. I go to her place every week to play Scrabble, talk languages, talk books. She loves... loved my visits, and not just for the regular bottle of sherry, though being diabetic she probably shouldn't have drunk it.'

'And what was her state of mind then?'

'She was in fine form. Three times she laid out seven-letter words. She always won. She was telling me all about a trip she was planning to Europe. So, as I said, there's no way she would commit suicide. How did...she?'

'It appears she shot herself in the head.'

'What?' *Not likely*. 'No way. Besides, where would an 86-year-old woman get a gun?'

'We have yet to establish that. Are you aware that she had terminal cancer?'

Oh, just hit me with more shit. My shoulders sagged. 'No. She didn't tell me that. But she was never one to complain.'

'She mentioned it in her note and we have established it from her doctor. Metastatic breast cancer.'

'Oh shit. Poor darling.' That news was almost worse to bear than the fact that she was now dead anyway. 'She never said a thing. The note. Can I see it?'

'We were intending for you to accompany us to the library. Detective Senior Sergeant Loddon wants to speak to you, given that Ms Grey mentioned you by name in the note.'

We pulled up down the street from the Athenaeum and, as usual, I paid homage to Athena, whose stone likeness presided over the library from the decorative niche above the second storey, before dashing under the cover of the veranda to avoid getting thoroughly drenched. The sergeant raised the crime scene tape for me to duck underneath and led me inside. It was familiar territory, of course, but I'd never entered its portal with such a heavy feeling. The scene as we entered the library and reading room was both sombre and frenetic. Forensics detectives and a host of uniformed officers and detectives milled about, mostly near the ten-seater table where I'd spent so much time reading and where I'd first met Ernie. I tried to get a glimpse of her. Was she still here?

Yes. There slumped over the table, her delicate silver hair congealed with blood. A spray of it across the table. She surely couldn't have done this to herself. I clung momentarily to the bolstered column, feeling lightheaded.

The sergeant supported my elbow. 'Might be best if you don't see that.' He guided me around to where a greying detective sat in a tub chair at a small round table. The detective stood and shook my hand. 'Miss Jordan, thank you for coming. Detective Senior Sergeant Jim Loddon. Homicide.' He pointed at the seat beside him.

'I can't believe it,' I blurted as I sat. 'I told the sergeant that I don't believe she killed herself.'

'But she wrote a note. And the gun is still in her hand.'

'I still don't believe it. And if you're from Homicide, what does that tell me?'

'It's usual procedure for us to be called if there's a firearm involved.'

'Can I see the note?'

'In a moment. Just some questions first.'

In answer to his first question, I reiterated my last encounter with Ernie. 'She never mentioned the cancer – though now I come to think of it, she did seem distracted.'

'In what way?'

I thought back. 'We were playing Scrabble and the phone rang. She took it into her bedroom, but I could hear her raising her voice. She looked a bit rattled when she came back out, but she didn't say anything. We carried on playing.'

'Do you know who it was? And what time?'

'I don't know who, but it would have been about 9.30. I thought it a bit odd that somebody would ring her that late.'

'We will, of course, check her phone records. See who it was. Do you know any of her relatives?'

'She doesn't have any. She never married, and her last remaining nephew died last year, I think. How long has she been here? Since Saturday?' Here, alone, all that time. Again, I fought back tears.

Loddon nodded. 'We haven't ascertained how she came to still be here after the library closed at two o'clock. The staffer who locked up isn't working today. I'm waiting for the guys to bring her in.'

'Helen Caulfield?' *Did she have something to do with this?*

'Yes.'

'Oh, I've just had a thought. Poor Bolshoi.'

'Bolshoi?'

'That's her cat. He's a Russian Blue and Ernie loved the ballet. He'll have been shut inside for two days.'

'My guys will look after him when they get there.'

'Thanks. But tell them to make sure he doesn't get out, or he'll do a runner.'

Loddon turned over the paper on the table. 'Don't touch it.'

I nodded and read. Ernie had such perfect writing; beautiful script and always in fountain pen.

I can go on no longer. Theirs nothing I can do. The pain is killing me. It has been worse since the Commencement of my treatment programme. Having diabeties is bad enough, but now cancer. Only those close to me will understand. Well, I have had a good life. And so I choose to die here. Here among the books I so treasure. The books, that have defined

my life, are on these shelves. A life devoted to Reading and further understanding is not a life wasted. I apologise to whomever finds me. My Dying wish is that it not be Alison Jordan.
Ernestene Grey

So many things were wrong with this. I reread it and then read it again. 'I can tell you one thing, Ernie did not write this voluntarily. Yes, it's her handwriting, but there's at least seven clues here that tell me – and maybe me alone – that she wrote it under duress.'

'You believe somebody compelled her to write it?'

I nodded. 'She was a languages and linguistics professor. What she didn't know about languages wasn't worth knowing. And she was such a stickler for correct spelling and grammar she could not have written this unless...she had a gun to her head.'

'Clues?'

'For starters, she most definitely knew the difference between "there", "their", and "they're" so there's no way she'd have written "theirs nothing I can do". The lack of an apostrophe is another dead giveaway.'

'Secondly, Ernie is, or should I say was, American, so under no circumstances would she spell program with the additional "me".'

Loddon looked dubious.

'Okay, third, she would never use the word "commence". She started out as a journalist and journalists avoid using commence where possible. Only ever start or begin, depending on the context. Fourth, having been diabetic for 50 years, she would know it's not spelled that way. Am I convincing you yet?'

'She might not have been entirely rational. She *was* 86...'

I gave him my best withering look. 'Ernie's mind was sharper than a stiletto. Better than most 30-year-olds.'

'So that's four clues.'

'Ah, but there's more. She was of the old school, the one that said you should never start a sentence with "and".' I studied the note again. 'Then, there's the fact that she has used the object form here – "whomever" – instead of the subject form, "whoever". She would never make that mistake.' Loddon looked like half the students in my VCE English class; disinterested and perplexed. He was about to speak when I raised my hand. 'Then, there's her signature. In case you hadn't noticed, she misspelled her own name. Ernestene with an E.'

Loddon finally looked like he might be convinced. 'So, you think she was murdered?'

'I can't imagine who would want to kill such a sweet darling, but yes, I believe she was murdered.'

'Well that puts a whole new slant on things.' Loddon beckoned to another detective. When the man approached, Loddon said to him, 'Get the forensics guys to check for trace evidence. I think we're looking at murder here, not suicide'.

'A couple of other things are bugging me about that note, but I can't put a finger on them at the moment. Any chance I could get a copy of it?'

'It's not the done thing, you realise, but then, you have already been a big help to the investigation.' Loddon had a constable run off a copy of the note and handed it to me with his own card. 'Please contact me if you come up with anything else'.

I was back at my desk, but no way could I concentrate on my notes for tomorrow's lecture. I pulled Ernie's note from my bag and studied it again. Oh. Another thing I'd missed – her use of the word "that". *The books, that have defined my life, are on these shelves.* Only a grammar Nazi would discern the subtle difference between using "that" and "which". Firstly, in this type of sentence, "that" would not be prefaced by a comma; and the use of "that" made it a defining clause, which intimated that only the books on the library shelves defined her life. Yet she had an incredible library at home. Had she written "which", I might not have picked up on it, as it would have been grammatically correct. But something else was there staring me in the face. I just wasn't picking up on it. I needed coffee. Coffee always did the trick.

I returned to my office ten minutes later with a double-shot long black and scanned the page again. There it was. The peculiar use of capitalised letters. Commencement, Reading, Dying. CRD. What was she trying to tell me?

I read it again and suddenly the letters jumped off the page. Commencement, Only, Well, And, Reading, Dying.

C.O.W.A.R.D.

My hair stood on end. Snatches of a conversation came to mind. Back in June, when a news report revealed that Anthony Bourdain had hanged himself. *You'd have to be brave to hang yourself,* I'd said. *No,* she'd said, *suicide is for cowards. You'd never see me do it.*

So now, was she telling me she *had* resorted to cowardice...or that she definitely didn't? *You'd never see me do it.* The latter, surely. Should I ring Loddon? It was nearly knock-off time. I'd ring him from home.

I alighted the tram in Fitzroy Street and decided to brave the weather to walk the few blocks down Canterbury Road to Ernie's house in Middle Park. Chances were that Loddon would be there. He'd mentioned that they'd be checking out her house. It would be awful, her not being there to greet me with her sparkling blue eyes and wicked wit.

Loddon was there, along with a half-dozen other detectives, some of whom were going door-to-door to speak to Ernie's neighbours. Loddon allowed me inside, though naturally I was instructed not to touch anything. Bolshoi came out of hiding and greeted me with his usual figure eights around my legs.

'Good timing,' he said. 'It transpires that none of her neighbours knew her very well or, at least, have never been inside. Maybe you can give us an idea whether anything is out of place. The lady next door said she was pretty sure that a man came to visit on Friday night, but it was too dark for her to get a look at him. Any idea who that might have been?'

I shook my head. 'Maybe the same person who rang Thursday night. Did you speak to Helen?'

'She's pretty shaken up. Blaming herself.'

'Why?'

'She was in a hurry to get to a party on Saturday. She said Miss Grey offered to lock up for her because she was still busy helping a man with some research or something.'

'A man?'

'She only saw him from the back. Fifty or sixtyish, she thought, and balding. Ring any bells?'

'No. I'd sure like to know who he was, though.'

'You and me both. Obviously, it's our first line of enquiry.'

I surveyed Ernie's lounge room. Nothing seemed out of place. All was as it had been on Thursday night; the Scrabble board still on the dining table. The forensics guys were dusting the room for prints.

'We might need to get your fingerprints, just to rule them out as foreign.'

'Yeah, sure.' Then it dawned on me. Something *was* missing. The book.

'Have you come across an old book? A dictionary about yay big, with a beaten-up leather cover?'

'Amongst all *those* books?' he said, pointing to the floor-to-ceiling bookshelf that lined the wall.

'No. She showed it to me on Thursday. It was on the coffee table. Very valuable, I believe. She bought it many years ago in Paris, but said she'd decided to sell it.'

'Maybe she needed the money. Cancer treatment doesn't come cheap.'

'We could check her computer. Maybe she'd already advertised it. May I?' I said, heading toward the niche she used as her home office. I opened the lid of her laptop and switched it on. 'Oh, password.'

'Do you know it?'

'No. But I can probably guess.' I typed "Athena" into the box and her home screen opened.

'Good guess,' Loddon said.

I searched her browser history and clicked on "Antiquarities". Evidently a site for rare antiquarian book sales. I scrolled through two or three pages of sales advertisements before I found it. '"Greyem" is a likely seller name for her.' I read the entry aloud in my best French. '*Dictionnaire Chinois, Français et Latin. Publié d'après l'ordre de sa majesté L'Empereur et Roi Napoléon le Grand.*'

'Translate please.'

'Okay. So it's a Chinese, French and Latin dictionary, written by Chrétien Louis Joseph de Guignes, and published at the order of Napoleon.'

'Bonaparte?'

'The one and only. It's a first edition. Printed 1813. She's got it advertised for $16,500.'

Loddon whistled. 'Phew.'

'My guess is someone wanted it but didn't want to pay the price.'

'It's certainly worth looking into.'

'I know you probably can't tell me, but did you trace that phone call?'

'A mobile, evidently purchased under a false name. But whoever it was rang three nights in a row.'

'Someone was harassing her then.'

'Looks like it.'

'Oh.' I pulled my copy of the suicide note from my pocket. 'I found a couple more clues. Perhaps a very big one.' I explained my findings to

Loddon and he agreed that the coward reference was most likely Ernie's way of telling us she was not about to kill herself.

I was just about to go to bed when the doorbell rang. I was surprised to see Loddon on the porch. 'Oh, hi. Have you found something out?' I invited him in.

'I'm sorry to bother you so late. But I have to ask you where you were on Saturday afternoon.'

'Why?' *What?* 'Am I a suspect?'

'Please just tell me where you were.'

'I was at my parents' place in Torquay for the weekend. Left here Friday night, left there last night.'

'And they will verify this?'

'Of course.'

'I'm sorry. I have no doubt that's true but it is usual practice to question the beneficiaries of murder victims.'

'But...I'm not a beneficiary.'

'As it happens, you are. Miss Grey revised her will a month ago, upon the cancer diagnosis, according to her solicitor. She has bequeathed her whole estate to you.'

'Holy cow. I didn't know.' My mouth was still gaping.

Loddon's eyes softened. 'No. I don't believe you did.'

I barely slept. Spent the whole night thinking about the fear Ernie must have felt. There, with a gun to her head, and no way of escaping it. There, with that incisive, academic, wonderful brain splattered across the reading table. So violent and incomprehensible. I would so miss our get-togethers. Aside from tomes about linguistics, the arts, politics and history, crime novels were Ernie's go-to reading. Mine too. We exchanged books all the time. Now I felt like we were the protagonists in our own murder mystery. In a selfish way, I'd have preferred her to die of cancer. At least then I could have visited more often, nursed her when needed, given her comfort. Told her how much I loved her. But some bastard had robbed me of the chance. I felt as though I had been violated too. And the old sausage had left me everything. I'd never bargained on that. It looked like beautiful, slinky Bolshoi, who'd spent the night on my chest purring like a motorbike, was mine now too.

A week went by in a blur of study for my Doctorate and half-hearted lectures, all the while hoping there'd be news that Ernie's murderer had been arrested. I'd done as much as I could think of to help, but I'd had just one call from Loddon, which was more to ask whether I'd heard any goss than to tell me anything he'd unearthed. It seemed they'd gone nowhere with their enquiries. I hoped Ernie's murder wouldn't turn into one of those unsolved cases that languished on the homicide squad's files until somebody got bored and thought to look into it again. After all, 86-year-olds died every day, didn't they?

I headed down the corridor of the School of Languages and Linguistics, past the imposing honour boards, intent on getting some fresh air and a bite to eat at the cafeteria. He was weird. One day something made me stop dead.

I backed up a couple of paces and stared at one of the boards. I'd walked past them hundreds of times and never really paid much attention to them. There it was.

Dr Graeme Coward, Lecturer in French Studies, 1998–2007.

Coward. She'd given me his name, I just hadn't twigged. I raced back up the hall to Angela's office. She'd been around here long enough to have known him. I popped my head in the door.

'Hi Ange. Tell me, do you remember Graeme Coward?'

'Sure do.' She rolled her eyes.

'What?'

'Nut job.'

'Really? Why?'

'Let's just say he had a propensity for wandering hands and inappropriate behaviour. But I went into his office one day and found him smelling and licking a book. He was politely asked to leave the faculty about ten years ago.'

'Is he still around, do you know?'

'Last I heard he was tutoring part time at Monash, and hopefully keeping his hands to himself. Though somebody mentioned him to me the other day. Said they'd bumped into him and he looked pretty crook.'

'So Ernestine would have known him?'

'For sure, although I don't recall them being buddy-buddy. She was much too clever. Besides, he didn't mingle much. Always too busy with his bloody books. Poor Ernestine. It's just awful what happened.'

'Yes, tragic. Any idea where he lives?'

Angela thought for a moment. 'Um…Elsternwick, Caulfield. Somewhere around there.'

'Thanks. Must catch up for a drink some time.'

'Yeah. See you.'

I rummaged through my bag for Loddon's card. Started to dial his number as I headed outside, then changed my mind. First I googled Monash University and dialled that number instead. After that enlightening conversation, and after I looked up the White Pages and got Coward's address, I rang Loddon.

'I think I've found us a suspect,' I said, once he'd acknowledged me.

'I'm all ears.'

'I'll meet you at 31 Gillespie St, Elsternwick, in 15 minutes.' I gave him no chance to reply. Didn't want him to talk me out of going there. I was glad I'd driven to work instead of catching the tram. It would save a lot of waiting and walking.

I pulled up in front of number 31, an immaculate Edwardian weatherboard with an attractive hedged garden. I waited until Loddon's car appeared behind me and he and another detective got out.

'So what's the story? Are you trying to do our job for us?'

'This is the home of one Doctor Graeme Coward, lecturer in languages and linguistics at Monash, who, I gather, has quite the collection of rare books.'

Loddon raised his eyebrows. 'What makes you think he's at home?'

'I rang Monash. He wasn't there. The faculty receptionist said he hadn't been for over a week. I got the impression no-one cared enough to find out where he was.'

'You really are doing our work for us.'

'Sorry. Yeah.'

I followed them up the path.

'Might be best if you stay outside,' Loddon instructed. He and the other detective climbed the steps and knocked on the front door. I, nosey Parker that I am, peered through the gap below the blind in the front window. The room was beautifully furnished with antiques. But protruding from behind a Rococo coffee table was a hand, flat on the carpet.

'You might need to call an ambulance,' I said. 'I think he's on the floor.'

Loddon was beside me immediately. He peered through and grabbed his radio to make the call, then directed his colleague, Jerry, to force the door. 'You, stay there. Wait for the ambulance,' he said to me. I looked through the window again. Ernie's dictionary was on the coffee table, though it looked greener than I remembered. I saw Loddon bend down to feel the pulse on the wrist, which I presumed was attached to Coward's body. He shook his head at Jerry. Jerry spoke into his radio, but I couldn't hear what he said. Loddon approached the window and pulled up the blind. I pointed to the book and he nodded. He looked at it closely, without touching it.

Before long, the place was swarming with police and forensics guys, among whom was a woman, which pleased me no end. I sat on the front porch, feeling like one of those sideshow clown games you pop ping-pong balls into, as I watched the comings and goings. Loddon emerged with the dictionary in a huge plastic evidence bag.

'Is this it?'

'I think so. But I thought it was brown, not green.'

'The green appears to be some sort of residue. It'll be taken to the forensics lab for analysis. It certainly connects Coward to Miss Grey. Good work, you. You should be a detective.'

I laughed. Coming from a Homicide veteran, that was quite the compliment. 'Oh, yeah. I'm a regular Miss Marple. Do they have any clue yet how he died?'

'There'll be an autopsy. I wouldn't want to speculate. But there's no sign of foul play. Of course, if it turns out to not be natural causes, there'll be a Coronial Inquest.'

'Do you think he's the guy from the library on Saturday?'

'Good chance. He's 50-something and balding.'

Loddon rang a few days later. 'The autopsy revealed that Coward had severe liver disease, but that wasn't the immediate cause of death. He was poisoned...with arsenic.'

'Shit.' I couldn't contain my surprise. All I could think of was the classic movie, *Arsenic and Old Lace*. 'The green stuff on the dictionary?'

'Yep.'

'Do you think Ernie put it there? I can't imagine her doing that.'

'Look, if she did – and we're not speculating on that at this time – then all I can say, is good for her. She probably didn't mean to kill him.

It's doubtful such a small amount of poison would have killed him if he hadn't had a preexisting liver disease. And we have no way of determining whether she knew about his condition. Besides, any crying for him would be crocodile tears.'

'Yes, I've heard about his proclivity for roaming hands among his students.'

'Hmm, that and the fact that he had a penchant for antiquarian books he didn't intend to pay for. We've traced a couple of other books from Coward's collection to an unsolved murder in Adelaide a year ago.'

'You're kidding.'

'No. We've been able to place him in Adelaide at the time of the guy's death. Dumb bugger had left the book plates with the victim's name on them inside the covers. So, we suspect that Miss Grey told him on Friday night that the book was at the library and told him to meet her there Saturday. She must have known that he was prepared to have it at all costs, so she took it somewhere public where she'd feel safe. Chances are that Coward had the gun trained on her without Helen Caulfield seeing it. And chances are that Ernie was too altruistic to let on to Helen, to avoid risking her life too.'

'That, I can believe. God, imagine her knowing that he might kill her for it. I can't bear to think about it.' *Ernie, Ernie, why didn't you tell me?*

'It will all probably come out in the inquest. September, it's set for.'

I thanked Loddon for the call and was about to hang up when he interrupted me.

'Oh, there's another reason I rang.'

'Yes?'

'Ever thought of branching into forensic linguistics? We could sure use somebody with your talent and expertise.'

'No, I hadn't. But now you've got me thinking.' Might beat lectures and endless papers. Might pay better too.

It wasn't until four months later, after Ernie's estate had passed through probate, and her house was legally mine, that I could face the ordeal of sorting through her belongings for what I would keep. Her book collection was a given, of course, but many of her personal effects were old and crusty and set for the op-shop. Bolshoi thought the packing boxes were his playground.

Also a given were her original paintings; a dozen or so oils, pastels and watercolours which adorned the walls. I'd packed her Scrabble game into a "keep" box. It would be a long time until it would see the light of day again. Playing with anyone else would feel like a betrayal.

I stepped into the tiny bungalow out the back, her erstwhile art studio when she was of a bent to crack out the paints. The shelves were coated in dust. She evidently hadn't ventured out here much of late. What to do with all this stuff? Maybe take it to a local art society? I'd come armed with boxes, so I started clearing the shelves of brushes, paints, tubes, canvasses, palettes and partly-finished works. I pulled a couple of spray cans of fixative off a shelf and noticed a rusted green tin behind. Looked like it belonged in a museum. I read the label: Berger's Pure Paris Green. But it was the word POISON, written in red capitals which really caught my eye.

I pulled out my phone and googled it. *Bloody hell.* A painter's pigment used by the likes of Renoir, Monet, Cézanne, Van Gogh. But also used as an insecticide. Highly toxic. Being a dill at chemistry, I couldn't comprehend the chemical formula, but the words *copper (II) acetate and arsenic trioxide* told me all I needed to know. It was more irony than coincidence – that her greedy murderer died the same way Napoleon Bonaparte did. Though his poison was mercury.

I laughed out loud. 'Ernestine Grey. You canny old cow.'

MYSTERIOUS MICHELANGELO

Mac Robertson Land 67° 36′ 10″ S, 62° 52′ 23″ E

IT'S A BALMY MINUS FIVE DEGREES CELSIUS. WARM REALLY, FOR late August in this frozen landscape. So conditioned am I to the vagaries of a warming Antarctica, I'm outside wearing thermals on my lower body, but stripped to a T-shirt on top. Given that it's my short-straw day to unload the slush pans – otherwise known as the shit bricks – from the compactor and into the sled, the exertion sure works up a sweat. With the slush sled harnessed to my waist – so one hand is free to hold the torch, the other to grip the guide wire – I'm heading down to the generator. Who'd have thought we'd ever have to resort to burning our own faecal waste to supplement our wind power? It's 10am, but that weird orange glimmer on the horizon casts only vague illumination; enough to see that Holme Bay is ice-free, and a new nunatak has emerged in the nearby Framnes Mountains; its granite peak dark and foreboding against the blinding icy whiteness.

It's quite the rigmarole and tough work, but hey, someone has to do it. It's not my favourite job, and a far cry from my erstwhile existence as an ER doctor at Melbourne's Alfred Hospital, but at least I'm still alive. And no longer under the autocratic rule of a Chinese dictator. The 2025 invasion took us all by surprise and demonstrated how piss-weak our government and defences were.

Okay, so I'm still a doctor, but I have to fit that in between the myriad other duties needed to sustain this frigid portable city. This last bastion of humanity. Volunteering as a ship's doctor, which included a free cruise for Mike, was the best decision I ever made. And perfect timing to avoid witnessing the world going to hell in a test tube. Those mad scientists who convinced the continents' six neo-fascist leaders that a global drop of toxic chemicals was the only way to eradicate that persistent Covid, have left this as the only refuge for at least 20 years.

Our surgery here – too rudimentary to be classified as a hospital – is the best we can hope for. The technology I relied upon before The Event has been relegated to history. Despite the equipment that was already here, and the gear we salvaged from the cruise ship's clinic, I'm like a missionary in a Third World field hospital, making do with what I have. Even Médecins Sans Frontières had it easier. The only upside here is that I don't have to deal with men.

The last remaining men, at last count 132, occupy an expanded Davis Station, euphemistically known as Davis City, while we women populate Mawson City. It's wishful thinking to classify our higgledy-piggledy assortment of domes and relocatables as a city, but somehow, it's comforting. It's all we've got, and for all we know, it's all we'll ever have.

Mind you, many of us regard it as Utopia. A life without men. No interference. No mansplaining. No harassment. We don't need them. Not their help, not their arrogance, not their sexual gratification.

We do, however, need their X chromosomes. But we've got that sorted, thanks to Melbourne Uni's groundbreaking method of separating out the Ys to assign gender when fertilising ova.

The gender treaty, signed three months after the *Endurance Princess* landed its fateful passengers on this icy wasteland, decreed that men and women should be segregated for the benefit of humanity. Clause to be reviewed in ten years, that is, 2049 – five years from now. The sexual politics began the moment we arrived, but the men hadn't counted on our resistance. We girls had had it up to our scalps with narcissistic, entitled, megalomaniac men. After all, *they* put the world in this shit. So far, it's worked well. We've proved how tough and resilient we are. They've proved that they have nothing to prove and nobody to impress. Though who knows what they get up to in Davis City, now they've surely run out of alcohol. Either that, or they'll have killed each other off in their selfish power struggles. Aside from the biennial semen delivery – that was the second of several contentious treaty clauses: no direct procreation – we never see them, and that suits us just fine. Imagine if they'd had to contend with the McLintock effect, that peculiar phenomenon of menstrual synchrony when women live together in close proximity. Sixty-something angry women suffering PMT together is one helluva force.

Anyway, better get cracking. Have to get these loaded into the generator, otherwise it's cold showers for the weekly quarter; that's 23 of our 90-strong Amazon populace. It's a three week wait for my monthly hot shower. Meantime, it's a tepid birdbath every other day.

Bricks unloaded, I'm distracted from my 300 metre return trek by the sudden manic squawking of a bunch of Adelie penguins. I can't resist the little darlings so I drop the guidewire and venture around the generator to see what the fuss is about. Startled by the torchlight, several scatter; their comical waddles hampering a speedy escape, but a half dozen appear transfixed by something orange protruding from the piled ice. What on earth is that?

I shoo the little birds away and bend to look more closely. Holy shit. It's a human arm. A human arm of the male variety. What the fuck? No points for guessing that the guy is dead, but how long has he been here? Could well be months, though in this cryogenic environment it could be longer. I unhook the sled harness, grab the brick shovel and dig around the frozen appendage to determine whether there's a body attached. It's tough going as the ice is rock hard, but before long I unearth the orange crown of a parka. I pull my finger scoops from my breast pocket, attach them to my gloved fingers and carefully gouge the ice away to reveal the frozen face. Dark eyebrows emerge but that's all I can see, as his face is buried in his knees. Not enough to recognise him, though my guess is he's pretty young. I'm relieved I can rule out it being Mike. I mean, I don't miss him, but I wouldn't wish him dead.

So, what is this boy doing here? Hasn't he been missed at Davis, presuming that's where he came from?

I can't unearth more of him myself, so I head back to the Red Shed to rally the troops. This'll blow them away.

'He's only young, and no, I have no idea how long he's been there. It'd have to be since last summer. Nobody would be so daft as to travel here in autumn or winter,' I whisper to the three selectively chosen women over morning tea.

"Lord Mayor" Jenny Ingle, our inimitable station leader – whose one-season stint prior to our arrival has now become six years – still looks stunned, as do nurses, Jessica and Wendy. 'I can't believe it,' Jen says. 'Why didn't the neighbours let us know he was missing?'

That's what we call the men – the "neighbours".

'I wondered the same,' I say. 'I'll have to radio Davis. Now, drink up and give me a hand to excavate him. I've got real work to do today.'

'Impregnation day?' Jen asks.

'Yes. Three today.' *Not to mention adding a post-mortem to my already overloaded agenda. Will have to pore over the medical library's forensic pathology book.* 'And listen girls, maybe keep mum about my find for the time being.'

Our mystery interloper looks like a Pompeii victim plaster cast; curled solid in the position in which he evidently froze to death; knees under his chin. I can't justify increasing the heating to thaw him out, so he'll have to wait until I can wrangle him flat on the autopsy bench. He'll be my first. I still don't know who he is, and my attempted radio call to Davis City didn't connect. For all I know, he might be the last surviving male, whose attempt to reach "civilization" failed at our doorstep.

I slip a slide under the microscope in the diagnostic lab to check that the first of three newly thawed samples is viable and am pleased to see a gazillion motile and eager spermatozoa. As the donor is indicated by only a number on the phial, so that we can track the gene pool, I can only hope that they're made of the right stuff. We may have the ability to exclude Y chromosomes, but we have no way of vetting good, bad or indifferent genes. Jessica and Wendy are in the adjoining room prepping our three young and somewhat intrepid hosts. Hannah and Jorja will be fine; they've experienced this impersonal and clinical impregnation before and have become superlative mothers, but Chloe is justifiably anxious and will require gentle coaxing. It's a lot to expect of a 16-year-old who's never experienced a sexual encounter. But I can hear laughter and loud chatter, so all sound nervously excited.

It's a relatively quick procedure. Hannah and Jorja are done in no time, but Chloe is full of questions, although her mum, Lara, should have explained all.

I tell Chloe to relax, bring her knees up, put her heels together and flop her knees apart.

'What if I want a boy?' she asks.

'Not going to happen. Sorry.'

'But how come everyone has girls?'

'There's a lot you won't understand, but back when it was the real world, a man could father any number of children in a year, while a woman usually bore one, maybe two if they're twins. Plus, women can only get pregnant until about 40, whereas men can produce sperm until they're maybe twice that age. So, to prevent a population explosion that we can't sustain here, we made a pact that for our first 10 years, we'd only allow female progeny.'

'Oh. I guess that makes sense.'

I keep Chloe talking so she barely notices me inserting the pipette, but one question surprises me.

'What's it like to have sex? You're old, you must have done it.'

'I'm not *that* old,' I say with mock umbrage. 'It largely depends who it's with, whether it's voluntary or forced on you. It can be euphoric, crazy, heart-stopping, or it can be frightening, brutal and painful. Maybe one day you'll get to experience it yourself, and hopefully the first version of it.'

Chloe shrugs. 'I think I'd be scared. I mean boys are pretty dumb, aren't they? The ones I knew...I couldn't imagine doing *that* with them.'

I snort. 'Some are, some aren't. Some get better when they grow up.' *And some don't. Get better – or grow up.*

'How much longer does this take?'

'We're done, actually. The rest takes nine months.'

She gives me a "d'oh!" look. 'That much I *do* know.'

'That's plenty of time to decide a name for your baby girl.'

'I want to name her after you, but two Laylas could get confusing here.'

I smile. 'I'd be honoured if you do, but not upset if you change your mind. Okay, you can get dressed now.'

I brush my fingers over the foetal-position statue on the trolley. Still frozen solid. It'd be like chiselling concrete to start on him now. Tomorrow, at the earliest. I eye my schedule on the wall. A first-trimester review of Caitlin is next, followed by a consultation with three-year-old Amber, our first Antarctic-born citizen, who apparently has a mysterious rash.

I wish for Caitlin's sake that the ultrasound hadn't packed up three years ago, but we manage to get by without it. It just involves some old-fashioned diagnostic techniques to determine potential abnormalities. Our only miscarriage in 17 pregnancies was Robyn's, but that may have been a blessing in disguise. I couldn't have detected spina bifida and if the child's case had been severe, we don't have the facilities to provide appropriate care. What I *could* do, was trash all sperm from Donor 68 to prevent it happening again. That, and console Robyn that at 39, she was off the host list. We consoled each other actually, as I'd taken myself off the list at age 32 after Em was born. Her exceptionally wide-apart eyes rang alarm bells and now that she's about to hit three and is so much taller than the others her age, I know my diagnosis of Triple X syndrome was correct. When she's old enough to understand, I'll tell her how special she is to have an extra X chromosome. But she'll have many future problems, not the least of which may be fertility issues.

While awaiting Caitlin's arrival, I tidy up and audit the sperm bank. All in order. More than enough samples to last until next summer. Enough, actually, to last five years.

'Have you gleaned anything about Michelangelo?' Jen asks, mid-chew of her Weddell seal steak.

I laugh at her nickname for our mystery man and shake my head. 'Can't even figure how to get his clothing off yet.'

'Try the plaster saw?'

I roll my eyes. 'Why didn't *I* think of that? Tomorrow. Give me a hand?'

'Yeah. I'm curious.'

'Still haven't raised the neighbours.'

'Maybe they've stoned each other to death.'

'Ha. Tough work digging up stones here. As tough as this bloody steak. So much for my former vegetarianism.'

'So much for fillet steak, mushrooms and a good red wine, *I* say.'

'Glad you allowed me to up the temperature last night, or we'd never get him flat.'

Jen peers over her glasses. 'Still going to be like wrestling a man-size ice cube that looks like he's saluting Hitler.'

She cracks me up, Jen. I'd have gone crazy here without her.

Jessica grunts with exertion. 'I can't get this boot off. It's like it's welded on.'

I ask Wendy to give her a hand. 'Just watch you don't pull his foot off with it.'

Jen fires up the plaster saw and carefully cuts around the neckline of Michelangelo's parka hood, stopping at the nape. 'I'll have to wait until we turn him over to cut the other side. Going to be tricky getting the saw between his neck and arm.'

I nod. 'Maybe run straight down his spine and then up and down this leg so we can prise his clothing off.' Meanwhile, I try to figure out how to separate his knees from his chin. His left arm is buried between his chest and thighs. 'Can't see any sign of injury so far, but that might change when we get him uncurled.'

Jess and Wendy are still struggling with his right boot. Jess looks perplexed. 'Why do you reckon his arm is up like that?'

'I'd say he was trying to draw attention while he was busily freezing to death. But nobody would have seen him round there.'

'Poor guy,' Jess says, 'what a horrible way to die. You'd think if he got this far, he could have made it inside.'

I have to agree with her. Another 300 metres and he'd have been safe.

It takes us two hours to peel, scrape and chisel away most of his clothing, though his legs are still welded together.

'You ought to see his backside,' Jen observes, 'it's like a great crimson bruise'.

I step around the table to look. 'That'll be lividity. It's where the blood pools at the lowest point after the heart stops. It's not surprising, given the position he died in.'

'Hah, now I remember that from that old *CSI* program. Remember that?'

'Sure do, Jen. I spent many a night yelling at the TV that stuff didn't happen that quickly. Okay, I think it's time to try some traction to straighten him out.'

That turns out to be no mean feat, but finally, we have him almost flat on the table, aside from his left hand which is stuck fast to his jacket-front. Finally, we get a good look at his face. He's maybe 20, meaning he'd have been about 15 when we landed here. From my recollection of the 14 children on board the *Endurance*, only two were teenage boys. Jess passes me another jug of hot water. I pour it over his hand and carefully prise it loose. That's when we see the blood. Well, more like a raspberry icy-pole really. I inspect his hand first. No injury, other than the skin I've pulled off in the separation process. But the blood-encrusted puncture through his jacket, just below his sternum, is telling.

I look at Jen. 'Something tells me our Michelangelo didn't die of natural causes.'

It's quiet now. Just Wendy and me. The moment I picked up the scalpel, Jen's bravado evaporated and she suddenly had a vital mission to attend to. Looking now at Michelangelo's naked cadaver, I see that X really does mark the spot: a perfectly round puncture surrounded by a cross-shaped impression within another circle. Witchcraft? Satanism? Surely not here. Beats me. I insert a long cotton bud into the hole and push it in, noting it's trajectory towards the heart. When I feel some resistance, I press my thumb and finger together on the bud to gauge the depth of the wound, then remove it and hold it against the body.

'Just as I suspected.'

'Into the heart?' Wendy says.

'Left ventricle, which means that what blood couldn't then be pumped into the aorta would have followed the exit wound out. That pooling in his backside, and the relatively small amount that bled externally, indicates to me that he didn't die instantly. He's either stemmed the flow of blood with his hand, or...what stabbed him was stuck in there, sealing the wound, for a while.'

'Any idea what it might have been?'

I shrug. 'Not a knife. A knife *sharpener* maybe. The right diameter. Or anything else round, pointy and deadly.'

'Do you need to open him up?'

'It's pretty obvious he bled to death – and froze – in the process. Not sure I see the point in investigating further. I'm no coroner. We might have to go out with the spotlights to see if we can find anything near the body.'

'I'll be in that.'

We search for an hour, clawing at the ice in a three-metre perimeter around the hole we pulled him from. Nothing. And not a damn thing to suggest how he got there. No skis, showshoes, stocks. Nothing. We head back inside; none the wiser.

'Still can't raise the neighbours,' Jen says, spinning a ski stock like a baton-twirler as she greets us in the foyer of the Red Shed. 'I'm starting to think they've all vanished. Or their radio's kaput or...'

'They don't want to communicate,' I offer.

'Chances are.'

I tell Jen about the suspected COD, and the mystery of the instrument of death. 'Can't tell whether he was stabbed, stabbed himself or fell on something. But if it was self-inflicted, where's the stabby thing?'

'I don't know, Miss Marple. By the way, do you remember you're on slushy duty? Jo covered breakfast for you, but you're on lunch and dinner, and it's Tiarna's and Bet Bet's birthday week, so you know what that means.'

'Yep.' *Caviar.* Among the mountain of food stores we'd ratted from the *Endurance,* before the neighbours absconded in it, was 1000 jars of caviar, of which we allow two for special occasions. That translates to about a Viagra-size portion each.

'Oh,' Jen says, 'and you need to check Brianna. She looks like she's ready to drop any minute. She's in her donga.'

'But she's not due for at least a month.'

'She's huge and really uncomfortable.'

Twins maybe? 'Okay.' I head off, then stop dead and turn. 'Show me that.' I grab the ski stock from Jen's hand and inspect the end.

Jen looks quizzical. 'What?'

I point to the tip and ridges on the underside of the basket. 'I think we've found our stabby thing, though not necessarily this one in particular.'

I find Brianna writhing and gasping on her bedroom floor.

'Mind if I check down below?'

'It's all wet.'

On inspection, I see her waters have broken and she's already four centimetres dilated. 'Come on, darling, I need to get you up.'

'It freaking hurts.'

'Yes, I know. Just take some deep breaths and I'll walk you to the delivery room. Your little girl's a bit early, but everything should be fine. Where's your mum?'

'Dunno. She's doing some plumbing somewhere.'

I poke my head out the door, spot Heather and ask her to find Louise. 'Tell her to go to the surgery.'

Louise holds her daughter's hand and tells her to relax. 'Eighteen hours I was in labour with you. Be grateful yours isn't taking so long.'

'I've decided on Rihanna, not Melanie,' Brianna says. 'Rihanna's so cool. I love her music.'

Louise, Wendy and I raise our eyebrows in unison. I daren't tell Brianna that if she were still alive, Rihanna would now be pushing 56 and maybe not so cool.

'And her name rhymes with yours,' I say.

'Didn't even think of that. Whoa...' The 16-year-old's body racks with another contraction.

'Okay, big push now. I can see the head.'

Brianna grips Louise's hand, screws up her face and screams as she pushes. The head is free. 'Now stop pushing, breathe slowly and on the next contraction, push even harder.'

Two minutes later the baby emerges. The shock stuns us all to silence.

Wendy's first to speak. 'How the hell?'

I'm still shaking my head. It's just not possible.

Somehow, inconceivably, it's a boy. That makes two mystery males in two days. It has me seriously doubting my efficacy at separating all the sperm samples. It should have been foolproof. It's times like this I wish Mike were here. Genetics specialist that he is, he'd have figured it in no time.

Word spreads around the Red Shed like wildfire, and boys' names are bandied around over afternoon tea until Jen wisely suggests Douglas – after Mawson himself of course. It's fitting. Jen allays Brianna's fears that Douglas might be removed from her and sent to Davis. She's right to ask what the men would do with a baby. I can see Douglas is going to be spoilt rotten due to his novelty status. I check my watch. It's five o'clock. I head to the kitchen.

It was a sad day that we reluctantly agreed to overturn the Antarctic treaty clause that protected all penguins, but without the occasional Adelie and Emperor meat, we'd be suffering from a lack of protein, vitamins and minerals since our meat stock ran out. Unfortunately, Emperor goulash is our birthday treat along with the aforementioned caviar. Tasting like a blend of beef, cod and duck, it's necessarily best served disguised in casserole gravy. I'm pleased to see that Roz has already diced the meat.

'Fancy that. A boy, of all things,' she says to me.

'I'm still astonished.'

'Yep. No rumpy pumpy around here.'

I nod. *Unless...unless!* The realisation hits me like a thunderbolt. At 4.6 kilos, I'd thought Douglas huge for a 35-week gestation. Was Brianna already pregnant? To Michelangelo? The timing could fit but it seems implausible. But then again, not. Two days ago, I'd have thought it impossible. I'll run it by Louise after dinner. But first things first. 'Sorry Roz, can you give me fifteen?'

'No dramas.'

I finally get through on the radio and thankfully, it's Mike, rather than *Endurance* Captain Geoff, now Davis City leader, who answers. He tells me their radio has been out for several days; the tower having been blown down by katabatic winds. They'd only just righted and repaired it. After satisfying each other that we're both okay, I ask him who's missing from Davis.

'Brad Kingston. Remember that little shit who told you to fuck off on the ship? Been gone what, 10-11 months. Why?'

'Because he's here.'

'You're kidding me. He got that far? When did he arrive?'

'That, we're not sure of. Possibly nine months ago.'

'Can't he tell you?'

'Nope. He's in the mortuary. We only found him yesterday.'

'Oh. Well, can't say I'm overcome with grief.'

'Did he leave there alone?'

'Yep.'

'Why?'

'We banished him.'

'You *banished* him? Why? Who do you guys think you are? King Arthur?'

'He was a problem from the moment we left Mawson. He tried to commandeer the ship and go back to Hobart, and his shitty behaviour escalated from there. After four years of threats, theft and...whatever, we gave him an ultimatum. Banishment or risk execution.'

'*Exe-bloody-cution?* Are you serious? Have you all gone primitive, feral, over there?'

'It wasn't like that. Trust me. Geoff had uncovered a plot by a dozen of the men to murder Brad. They feared it was either him or them. You know, there's an arsehole, an idiot, a saboteur, a would-be killer, in every crowd.'

'Not here, there's not. But I won't start *that* discussion. What's the *whatever*?'

'Yeah, well that was the final straw. Rape. At least two boys that we know of.'

'Jesus. So, what did you do? You sent him *here*.'

'No, we didn't. We banished him to the ship. It wasn't until a week later we noticed all the missing gear, the snowmobile and solar sled. We figured he wouldn't get far; that he'd either kowtow back, or perish somewhere we'd never find him. Not for a minute did we think he'd turn up there. That's why we didn't tell you. I mean, what are the odds?'

'He was evidently more resourceful than you gave him credit for.'

'How did he die?'

'Still trying to establish that. He either fell on his stock, or...someone stabbed him with it.'

After dinner, I beckon to Louise, who's carrying Douglas so that an exhausted Brianna can sleep, and lead her to the unheated makeshift mortuary adjoining the surgery. Louise gasps as I unveil Brad's head.

Her hand still covering her mouth, she stares at me wide-eyed. 'Where did he come from?'

'I found him out near the generator.'

'Why are you showing me, in particular?'

'He possibly explains Douglas's unexpected...gender.'

'How?' A long pause as the penny drops. 'Oh.'

'Yes. *Oh*. Brianna never mentioned him to you? Never told you what happened?'

Louise shakes her head in disbelief. 'You think...what do you think?'

'Intercourse, obviously. But voluntary or involuntary is the question. I suspect the latter. She couldn't have kept a sneaky tryst a secret, and surely she'd have brought him in. He'd have been starving, for starters.'

'Must have been before you impregnated her.'

I nod. 'About a month, I'm guessing.'

I straddle Brianna's desk chair and wait until she and Louise stop fussing over Douglas.

'He's a handsome boy,' I say. 'A great head of hair.'

Brianna beams with motherly affection, but a faraway look then transforms her face.

'Brianna, do you want to tell us about Brad?'

Brianna tries to disguise her astonishment with a questioning expression. 'Who's Brad?'

'Come on Brianna. The young man you had an *encounter* with nine months ago.'

She knows she's cornered. 'Oh. Him. Didn't know his name.'

Louise puts her arm around her. 'It's okay darling. Tell us what happened.'

'He staggered into the hydroponics shed while I was picking lettuces. I couldn't freaking believe it. Last thing I expected was to see a *boy*.'

'What condition was he in?' I ask.

'Pretty good, since he reckoned he'd walked a hundred Ks after his solar sled broke down. Said he'd pinched a shit-load of food and a whole bunch of stuff and skewered a few penguins here and there. We yacked for a while and he seemed okay, nice even – apart from staring at my boobs the whole time – until I said I'd bring him over here. I was trying to help him, but–' Brianna stares at her feet. When she lifts her head, I see watery eyes.

'But? Did he force himself on you?'

Brianna nods almost imperceptibly. 'He just went crazy. Like an animal. I couldn't stop him. I was so scared.'

Louise embraces her daughter. 'Oh darling, why didn't you tell me?'

'I don't know Mum. I wanted to but I–' She breaks into sobs. 'I was embarrassed, confused. I didn't think anyone would believe me.'

It dawns on me. 'Is that why you were so eager to volunteer for impregnation? Because you thought you might already be pregnant.'

Her shoulders sag. 'Yeah.'

'What happened to him then?'

Brianna squirms. Avoids eye contact. 'I don't know. I don't care. He just took off, I think. I was still on the ground. I stayed there for ages. I don't know how long. Roz was pissed off I took so long with the lettuces.'

Louise sighs. 'God, you'd think someone who'd struggled for 800K would want to find people, help, food, a comfortable bed. But what does he do? He fucking rapes the first person he sees. What a mongrel.'

'Desperado too,' I add.

'How do you know about him, anyway?' Brianna asks.

'We found him yesterday.'

'Shit.' Brianna looks panicky. 'He's still here? Where's he been all this time?'

'Buried in ice.'

'You mean he's dead? Good.'

I'm inclined to agree, though I say nothing. I'm also sure she's not telling the whole story, but I'll broach that some other time. *Did she stab him? Or did he fall on his own sword, so to speak? Either way, who cares? But if he fell on his stock, where is it?*

It's early October and Jen and I revel in plus three degrees as we enter the hydroponics shed to check the nutrient solutions and pH balance and prepare the net pots for the wheat seeds.

'Y'know,' Jen says, 'first time I came here, in 2022, the highest October temperature was minus two, so this is like a heatwave.'

'If only all those climate change deniers were here now.'

'Give me a hand to pull this bench across, will you?' she says.

As I put my hands under the timber frame to pull, something long and cylindrical clatters onto the floor.

A ski stock; its tip and basket stained with blood. We look at each other as the significance dawns on us. The fact that it had been hidden speaks volumes, but why did Brianna never tell anyone? It's not like any of us wouldn't have cheered about one fewer rapist in the world.

'Ha!' we both say. 'You go girl.'

THE VOTOS SOLUTION

JANE AND LINDA COULD NEVER HAVE ANTICIPATED HOW successful their educational program for men would be. After several years working together at the family resources centre listening to women talking about their insensitive, lazy, good-for-nothing husbands, the two social workers had had a meeting of minds over end-of-week drinkies one Friday night. Then, after several months of deliberation, planning and a good deal of lobbying the local council, DOCS and State and Federal pollies, the pair had finally succeeded in gaining a grant to put their course into action.

Their "students" were welcome to join the program of their own volition, could be prodded into it by their wives, or could be referred from outside agencies such as police, the family court or DOCS itself. The multi-faceted program would draw on a range of subjects in a bid to turn errant, ignorant and abusive husbands into useful, loving and supportive ones – with the ultimate aim of salvaging impaired marriages. With a variety of guest presenters, topics included "How to communicate without resorting to condescension", "How to make your wife feel special", "How to read and react to potential spousal meltdowns", "Situations to avoid", "What impact does your appearance have on your relationship?", "Spend a day in your wife's shoes", "Planning and cooking a dinner fit for a Queen", "You both own the remote", and "Ten things guaranteed to infuriate your wife".

Of course at first they'd agonised over what to call the program – both agreeing it needed a catchy acronym but also realising it needed to be something that would appeal to men in a basic, blokey way. It was, after all, blokes – not real men – who most needed their special insight.

'What about BAGH – Becoming a Good Husband?' Jane had suggested at another after-work drink session. 'Nah, too soppy and potentially likely to be used against their wives – as in the old bag.'

'I know...what about He Man?' Linda suggested, tongue in cheek.

'Which means what?'

'Um. Helping Educate Misogynists and Neanderthals, maybe?'

When she'd finished laughing at that one, Jane offered, 'I know – what about, hang on – it's coming. HELP. Husbands Experiencing Love Problems!'

'Or HEMP – Husbands Experiencing Marital Problems.'

'Ha. No I reckon our prospective clientele would rather smoke it than come to a class.'

'Okay, so what about we just call it The PUB program, as in Precluding Undesirable Behaviour – the acronym makes passable sense and guys would identify with it – they could truthfully tell their mates they're going "to the pub" without any stigma attached and it would give the program a public persona,' Linda proclaimed. 'But, of course, we'll know what it really means.'

'Which is what?'

'Pathetic...Useless...Bastards.'

'Oh, of course. How did I not guess that?'

Jane and Linda had realised, very early in their planning, that they'd never get men to attend such a course if they looked, sounded or dressed like the men's mothers – or wives for that matter. They had to ooze sex appeal – which they both agreed might be fun as a change from their so politically correct nine-to-five dress and behaviour code – and they had to make each guy think he was "the one" commanding their attention. The concept, they acknowledged, was fraught with complications, especially when it came to dealing with delicate male egos and the intrinsic need for each man in a group to assert himself as the alpha male, but they figured that if they could save even one marriage it would be worth it. And it might be fun in the process.

In the two years since the program had been launched, they had been surprised to find that men were recommending it to each other and that some wanted to return for an advanced course. They even had a waiting list. Over time, they had added other subjects to the course, including some of a more intimate nature in which appropriately credentialed tutors (all of whom had to meet Jane and Linda's criteria of being enticingly clad and appealing to men) presented their top ten tips on how to pleasure a woman, which had proven incredibly popular.

The best thing about this, from Jane and Linda's point of view, was the number of women they'd noticed around town who were smiling more than usual. It was apparent that their classes were having the desired effect – at least in some households.

But Jane and Linda were still perturbed to discover that some men were simply beyond redemption. All the classes and courses, grooming and cajoling, persuasive discussion and blunt observations were not going to save these men from their own complete, unmitigated fuckwittedness.

It was time for Plan B. Jane and Linda felt it was their duty to offer total satisfaction to the women who were on the receiving end of their husbands' recalcitrance.

They'd come to this realisation in the wine bar on yet another Friday night post-work session. It seemed they made all their best decisions there. Gavin had given them the idea. They simply had to do something to put him out of his poor wife, Sue's misery. After six months on the PUB Program, it was evident he hadn't learned a thing. They formulated a plan – henceforth to be known as Elevation to the VOTOS Solution – which would remain a secret between the two of them.

Gavin was a nuff-nuff. Too stupid to have ever been allowed to become a husband – let alone a father. Unfortunately, he was that twice over. But being a nuff-nuff wasn't his greatest problem. He was violent as well. He had started The PUB course, kicking and screaming, at the behest of the local magistrate who, in determining punishment for a minor domestic violence episode, deemed that it would be more beneficial to him than a jail sentence. Jane and Linda had taken him on board on the understanding that particular attention should be paid to his misogynistic tendencies. He'd been a handful from the get-go and had railed vociferously at Jane and Linda's suggestions about how a husband should behave – especially in the presence of young children. Jane and Linda were confident that without their intervention there was a real risk that, despite Sue's tireless efforts, her two sons would become Gavin-induced violent nuff-nuffs too. Something had to be done. But it had to be something that would still see Sue and the boys right financially. Divorce was therefore not an option. Besides, a decree absolute simply wasn't absolute enough.

Jane and Linda had spent a lot of time trying to figure out what to do. VOTOS – Victims of Their Own Stupidity – was the answer. All they had to do was devise a death that was so stupid or unlikely that nobody would suspect it was anything other than an accident of the victim's own making. Then came the fun part. It had taken a bit of surreptitious research into Gavin's behaviour, but Linda had ultimately come up with the plan. She had never expected that, aside from being a violent nuff-nuff, he was a sexually impotent nuff-nuff as well.

When Gavin the Gormless suffered a mammoth heart attack after popping eight Viagras, the Coroner had labelled it Death by Misadventure. Linda and Jane agreed that that was a satisfactory outcome. It had been so easy. Linda had known that the best way to ensure a nuff-nuff *would* do something was to advise them, in the most authoritative manner you could muster, *not to do* that something.

'No,' she'd said when he'd asked her during a private session, 'I wouldn't suggest taking more than two at a time or you might end up with a permanent erection'. How was she to know when she handed him the sample packets that he was also taking nitroglycerin to treat his angina? After all, most people should know the two didn't mix. And naturally he wasn't going to tell anybody else about such a private discussion.

It had happened quicker and sooner than even Linda had suspected. Just a week later, she and Jane were attending his funeral - to offer their condolences to Sue and the boys, of course.

Dick turned out to be almost as easy to dispatch. The MO was different but the applied logic was the same.

He'd only just started the program, but Jane had determined, in her preliminary interview, that his belligerence knew no bounds. She'd asked Dick why his marriage to Bernadette seemed such a struggle.

'I dunno. Nuffin I ever do seems to be good enough for 'er. Y'know I spend so much time tellin' 'er how to do things and she just gets stroppy. I mean I must've told 'er 27 times how to start the lawnmower and I seem to spend all my time pickin' what to watch on TV so we don't have to watch fuckin' wildlife documentaries and she just cracks the shits and disappears into the bedroom to read or talk to her girlfriends on her fuckin' Facebook phone. And geez, when I told her that I thought I'd save us some money by not buyin' her a friggin' birthday present, well, she just went fuckin' ballistic, y'know.'

'Hmm. So, what do you do to help around the house?'

'Me? Well fuck, nothin'. Why the fuck should I? That's 'er domain. Y'know I go out an' work three days a bloody week, why the hell would I do anythin' around the house?'

'Yes. Point taken.' Jane nodded as though she sympathised and understood perfectly where this useless excuse for a man was coming from.

'Yes, I think you could benefit from our course. We can show you a few things that might improve your home life and score you some points with your wife. Now, just another question and excuse me that it's a bit more personal. But what about sex?'

Jane wanted to vomit the moment Dick opened his mouth.

'Oh geez, I don't know what's wrong with me. I just, you know, I just can't get it up any more. And doesn't that just drive her mental. Y'know I'll try to get on 'er in bed 'n'all and she'll just kick me off. Tell me I'm useless.'

'Hmm. So, what about foreplay?'

'Huh. You've gotta be jokin'. I'm not havin' anyone else get in bed with us. It'd be pretty fuckin' crowded with four.'

Jesus. A total moron. Looks like the full treatment is the only option. We have to save the poor woman from this complete Neanderthal. Don't even need to discuss this one with Linda.

'Dick, I think I know just the thing for you. I don't know whether you're into crystals and all that stuff, but I have a friend who's an amateur gemologist and she swears that since her husband started handling some of her minerals, he's...shall we say, transformed. He'd been a bit, you know, disinterested, shall we say, and a bit on the limp side. But since he's started rubbing in one particular mineral each day he's, without giving away any personal secrets, he's become – as she calls it – a stud muffin. It only took a week or two. She's really impressed, believe me.

'You're kidding me. So how can I get hold of some of this...mineral or whatever?'

'Well, as it happens, I've got some here. Just between you and me and the gatepost,' she whispered to him conspiratorially, 'I thought I might get my husband to try it, too. But hey, I can get some more.' She opened the bottom drawer of her desk and plucked out a small plastic bag containing a shard of pretty blue rock. 'But on the understanding that you don't tell anyone about it, because naturally, I don't have any clinical expertise in this. You know, I'm not an expert.'

Over drinks that evening Jane told Linda about their new VOTOS candidate. Linda understood perfectly that Jane had made what was clearly a necessary decision without consulting her.

'Of course I didn't tell him what it was, in case he got it in his head to google it. I've seen him in there in the library on the computer sometimes and Bernadette told me that's because he's too stingy to buy his own computer. Stupid bastard. Of course I told him under no circumstances to lick it. That that might be tantamount to an overdose of Viagra.'

'Ha ha. So you think he's hooked?'

'Totally.'

'How long do you think?'

'I'm guessing not very long.'

Linda smiled. 'You know, I can't help feeling we're doing a real good. We ought to get a medal for services to humanity.'

'Yeah, or huwomanity, more to the point.'

Two weeks later, Jane found her regular parking spot blocked by an ambulance when she arrived for her Tuesday afternoon counselling session. Linda emerged from inside the community-cum-library centre with a solemn expression on her face and Verity, the centre's bookkeeper, by her side.

'What's going on?' Jane asked.

'Oh, haven't you heard about the body in the library? It's just awful,' Verity had blurted. 'It's that guy that comes to your PUB classes.'

Jane looked at Linda quizzically.

'Dick Freeman,' Linda said with a who-would-have-guessed face. 'He just dropped dead sitting there at the computer. Nobody even noticed for a while. It's weird though, apparently his tongue was sticking out and it was bright blue.'

'Really?' Jane tried hard to feign astonishment.

Most of Dick's family were perplexed and intrigued by the Coroner's report, several months later, which determined that he had died of copper sulphate poisoning. The coroner had been unable, however, to determine why Dick had been sucking Chalcanthite and where he had got the extremely rare and toxic mineral.

Jane and Linda had breathed a sigh of relief. Fortunately, nobody had connected the dots and learned that Jane's late Uncle Fred, an eminent geologist, had left her his collection of volcanic stones. They knew, however, that this methodology in implementing the VOTOS Solution could only be a single-use application in such a small community, otherwise people might get suspicious. But Jane and Linda knew they'd done Bernadette a great service. She was already in another very fulfilling relationship with a veritable SNAG, and, it seemed, never stopped smiling these days.

They had to get more creative.

They had a new candidate on the list for elevation to the VOTOS Solution. John Hiscock – an appropriate name really, since that was all he ever thought about. John and his wife, Ella, had not long moved into the town, but Linda had come across the hapless wife in a café one day. Linda could tell that Ella had been crying and approached her cautiously and with genuine concern to ask if she was all right. Two hours and three chai lattes later, Linda had gleaned that Ella too was a victim of HISS – Husband Invoking Spousal Stupidity.

'It's just so frustrating,' Ella had confessed to her newfound confidante. 'You know, I'll ask him to help me do something and he'll either tell me what to do or, worse, he'll try to reinvent the wheel. He'll never simply roll up his sleeves and get in and help. And unfortunately he resents me for being smarter than him so he devises all these irritating things to make me look dumb, especially in front of other people. He also seems to just like antagonising me into an argument. I think he thrives on it. I know I shouldn't take the bait but sometimes I just can't help it. It's so irritating.'

'That's sort of like small man syndrome,' Linda had suggested.

'Dumb man syndrome's more like it,' Ella had said with a laugh. 'But that's not it really. It's the sex. He never stops thinking about it, talking about it, watching it...'

'Doing it?'

'Well not with me, thankfully, because frankly I'd rather watch paint dry. But he spends an inordinate amount of time in the toilet and bathroom, usually with magazines. You know...'

'A wanker then?'

'In every sense of the word.' Ella had put her hand to her mouth as though covering the unseemliness of making a joke.

So Linda made a suggestion to Ella and she readily accepted the offer, but was cautious about how to broach the subject with John.

It was decided that Linda would visit them at home one day, like a friend dropping in for a casual visit. She'd made sure that she looked tarty enough to attract John's attention, which had immediately had the desired effect, and she'd observed how he condescended to and demeaned his wife without even realising he was doing it. She'd managed to get him alone – following a prearranged signal that sent Ella to the bathroom – and had suggested in her most seductive manner how he might benefit from becoming a part of her special program. It would help unleash the devil in him, she'd promised. He was hooked like a flaccid mullet.

He religiously attended all the PUB sessions, making Jane and Linda cringe with his sexual innuendos. Why was it, they wondered, that the ugliest men always thought of themselves as sexy – as God's gift to virility? God, the man had barely any hair, dreadful taste in clothing, half a complement of teeth and even less machismo. On the Don't-Even-Think-About-Coming-Near-Me scale he was a nine-point-five at least. And on certain days, when it was evident he hadn't cleaned those picket-fence teeth, he ranked a nine-point-nine.

Poor Ella. All the grooming in the world wasn't going to turn John into a likeable human being – let alone a sustainable husband.

What to do?

Over more chai lattes on a Friday morning off, Linda gleaned some useful information from her now firm friend, Ella. Aside from his preoccupation with sex, John's secondary vice was hunting. He and his troglodyte mate, Kevin, satisfied their bloodthirsty tendencies once a month when they absconded together for a weekend camping-hunting expedition. This involved loading Kevin's ute with their rifles, ammo, tent, loaded Esky, Primus and cans of stew and baked beans, and pissing off into the bush. They didn't much care what they shot: deer, rabbits, wild dogs, wild boar, ducks, kookaburras. Anything. As long as it had a pulse it was fair game in their book. Mostly they were too pissed to give a shit.

Hmm.

Linda passed this information to Jane and they conspired. They might be able to save some defenceless wildlife into the bargain.

At the Thursday night PUB session before his next hunting foray, John had inadvertently provided Jane and Linda with a possible, albeit by no means infallible, strategy. Despite complaining of a head cold all night, John had been yabbering on excitedly about the fact that his usual weekend trip was being extended to five days, since both he and Kevin had managed to get time off work. Linda remembered something she'd seen on the news some time ago. It was worth a try. Having wised-up Jane so that she wouldn't put her foot in it, Linda called John aside after the class and invited him to share a scotch with the teachers. He thought all his Christmases had come at once. He was the Chosen One. Little did he realise what he was being chosen for. He'd been fascinated to learn from them that not only was Tylenol excellent for relieving the symptoms of colds but it was a little-known fact that it greatly enhanced the effects of alcohol and, in the right dosage, could lead to unimaginably heightened sexual pleasure; especially if one was on one's own... It was just a suggestion.

They could never have dreamed that their plot would take out two dodo birds with one stone. When Ella, and Kevin's wife Sarah, reported to police the following Thursday that their husbands hadn't returned home from their hunting trip, the search was on. They were found by two park rangers the following day. They were both lying around their long-dead campfire. Flies open and flies humming around their comatose bodies. Surrounding them were two slabs worth of empty Jim Beam cans and a pile of empty packets of Tylenol. They'd had a lot of fun...until they'd both started feeling decidedly seedy.

Kevin died of liver failure in the ambulance. John's liver gave out the following day in hospital. Their deaths hit the news big-time. For weeks afterwards, current affairs programs reported on the dangers of mixing alcohol and prescription medicines.

The results of their inquests were foregone conclusions – Death by Misadventure.

Ella and Sarah were united in mourning. For all of about a month. Then they joined the tennis club together, they took out gym memberships, they spent a day in a day spa having makeovers, they joined a book club and a bushwalking club. They went to the movies together and were planning a holiday together. They got a life. And from all reports, they never looked back.

For a while, there was some speculation in Jane and Linda's community about the coincidence that three of the PUB Program's students had died in peculiar circumstances in a relatively short period of time. Jane and Linda were at a complete loss to explain it. They, it appeared, were just as surprised and perplexed as everybody else. But they decided that maybe the VOTOS program should hibernate for a while.

And it did.

For all of seven months.

Then Craig appeared for his preliminary interview. Jane and Linda conducted the evaluation together. Within two minutes, there was a tacit agreement between them. Craig's answer to almost every question they asked was, 'dunno'. Definitely not a thinking man. If he'd maybe answered 'I don't know' at least once, they might have given him credit for having one marble rolling around in his vacuous head. They wondered whether he'd ever even tried to make a decision. Like using a condom, maybe. They decided that Forrest Gump's expression 'Stupid is as stupid does' should have been coined for Craig. He actually made Gavin the Gormless look clever.

'There should be a law against idiots like that being allowed to procreate,' Linda had said afterwards.

'Yep,' Jane had agreed, 'but then Carol's no mastermind either'.

'You're right about that. Any mother who thinks that Macca's is a healthy diet for anyone, let alone infants, and whose favourite pastime is dressing her kids' teddies while watching cartoons in her pink fluffy-bunny flannelette pyjamas in the *absence* of her kids – is no Mensa candidate.'

'Oh, now you're just getting bitchy,' Jane laughed, casually slapping Linda on the arm. 'I happen to love my pink fluffy-bunny flannelette pyjamas.'

'Ha, the day I see you trading your sexy negligees for flannelette fat-Albert coveralls is the day I'll have to commit you to a funny farm for faded floozies.'

'Nevertheless, I feel we have an obligation to save Carol. Don't you?' Jane asked.

'It shouldn't be too hard. Craig should be easy to dispatch. I'm surprised he even remembers to breathe. If it had to be a conscious decision I doubt he'd have made it past the age of eight.'

So the women were back into research mode.

They were able to glean that Craig's only interest was playing video or Xbox games and that it was not uncommon for him to sit in front of the TV (not the same one Carol reserved for her cartoon-watching) for hours on end, fighting fights with predictable two-dimensional enemies. Apparently, his only forays into the big, wide real world were his Friday Disability Pension day grocery shopping expedition with Carol and his, now regular, Thursday night PUB classes.

The former gave Jane and Linda no inspiration and the latter would be too suspicious, so the women had to think laterally.

'Why is he on the Disability Pension?' Linda asked Jane. 'What condition does he have?'

'Nothing serious that I know of. Just fat and lazy I think'.

'Simon plays some of those video games, doesn't he?' Linda asked, referring to Jane's 15-year-old son.

'Half an hour a day. That's all he's allowed. And he's not allowed to have the Xbox in his bedroom – only in the lounge. But he's pretty good. There's no way on earth my reflexes could ever be that quick. His latest game is *Dragon Age: Inquisition*. He's only had it a week but he's already up to Level Six – so he was bragging at breakfast this morning. I had to look interested and impressed of course. Anyway, what have you got in mind?'

'Hmm. Thinking, thinking. What would rile a 35-year-old Xbox addict more than anything?'

'Being beaten by a 15-year-old would be my guess.'

'Exactly.'

'But how...?'

'Well Craig's flabbier than a Right Whale with enough chins to fill a Chinese phone book, isn't he?'

'Yep. And he chain smokes.'

'So...if he happened to be lent a copy of *Dragon Age: Inquisition* and happened to be told that your 15-year-old son reached level six in – shall we say – *two* days, what do you think he'd be likely to do?'

'Play it non-stop until he gets there too. But I don't see how...'

'Ever heard of deep vein thrombosis? It's just a vague possibility, but you never know.'

'Hmm. Good one. Nobody would ever suspect anything.'

Linda spoke in a suitably mortified voice the following Monday when she received a panicked phone call from Carol.

'I can't believe it, Linda,' she confided. 'That he could be sitting there perfectly all right one minute and then the next minute, he gets up and keels over. Dead. Just like that. I mean, he was only 35. It was only because the pee bottle he'd kept beside him so he wouldn't have to get up was full and he didn't have any choice, since I was in the laundry doing the ironing with my earbuds in and didn't hear him calling.'

'Unbelievable,' Linda had commented. 'Who'd have thought? But how long had he been sitting there?'

'From five o'clock Friday afternoon until when it happened at about seven o'clock last night. The ambos said it can be that quick. They reckoned the clot must have gone straight from his leg to his pulmonary artery. Bang. Just like that.'

'So, 50 hours. But what possessed him to sit that long?'

'He was absolutely determined to get to Level Six of that stupid game someone lent him. Buggered if I could figure out why. Waste of bloody time, if you ask me.'

Despite the tragic loss of Craig to society and the bodily hole it left in the current PUB Program lineup, his passing had little impact on the success of the course.

Women were now stopping Jane and Linda in the street to expound at length at how their lives and relationships had improved and on the newfound virtues of their heretofore antagonistic, lame husbands.

They began to wonder about the potential of franchising the PUB Program. It would take a lot of effort to get off the ground, with training programs to establish and marketing literature to produce. And it would require a highly confidential interview process to find suitable candidates to roll out a nationwide program, but the idea certainly had merit. And who knew? Maybe some of those new coordinators might realise, in their own good time of course, the need for an advanced solution. And maybe, just maybe, Jane and Linda would let them in on their secret.

Some time later, Linda and Jane were sharing a morning coffee in their office when the phone rang. It was Jess, coordinator of the PUB Program at a northern Queensland community centre. Linda turned on the speaker phone for Jane's benefit. Jess advised her mentors that two of her students had died in very peculiar circumstances, within a month of each other. One, for some inexplicable reason, had overdosed on Viagra. The other, it seemed, had been poisoned by a strange stone he'd been sucking. Her community was awaiting the coroners' inquests. Jess acknowledged that she was at a complete loss to explain it.

Linda consoled her and told her not to worry. In fact she told Jess that, by extraordinary coincidence, one of the programs in WA and another in South Australia had recently reported not dissimilar turns of events. It was baffling. Those inquests had already been held and the coroner's findings? Death by Misadventure.

Jane and Linda merely looked at each other and wondered why no coroner had coined the acronym VOTOS.

ECHO WREN

ECHO WREN KICKED OFF HER SHOES, PRESSED THE MUTE BUTTON on the seat-back television screen and reclined the seat. It was going to be a long flight. The trip from Sydney to Copenhagen was over 20 hours, and stuck in a centre seat she had no view of the landscape below. Sleep was her best option. She'd just downed a Courvoisier to help with that. It usually did the trick.

Half an hour later she was still maddeningly awake: the in-flight magazine read from cover to cover, a second cognac put to bed and an unknown symphony tapped out on the armrest. The only consolation for insomnia was enduring it in first class instead of cattle class – she was grateful to her employer for that. Actually, she was grateful to her quarry for that.

She glanced up the aisle. Linda Falcon or Lauren Fairley or Lana Foster – whatever her name was today – was two rows up on the left side. Not that she could go anywhere 30,000 feet over the Indian Ocean, but Echo still needed to keep an eye on her. Problem was, it was hard *not* to keep an eye on her. She was tall, leggy, ridiculously attractive. And deadly. Jennifer Hawkins with a gun. She could be easily mistaken for a fashion model; her wardrobe was certainly the envy of one.

Echo wondered what made her tick. Surely it wasn't just the money – which would be vast. Obscene even. Was it an adrenaline rush, to line up a stranger in your sights and pull the trigger? Was there some political motivation? Did she just like killing people? Was it genetics that made one person carry a gun for evil intent and another for good? Sure, *she'd* shot people but that was for survival or the greater good – not money or for the thrill of it. And Echo's brief was never to kill – only to thwart, incapacitate and capture.

Fitzy hadn't told her who The Falcon's target was. That was her quarry's tag – The Falcon – which Echo thought ironic, given her own name. A Wren pursuing a Falcon. Improbable in the wild. But Echo was highly trained in counter-terrorism and anti-assassination. Her job was to foil assassination attempts, or hits on targets of lesser political significance, any way she could. The politics didn't interest her. She'd stymied more than one political murder in which the target probably deserved to be taken out for the sake of mankind. Like Tony Abbott. Aside from her ASIO colleagues, no other Australians even *knew* about the attempt on the Prime Minister's life. Because of her. She'd taken down the sniper with a perfectly aimed shot in the arm, before *he'd* even taken aim. And she had to live with that, while the rest of Australia continued to live with Tony Abbott. Her colleagues had applauded her for uncovering the plot to kidnap Gina Rinehart and snookering an assassination attempt on Clive Palmer. But when you were dedicated to your job, you couldn't help bad luck.

It was because of her dogged surveillance skills that she'd been assigned this case. To follow The Falcon wherever she went. So if that meant a first-class trip to Denmark – great. She knew stuff-all about Denmark – let alone Danish politics – and struggled to even name a Danish person, except maybe Crown Prince Frederick. And she only knew *his* name because he had married an Australian. She hoped that Fred and Mary weren't the Falcon's targets. Unlikely. Despite her wishful thinking for sexual equality in the world of international intrigue, she conceded it was unlikely that a female "button man" would ever be assigned such prominent targets, no matter how good her credentials. Besides, why would anybody want to kill such nice people?

Her usual MO was to surreptitiously follow her target and use her wrist phone and lapel camera to relay pertinent information to Fitzy and the team. Few people, even world-class assassins, were suspicious of women following them, especially if their shadows were as ordinary looking as Echo was. She had made a fine art of blending into crowds; behaving with such insouciance as to be invisible. In fact she often felt transparent when waiting for service in cafés or at shop counters. People seemed to see right through her. Maybe that explained why she was still single.

She'd been tailing The Falcon for six weeks, trying to link her to the death of Fabrizio Longhi, the Sydney Mafia boss found dead in bed with a syringe sticking out his neck a couple of months earlier. It had been a dull surveillance op. Echo hadn't uncovered a thing to connect Linda Falcon to the hit. Instead, she'd spent countless hours sitting outside hairdressers, drinking endless lattés at Sydney cafés, traipsing a block behind on shopping expeditions and gazing at Falcon's third-storey apartment windows through binoculars. The woman hadn't put a foot wrong.

But Fitzy had advised her, in this instance, to stick to The Falcon like glue – even if it meant actually making herself known to the assassin. Maybe even intimately. It might, he'd said, be the only way to get the information they needed. Echo understood this to mean that they didn't know exactly who The Falcon's target was. Their intelligence – gleaned from monitoring her phone and bank accounts – revealed an international bank transfer of $50,000 into her account on June 22. The fact that she had booked the flight to Copenhagen the same day was the clincher. She was going global. But who was paying her? And who was the prey?

Echo pulled her tablet out of her bag and opened Facebook. A few minutes scrolling might send her to sleep. Terri was enjoying dinner with Dave and Maddy (*without her*); a funny clip of cats falling off shit (*LOL*); police were questioning a man about the stabbing murder of his wife (*what, again?*); scientists were contemplating naming two craters on Charon, one of Pluto's five moons, Kirk and Spock (*whoot*); her mother was showing off one of her incredible birthday cakes (*brilliant, Mum*), apparently – according to the I Fucking Love Science website – burning NH4Cr207 with HgSCN opens a portal to hell (*who knew?*) and Grammarly was imploring people to 'Stop abusing the ellipsis...I mean it' (*too right*).

It did the trick – her eyelids started to droop.

The clatter of the food trolley jolted her awake. She checked her watch. She'd been asleep for seven hours. It was daylight outside. The sight of the hostess holding a pot of coffee was bliss. She tipped her head to look up the aisle. The Falcon was gone.

She didn't panic.

As the hostess handed her a coffee, she spotted The Falcon heading towards her from the toilet. Their eyes locked momentarily. The Falcon smiled; a genuine eye-creasing smile. Seductive maybe? Surely not. Echo smiled back. An opportunity? Or just a tacit agreement that they wished the flight would be over?

Echo almost mistook the vibration of her phone for the soporific droning of the engines. She pulled it from her jacket pocket. A coded text message from Fitzy: Booking Hotel Kong Arthur, Nørre Søgade 11.

She replied in code. Kong Arthur?

Yes, Kong Arthur.

Whatever. Echo shrugged. *Does it have round tables?* The phone vibrated again.

Flight 7am Sat Copenhagen-Faroe Islands. Falcon on board. Be on it.

Faroe Islands, where the fuck are the Faroe Islands? Echo checked Google Maps. *Holy shit. Halfway to friggin Iceland. Way to buggery off the north coast of Scotland. What the hell is The Falcon going there for?*

She texted Fitzy: WTF?

YGIAGAM

Fortunately, Echo knew Fitzy well enough to know that meant, 'your guess is as good as mine'. *Saturday at sparrow fart – why so frigging early?* Echo excelled at many things – but not mornings. But at least she'd have all Friday to look around Copenhagen – allowing for having to tail The Falcon.

Now, however, according to the captain, they were about to descend into Dubai. 'If you look out the left windows, passengers, you will see the Palm Jumeirah, Palm Jebel Ali and The World Islands off the coastline of Dubai.' *Bugger.* Just her luck that her seat was in the middle. She stood up and shuffled forward. The Falcon had two seats to herself. She bumped The Falcon's elbow.

'Oh, sorry, do you mind?'

'No, go right ahead. I've seen it before.' She pulled her legs in to let Echo through to the window seat. Echo wasn't feigning interest in the view – she really *did* want to see it. But she hadn't expected to be blinded by those mesmerising green eyes. She looked out and was truly impressed at the sight of the man-made sand islands contrasting with the azure water of the Persian Gulf. The Palms, however, looked more like the creatures from *Alien* to her.

'Incredible, isn't it?' She said it casually and turned to look at The Falcon.

'Mmm.'

'Well it is to me, given that I've never seen it before.' She wanted to engage The Falcon in conversation. To hear her voice.

'Okay, I confess, I was pretty blown away the first time I saw it. But I've been here several times, so it's nothing new to me.'

'So are you getting off here? Or going on to Copenhagen?'

'Hmm?' *Distracted. She is distracted.*

'Sorry, not that it's any of my business.'

'Oh, sorry. I've got a lot on my mind. No, I'm going on to Denmark. *That* will be new to me.' Her voice was as sexy as her body.

'Yes, me too.' Echo decided to push a little more. 'So, are you just on a holiday? Or business?'

'Ah...' *she is choosing her words carefully,* 'a bit of both.' *She isn't going to elaborate. And she didn't mention the Faroe Islands.*

'You?'

Echo could tell she wasn't interested in her reply. 'Bit of a holiday, but I'm a writer,' she lied, 'doing some research.'

'Yeah?' *She doesn't want to know. Not interested in what sort of writing.*

The stewardess leant across The Falcon and told Echo to fasten her seat belt. Echo looked out the window. The airport terminals looked like giant sausage rolls. She didn't comment. The Falcon wasn't interested.

Eight hours later, after an uneventful stopover in Dubai, the Emirates flight was circling Copenhagen. Half an hour later, Echo hailed a taxi and 20 minutes after that, she arrived at the Hotel Køng Arthur. Her timing was perfect. The Falcon was standing at the check-in counter. Echo sidled up beside her and tried to act surprised. 'Oh, hi. Fancy meeting you here. Gosh, if I'd known you were staying here too, we could have shared a taxi.'

'Mm...could have.' *This woman is no conversationalist, even 16,000km from home with a fellow Aussie of the same age and sex.*

'Maybe we could have a drink later, or dinner. That's if you don't have plans already.'

'I do.'

'Oh, okay. Maybe a coffee tomorrow then.'

'Maybe. See ya.' *Noncommittal.*

'Yeah...okay.'

Echo watched her walk to the elevator pulling a Bluesmart wheelie case with her right hand and toting a matching overnight bag. *How could she even have these? They haven't been released onto the market yet.* Echo had seen them online a week ago. They cost a bomb. Referred to as smart bags, they hooked up to a phone app to protect themselves from theft. They had a built-in phone charger and internal weighing system. *Neat. I'm envious.* What they didn't have, however, was a means of detecting a miniature recording and tracking device like the one Echo had surreptitiously stuck to the case as The Falcon passed her.

When Echo checked in, the concierge handed her a parcel. 'This arrived earlier today, Ms Wren. Enjoy your stay.'

Half an hour later, Echo was revelling under a hot shower. She had secured the room next to The Falcon. She figured that *she* would be showering and vegging out too. It was unlikely she would be in assassination mode tonight – especially with jet lag, so Echo felt she could relax. She emerged from the bathroom wrapped in the robe provided and with a fluffy towel around her head. She grabbed a Carlsberg from the bar fridge and plopped on the bed. She placed the receiver into her ear and lay back.

All was quiet in the adjoining room. *Is she napping? No.* Echo heard her voice.

'Hello, room service? Yes, I'd like to order a meal please. Spanish thank you.' She ordered something Echo had never heard of. *So, she is staying in.* Despite her tiredness, Echo couldn't help thinking about the happy hour down in the bar and the prospect of something exotic at the Sticks 'n' Sushi Japanese restaurant downstairs.

Replete with sushi and a scrumptious vegetarian meal, Echo lay back on the bed to check her phone. A message: *grindadráp* – Google it.

What came up on her screen appalled her. She wanted to vomit. A picture from hell. Dozens of pilot whales slaughtered on a beach – the water scarlet with their blood. As she read, any notion she'd ever had of the human race being humane was gone forever in a sea of whale gore. The Faroese people embarked every year on a sea-chase to round up passing whales and dolphins, drive them into one of 23 "grind" bays around their islands and slaughter them. For sustenance? No. Their meat was so full of mercury, the Faroese were advised to eat it only once a month. It was for tradition. The Faroese had been doing it since the 1300s and didn't want to stop. Echo read on; sick to the stomach. According to Faroese laws governing the *grindadráp*, all Faroese and any person visiting the islands during the grind season had to report all sightings of whales and dolphins to local authorities so that the cetaceans could be targeted for slaughter. Those who didn't, could be arrested, prosecuted and even imprisoned.

She was more appalled to learn that not only did the Danish government condone the *grindadráp*, it sent warships to the islands to protect the Faroese from those who might interfere with their massacre. That did not stop the Sea Shepherd organisation from trying to stop the slaughter each year. This year, more than 500 volunteers were surrounding the islands in all manner of watercraft to interfere with the round-up.

So why is The Falcon going there? Who is she being paid to kill?

Echo typed: Holy shit. Who's the target? One of these butchers?

Fitzy replied: Still working on it. Could be Hogni Hoydal, leader of the Faroe Island Republic Party, just reelected to the Danish Folketing. Could be the Foreign Affairs Minister, Kristian Jensen, or Environment Minister, Eva Kjer Hansen, or even the new Prime Minister himself, Lars Løkke Rasmussen. Bank transfer came from Faroe Islands, via Copenhagen.

Hmm. Any of these against the grind?

Fitzy: Will check. Could be Paul Watson, founder of Sea Shepherd. On his way to Faroes.

Echo typed Sea Shepherd into her Facebook search. Usually Facebook posts were more up to date than websites. She "liked" the page so that she could see more posts. More gruesome pictures of blood and whales with partially severed heads. Thirty-two of them lined along a beach. Fifty-seven in another bay. This was happening right now.

Echo wished she could be there – to defend them. To talk sense into these people. Like they would listen to her. Hell, she didn't even know their language.

How was she going to sleep now? With these images burnt into her psyche. But she did need to sleep. Who knew what tomorrow would bring?

Echo was roused from a fitful sleep by a beeping noise. Alarm? Phone?

Shit! The tracking device. The Falcon is on the move. Fuck...at this hour. Two friggin' thirty. What is she up to? Echo had no alternative but to jump out of bed, pull her jeans and jacket on, pop the tracker into her pocket and grab her gun from the parcel she'd opened earlier.

She got down to the lobby just in time to see The Falcon getting into a black Mercedes outside. Shit. She hurried to the reception counter and was told by the night manager that it would take five minutes for a taxi to arrive. *Thank God for the tracker. And thank goodness she took that case with her. Where the fuck is she going?*

Unfamiliar with the layout of Copenhagen and having no clue where she was going, Echo could only give the taxi driver directions to turn left or right. They travelled south-east along H.C. Andersens Blvd, past the town hall and Tivoli Gardens, before turning right into Christians Brygge. It took Echo a while to adjust to being on the wrong side of the road. She thought she saw occasional glimpses of water out the left window. They passed a shopping centre, Fisketorvet Byens, on the left and travelled another kilometre or so before merging into another road. Echo looked at the tracker. The Falcon had stopped somewhere up ahead. The taxi driver explained to her, in perfect English, that they were in the Sydhavnen – South Harbour – area. The wide thoroughfare sliced through a light industrial, business streetscape.

'Please turn left here and then right a...about here,' she instructed the driver. 'I'm looking for a black Mercedes'.

'Not easy in the dark,' the driver replied. 'Wait a minute, there – is that it?'

'Could be. Not sure. Would you mind just parking here for a while?'

'Your money. The meter's still running.'

'Do you have any idea what that building is? The one with the lights on in the window. Is it a nightclub or something?'

'Not likely. Office buildings here mostly.'

Echo was perplexed. Why would The Falcon go to an office building in a foreign city in the middle of the night?

She texted Fitzy: Check out 29 Teglholmsgard and black Mercedes coupé, AP 53945. Fitzy would get the Copenhagen contact to check them out.

About ten minutes later, as Echo rubbed the tired from her eyes, the driver made her start. 'Is that who you're following?'

She looked up as The Falcon emerged from the building, pulling her wheelie case and with a long object in a bag slung over her shoulder. She got into the passenger side of the Mercedes. Echo couldn't see the driver.

A weapon. Of course. She needs a weapon and even in the bag it looks ominous. Big, bulky, presumably high-powered and freaking serious.

'Can you follow her please – ah, without being obvious?'

'Are you a cop or something?'

'Something.'

'Oh...okay.'

Echo waited in the hotel lobby for ten minutes before taking the elevator to her room. She'd had to stay well back so The Falcon wouldn't see her. Once back in her room, she sent a message to Fitzy: Big weapon collected. Sleep now.

Echo poured herself another coffee and took a bite from her Danish pastry. She was dog-tired and the bright sunlight streaming through the atrium above the breakfast room did little to enhance the morning. She hated mornings. Not so The Falcon, it seemed. Echo stifled a grumble when she spotted her sashaying into the restaurant in jeans and a skimpy aqua singlet. She could have been on a catwalk. Her face smileless, her hair perfectly tousled, her makeup immaculate. Echo tried not to stare.

Their eyes met across the buffet table. The Falcon smiled wanly. Something was bothering her. Echo waved pathetically and was astonished when The Falcon collected a cup, poured some coffee and approached her table.

'Hi. Let's have that coffee.'

Echo tried not to look stunned. 'Sure. Is everything okay? You looked a bit upset.'

'Travel plans are all fucked up, that's all.'

'Why, what...?'

'Supposed to be flying out of here tomorrow but a fucking volcano's erupted. Did you see it on the news?'

'No. Where?'

'Frigging Iceland. That fucking unpronounceable volcano that erupted in 2010 – remember all those flights that were cancelled? – has blown it's flipping top again.'

'Shit. I was supposed to be flying tomorrow too. So have all flights been cancelled?'

'Pretty well everything within cooee of Iceland. Where were you going?'

Echo wasn't sure whether to lie or tell the truth. But it could have a major bearing on her pursuit of this woman. 'A place called the Faroe Islands. You probably haven't…'

'Shit. That's where I'm going.'

Echo donned surprise. 'Really? You're kidding. So can we still get there?'

'There's a ferry – only goes on Saturdays and Tuesdays. Might be a fat chance of getting on board at such short notice and it leaves from Hirtshals, which is a few hours' drive away.'

'We could go together, if you wanted to – share the ride and maybe a cabin. Does it have cabins?'

'Yeah, sure. The ferry takes over 30 hours, so you'd definitely want to sleep. I'll see if I can book online. Have you got your credit card handy?' The Falcon pulled out her iPhone and before long had booked a double berth on the MS Norröna. 'It leaves Hirtshals at 3.30 tomorrow.'

'I hope you mean 3.30pm.'

'Oh, yeah. Afternoon.'

'Thank God for that.'

'Not a morning person?' *Suddenly very chatty.*

'Nope.'

Echo's phone vibrated. She held it under the table and casually checked the screen. Mercedes belongs to Torkild Vestergaard. Get this, nephew of Danish Prime Minister. Sydhavnen address – weapons dealer. No surprise.

Holy shit. Echo almost said it out loud. *So what the fuck are they up to?* The Falcon interrupted her thoughts.

'I've gotta go. Things to do. How about I organise transport for tomorrow and we'll leave here about 10 o'clock?'

'Sure, great. Thanks. Oh, I'm Elly by the way,' Echo lied.

'Yeah, hi. I'm Lauren.' *Today, anyway.*

Echo messaged Fitzy. On board Norröna tomorrow pm. Shared cabin. Will I tail today?

Reply: Nup. Might as well sightsee. We're on it.

A whopping great motorbike was not what Echo had had in mind for transport, but she acquiesced when The Falcon handed her a helmet. Riding pillion behind an obviously experienced rider was both terrifying and exhilarating. Echo hoped The Falcon wasn't too uncomfortable with her gripping on like a koala up a gum tree. Fancy that, she was worrying about the welfare of a hired assassin. It was all the more uncomfortable because of the "telescope" slung over The Falcon's shoulder. The ride took the best part of four and a half hours – most of which was a blur to Echo. It left her with a stiff neck and no lingering impression of the Danish countryside.

Echo was relieved to sit at a table and relax in the ferry's Saga Café, with a Carlsberg in one hand and a tempting menu in the other. Her hair looked like a bird's nest – befitting a wren. By contrast, The Falcon looked freakily demure and relaxed for someone on a murder mission. Echo decided to probe her a bit.

'Are you just going to the Faroes for a holiday? Is it good for stargazing or something?'

'Huh? Oh, you mean the telescope? No, that's a gift actually. For my cousin – he lives there.'

Echo hadn't seen *that* coming. She'd wondered how The Falcon could have become known to somebody wanting an assassin in a place as remote as the Faroe Islands. Sure, the "gift" had a scope but it wasn't for looking at the stars. Echo had unzipped the bag and taken a peek while The Falcon was in the toilet. 'Oh, really? Is he Danish or Faroese?'

'No, no. But he married a Faroese woman. Nicoline.'

'So I guess you'll be staying with them.'

'Yep.'

'What do you think about the *grindadráp*?'

She shrugged. 'I don't think about it. I guess it's pretty horrible if you *do* think about it. You?'

'Makes me sick. It's appalling.'

'So why are *you* going there?'

'Research for a book I'm writing.'

'You're not writing about the "grind" are you?'

'No – it's a Viking adventure thing. The Faroes were a staging point for a lot of Viking invasions.' Doubtlessly crap, but Echo made it sound legit.

'Yeah? I love the TV show. *The Vikings*.'

'It's great, isn't it? And reasonably authentic.' *What would I know?*

Despite her efforts at drawing out The Falcon and discovering that she was interesting, witty and surprisingly gentle, Echo had been unable to glean any leading information about the target from her during the trip. She had actually enjoyed her company. Perhaps too much. And she'd looked incredibly sexy asleep. It had been a first for her to share sleeping quarters with a suspect.

They arrived at Tórshavn, capital of the Faroe Islands, at 11.30pm on Sunday. Echo was still nonplussed at having watched the sun set only an hour and a half earlier. Daylight at night was truly doing her head in and compounding her jet lag. "Lauren" had kindly dropped her off at the Hotel Streym which, as it happened, was only 350 metres from the ferry terminal. She'd said goodbye in a manner which didn't invite or expect reacquaintance. That was fine. Echo had moved the tracking device from The Falcon's trolley case to the rifle case.

Echo checked Sea Shepherd's Facebook page as she ate her breakfast and was stunned to see that a "grind" was underway not far away. Dozens of Sea Shepherd volunteers were trying to block an armada of Faroese watercraft herding a pod of pilot whales into Sandagero harbour. She checked the tracker. The Falcon was about two kilometres away in the vicinity of Torshavn's hospital. Echo doubted she was sick. One didn't take a high-powered sniper's weapon on a visit to the doctor. While waiting outside the hotel for a taxi, Echo checked Google maps. The hospital overlooked Sandagero harbour.

Echo was there in five minutes. The hospital sat atop rocky cliffs. The tracker showed that The Falcon was closer to the water. Echo walked down the road towards the helipad which perched on the clifftop. She pulled her mini binoculars from her pocket and looked down at the cove. The images she'd seen on the internet were there – in real life. Dozens of people lined the beach. A flotilla of small boats hummed and manoeuvred offshore. The water was crimson. Whales were dying en masse right in front of her. She was helpless to do anything. She wanted to die a bloody death to absolve mankind of its sins.

Then she saw The Falcon. Her hair raised in tendrils by the wind. Prone on the edge of the cliff. Her weapon aimed. Echo crept through the grass behind her. When she was about five metres away, she realised The Falcon was talking to somebody. Echo spotted the earpiece in her right ear.

'Yes, yes. I think I have it. The white boat with the black stripe down the side. Is he the driver or the passenger? Huh? Yeah, white hair and beard. Got him.'

Echo froze. Should she stop her now or wait a moment longer. The Falcon was looking through the sight – finger on trigger. She was aiming at one of the boats. Echo realised she couldn't hesitate.

But she did.

And in that moment, The Falcon pulled her head away from the gun sight and shifted her gaze to the beach.

Is she shaking her head? Holy shit – is she sniffing? Crying?

Echo crept closer, aiming her gun at The Falcon's head. She stopped dead.

'I was wondering when you were going to appear,' The Falcon said calmly, without turning her head.

Echo was stunned. Had she known all along? Was she losing her touch? 'Who's the target?' She tried to sound calm.

'You mean you don't know?'

'I'm guessing Paul Watson.'

'Yep – and some. But I can't do it. How can I witness what those bastards are doing down there and be on *their* side? It's so awful. I want to shoot the lot of them.' The Falcon wiped her eyes.

'Me too.' Echo had a lump in her throat. 'Maybe we *should*...shoot them.'

'Are you kidding me?'

'Yes. But I wish I wasn't.'

'I'd rather be out there with Watson and the Sea Shepherd crew, defending the poor creatures.'

'You and me both. But who hired you? Your cousin? Or Torkild Vestergaard?'

'Not my cousin, although he was the link to me, without knowing what they wanted me for. Torkild.'

'So is he acting for the Prime Minister?'

'Yep. They want to send a message to Sea Shepherd. A big you'd-better-fucking-back-off message. The Prime Minister's wife is Faroese. He's got blood on his hands, big time.'

'You should shoot *him* then.' *Shit, did I really just say that?* 'Where's Vestergaard?'

'Copenhagen. So what are you going to do with me? Are you wired, by the way?'

'Yep, I am. We'll have to extradite you to Australia.'

'But I'll go back willingly. Save all the bullshit. So long as you leave my cousin out of this. He's not involved. Besides, I haven't actually done anything. And you've got nothing on me in Australia. I know that.'

Echo hated to admit that The Falcon was right.

'What do you think?' She directed the question to her wrist watch.

'Get your arses back to Copenhagen ASAP,' Fitzy replied. 'We'll have to debrief you there. Leave the rest to us. We'll get the Danes to pick up Vestergaard. The political ramifications of this are going to blow the jam out of the Danish population's...danishes.'

The Falcon nodded. 'That's not going to help *those* whales now. Here, help me up.'

'Wish we could go down there and do something positive,' Echo said.

'We'd get arrested. Trust me. They've already arrested six Sea Shepherd volunteers, which is so stupid because all that does is draw more attention to it.'

'I know.' Echo grinned. 'So it's worth it, don't you think?'

Fitzy was ropable. 'How the fuck did you lose her?' he shouted down the phone.

'Beats me. She must have found the tracking device and got off the ferry before it docked.'

'Well, you'd better bloody find her.'

'Trust me. I'll track her down somehow. Give me a week. You could, at least, be glad that I foiled the attempt on Watson.'

Echo pondered the plans she and the Falcon had made over cocktails in the ferry's bar. Echo couldn't help liking her. But was the Falcon's seemingly reciprocal attraction merely subterfuge? Only time would tell.

The Falcon had floored Echo with her remarks. 'I do have scruples, you know. Sometimes it's the wrong target, but I've been paid to do a job. Doesn't mean I can't decide how to better spend the money.'

Echo wasn't sure she'd got her gist. 'Do you mean–?

'I do.'

Hang the professional ethics, Echo had thought as the two birds had clinked glasses at the notion, and planned where they'd meet for dinner afterwards.

Eight hours later, Fitzy was on the blower again. This time, "ropable" was an understatement. 'She's taken out Vestergaard!'

Echo feigned shock. 'What?'

'The Danish Security and Intelligence Service were taking him into custody when *thwack,* bullet to the head.'

'Holy shit. But how do you know it was her? Did they catch her?'

'Nope. Vanished into thin air.'

Yep, Echo thought. She flew off, as birds do.

MURGATROYD TO THE RESCUE

June 21, 1897

Honestly, how's a woman to think, with all that pacing upstairs? Once again, there's dust drifting down onto the scone mix. If it's not the creaking of the floorboards, it's the caterwaul of that darn violin. Sombre strains if he's maudlin; marginally more mellow if he's analysing. Enough to make a respectable woman run into the street and holler unseemly profanities. And all the coming and going, day and night. Shady, distressed individuals whose visitations are invariably urgent. He has me going upstairs and down like a yoyo; a veritable puppet on a string. I'm messenger, secretary, watchdog, cleaner, cook, slave to every whim.

But you won't hear me harp, leastways not out loud. Think how dull life would be without his Lordship upstairs fretting little details. Besides, he's like a son, my Sherl. I'd expect him to regard me as a mother in the absence of his own.

Astonishing, the things I've heard when there's a client up there. Amazing how much one can hear with a tumbler pressed against the door. Wonder if *he's* conversant with that tactic.

Guess he's up there cogitating over the case of his late-night caller. No decency in a man, especially one in such an agitated state, turning up on the doorstep at one in the morning. Folkestone, he hailed from, according to his card. Come in on the late train. Urgent, he said, standing there jiggling like a fish on a hook. Fortunately, Sherl was still up, though Dr Watson was a tad perturbed at the intrusion to his slumber. Softly spoken the man was, though. I couldn't hear a blessed word – tumbler or not.

Breakfast tray is ready. Scones in the oven. Time to get his Lordship out of bed.

'Mrs Hudson!'

'Golly gosh, Mr Holmes. I didn't hear you come down. Half scared me out of my pinny, you did.'

'No time for breakfast. I'm off to–'

'Folkestone?'

'Why, yes. A singular case, if I'm not mistaken. I expect to be absent for two, maybe three days.'

'But Mr Holmes, you'll miss the Jubilee celebrations.'

'Mrs Hudson, you think that I, who have had private audiences with Ma'am more than once, would deign to join a throng of the great unwashed to pay respects?'

'But 60 years, Mr Holmes.'

He flicks up his hands; his signal of nonchalance.

'And Dr Watson?'

'Will accompany me.'

'That's more eggs for me, then.'

He's already out the door when I hear Watson's footfalls on the stairs. I reciprocate his lapdog expression with a shrug.

I'm replete – who wouldn't be after eating six eggs – when there's a knock at the front door. I barely have the door open when a young man, clad in dark clothes and cap and reeking of horse manure, brushes past me into the entry.

'I need to see Sherlock 'olmes on a pressin' matter.' He's panting like a steam train.

'You've just missed him. He won't be back for three days.'

The chappy looks set to crumple, falls against the wall to support himself. 'Oh, wot?? 'e's 'er only 'ope.'

'Her? Who?'

''er Majesty's.'

'Victoria herself? Goodness. You'd better come in, sit, calm down. I'll brew some tea.'

'No time for that. I 'aveta–'

'Come now. Ten minutes for a cuppa will calm those nerves.' He sits, wild-eyed, wringing his hands. 'Now, I'll have you know that one cannot live in such proximity to England's foremost detective, without some of his expertise rubbing off. Tell me all.'

'I fink there's trouble brewin' for the Queen's Diamond Jubilee tomorrah.'

'How could you know this?'

'I'm a groom at the Royal Mews. This mornin' all the Lord Chamberlain's Department and the Master of the 'Orse 'ad to gather behind the palace. A nuisance too, 'cos we're all working flat ah to get sorted for the procession.'

'What was the import of this congregation?'

'Someone half-inched one of the Queen's jewels.'

'And a member of the staff is suspected?'

'Yer.'

'How does this involve you? Should not the Queen's guards investigate?'

'Prob'ly, but if I could finish...'

'Ah huh.'

'I couldn't sleep last night, worried about today, so went to check on the stables and I heard two folks talkin'. That dodgy beggar, Georgie Bent, havin' a chinwag with a miss out in the forecourt. She says, "I got it and Ma'am hasn't missed it." Then Georgie says, "serves 'er right. I could kill 'er, for treatin' you so poor". Then she gave 'im somethin' real small. He kisses 'er and off she trots.'

'Which way did she go?'

'Back to the palace.'

'Did you know this girl?'

'Not to speak to, but I think she's one o' the Queen's ladies.'

'Can you describe her?'

'Tall, skinny. It was dark, but she 'ad a blotch on 'er cheek.'

'What happened then?'

'I followed Bent back to the Mews. I snuck up be'ind 'im at the stables and asked, "Whatcha got there, Georgie?" He jumps like spring-heeled Jack and stuffs whatever she gave 'im into 'is mouth.'

'Goodness. Did he swallow it?'

'I dunno, 'cos he clobbered me. Next thing I knew, I woke up in the stables in time for this mornin's muster.'

'Was Georgie there?'

'Nah. I reckon he done a bunk. But his girl was there, lookin' guilty as sin.'

'Did you tell anyone?'

'Only me Dad. I worried I'd get in trouble, but Dad's a high-up coachman in the Mews, so I thought 'e'd know what to do. Dad said 'e'd look round for Bent, and sent me to fetch Mr 'olmes. The Great Detective 'elped the old man out of a pickle, once, so Dad trusts 'im. I ran the whole way 'ere and I gotta be back quick smart or they might think I 'ad a hand in it.'

'I see how Mr Holmes would be of service. But in his absence, we shall resort to the closest option. Now lad, you be off back to work assured that I'm on the case.'

'But what can *you* do?'

'You'd be surprised. As it happens, I'm no stranger to the palace. Sometimes lad, it's not what you know, but *who* you know. One more thing. Your name?'

'William Churcher.'

'And your father?'

'He's William Churcher too.'

I dash off a telegram to my favourite former subordinate, Lily Martin, bidding her to meet me at Grosvenor Square at one o'clock. One does not serve as a Lady of the Bedchamber for five years without maintaining close acquaintance with those still in service. Lily, astute as she is, will doubtlessly be happy to impart any inside gossip, given the circumstances. I *should* send another to Folkestone, ahead of Sherl's arrival, but where's the fun in that? I *do* send one to Mr William Churcher Senior, care of The Royal Mews.

Now, I have investigating to do.

As I enter the upstairs quarters, I'm overcome with the smell. Another of Sherl's noxious experiments left gurgling on his desk. I snuff out the Bunsen burner. I swear that one of these days he'll burn the house down or blind an eye in an explosion like Bunsen himself. Even Dr Watson hadn't thought to douse it. I'm hoping Sherl didn't take his morning newspaper.

Ah, there it is. Plenty about the Jubilee. I see the Queen will be entertaining Archduke Franz Ferdinand, among other dignitaries, at a banquet this evening, and there's all the details of tomorrow's procession. No mention of anything amiss in the Royal Household though. I nod my respects to Victoria, framed on the wall, before I head downstairs.

I arrive at Grosvenor Square, a little puffed from the 20-minute walk. Lily's there already, in our usual seat.

'Whatever's the matter, Mrs Hudson? Your telegram was urgent, but I can spare only half an hour. Her Majesty is in quite a dither.'

'So I believe. Something precious has been stolen, I gather.'

'How could you know?'

'I'll get to that. What was it?'

'Her sapphire brooch. The one Prince Albert gave her for their wedding. She was planning to wear it tomorrow. It's her favourite piece. Must be worth a few bob.'

'Goodness. Thousands of bobs, I should think. Now, tell me, is there a girl in the Queen's employ with a birthmark on her cheek?'

'That'd be Mary Havers. She's the newest Lady of the Bedchamber. Only been there a month. Clumsy girl. Not at all to Ma'am's liking. I believe she was threatened with dismissal just yesterday.'

'Do you know if she is acquainted with one of the grooms? A young man named Georgie Bent.'

'Couldn't say, though I had to give her a talking-to last week. A strand of hay she had in her hair.'

'Interesting. Now, I need your help. Keep your eyes on Miss Havers like a hawk. Let me know, post-haste, if she behaves curiously.'

I'm almost clear out of breath when I reach The Mews, but I'm right on time. I presume the man loitering there is Mr Churcher. When he addresses me by name, I'm proved correct.

'My son was right, Mrs Hudson. Georgie Bent has scarpered. I've searched the entire Mews. Such a shame that Mr Holmes ain't here to investigate. He's an expert in averting scandals.'

'True. But unbeknownst to him, I have considerable investigative talent myself. Might you know where Georgie lived before joining the Royal staff?'

'He's at Lennox Gardens– number 43.'

'Thank you. Please inform me should he return to the Royal Mews.'

My steps are positively flagging as I approach the Bent residence – a slim three-storey building with an arched portal – but I get no reply to my knock. Luckily, a neighbour leaving his house renders assistance.

'If he's not at home or at The Mews, most likely he's at Newhaven Tavern,' he says.

I swear I'll have worn my shoes out by the time I'm home again, but fortunately, the tavern is along my northerly route. I'm in need of an ale myself once I arrive. I'm smattered with queer looks as I enter; after all, it's unfitting for a woman to be in a hotel alone. But I'm a brave one. The bartender eyes me with contempt, and refuses my request for an ale, but when I tell him I'm an emissary of the great Sherlock Holmes, he's all ears.

'You've not long missed Bent,' he says. 'Left twenty minutes ago after downing two pints and nattering about seeing a man about a dog.'

'Do you know where?'

'Nah.'

He's not far away then, but he could have gone anywhere. The trail has run cold.

I unlock the door and wonder about the smell. Goodness. The scones. I dash to the stove, armed with a cloth, and open the door. I wave my hands wildly to dissipate the smoke, and pull out the tray. Appears I've invented charcoal dumplings. Won't be telling Sherl that *I* nearly burned the house down.

Revived by a cuppa, I head upstairs. I've got to thinking about the adventure of the Blue Carbuncle, so entertainingly retold by Dr Watson. Perhaps, like the errant goose in Watson's account, young Georgie *did* swallow the gem, though I imagine doing so might cause some discomfort. I rummage through Sherl's archives and find his notebook on famous jewels. He does like to be in the know about such things, and *I* need to know what I'm looking for. I skim past his entries for the Blue Carbuncle, the Hope Diamond, the Koh-i-Noor Diamond and the Black Prince's Ruby to find his entry on Her Majesty's sapphire brooch. It must be a beauty. *A deep blue oval sapphire, surrounded by 12 brilliant diamonds set in gold. Measuring more than one-and-a-half inches long and almost as wide.* And, as Lily said, a wedding gift from her late husband.

Of course! I look at her portrait, and there it is, sparkling on her ample bosom. A beauty indeed.

What to do now? What would Sherl do now? I can't solve the case here. Aha. I have it. I know Dr Watson won't mind my snooping in his room. No point trying Sherl's wardrobe; he's too tall and slim. I pull a tired pair of trousers, Watson's old, favourite tweed coat and his scuffed brogues from the wardrobe and search in his drawers for a flannel shirt. Satisfied, I head into Sherl's ever-messy room and select a moustache from his box of theatrical disguises atop his tallboy and snatch his deerstalker from the hatstand. Somebody might as well get use of it.

Back downstairs, I nod to myself in the mirror. I dab my fingers into the freshly baked charcoal and spread some on my cheeks.

The cab deposits me at the end of Lennox Gardens Mews – no way was I walking again – and I saunter, head down, towards number 43. Who's to know when, or if, the lad might appear? I could be in for a long night. I perch on a low fence, overhung with shrubbery, opposite, as though taking a breather, but with eyes darting in all directions. There's not much activity on the street. Fortunately, I've brought a book.

Ten minutes go by. I see a man approach from Milner Street – too old to be my quarry. He nods. 'Evening sir,' he says as he passes. I say 'evening' back in the deepest voice I can muster. He doesn't break his stride; my disguise must be convincing.

Three hours pass with no sign of Bent, though others bid me good evening. I marvel at Sherl's patience at endless hours of surveillance. I can't help being a bit fidgety. It's near nine o'clock; the sky darkening into night.

Aha! Someone's coming. Slouching and weaving like a tosspot. He props in front of number 43 and fumbles for a key. I spring from my roost and cross the street in six paces. Hearing my footsteps, he turns. Bleary eyes can't focus on me.

'Georgie Bent,' I say, most authoritatively. 'Hand over the jewel!'

'Huh? is all he can say.

'The brooch. I know you have it.'

The sharp kick in my crotch has me doubled over. As I regain my composure, he bolts down the street, fast as a jackrabbit.

Blast. No way I'll catch him; not in these sloppy shoes. And not likely that he'll return now he knows I'm onto him. At least I got a look at his face; dark hair, dark eyes, crook nose and two-day stubble. Nothing for it now but to retire home and await tomorrow.

Being that it's a right royal day, I'm up early. I open the front door and call out to young Billy, the page, for the morning paper, then scan it while tucking into my porridge. I'm thinking that Her Majesty might be a target – a sitting duck, if you will – during her procession from Buckingham Palace to St Paul's Cathedral. Paper says thousands of onlookers slept in the parks outside the palace walls or took up position along the route last night. Thousands more will join them later this morning. I respond to a knock on the door and take delivery of a telegram. Some intelligence perhaps.

Lily's brief message is telling.

Mary Havers dismissed this morning. Swears retribution! Lily.

Dressed in my finest outfit, I hail a cab outside number 221B and direct the driver to take me to Holborn Road. I can't be everywhere and can only pray that no injury befalls Ma'am en route. I had prayed for sunshine for Ma'am, but alas the clouds hang like shrouds.

I alight from the cab near Farringdon Street, which is choked with spectators. I employ my elbows to bustle through – all the way down to Ludgate Hill. It's a festive sight, with Union Jacks draped from balconies, bunting rainbows and festoons of flowers overhead, upper-storey windows filled with beaming faces. An explosion of colour to rob the city of its usual soot-grey hues. Much chanting of God Save the Queen. I struggle to acknowledge that it's ten years since the pomp of Her Majesty's Golden Jubilee. I press my way left into Ludgate Hill, with barely room to move; the crowd lining the street is held at bay by a fence of red-jacketed soldiers, their bayonets forming an impenetrable palisade.

Twenty minutes of shoving, grunting, puffing – toes smarting from being stepped upon – I finally take up a splendid vantage point opposite St Paul's west steps, though eye-to-eye with a horse's behind. I'll have to wait an hour. I scan the crowd for possible suspects, though it's difficult to see past the press of horse flesh and waving Union Jacks. The cathedral steps are choked with clergy, Tower of London Warders and white-gowned choristers, some poised atop pedestals halfway up. I feel the comfort of the weapon in my deep pocket; knowing I'll be ready to deploy it in defence of the Queen should the situation warrant – regardless of the consequences to me. I ponder what Sherl would do in such an instance. I pray that my return telegram to the palace, earlier pressed into the hand of the Telegraph Office's delivery boy, has the Queen's guards on high alert.

At 11.15 on the dot, just as the paper had said, a great boom startles the crowd into silence and then immediately draws cheers. A cannon fired from the palace heralds the departure of the Queen's procession. As though dispelled by the sound, the clouds lift and the sun emerges, bathing the scene in sunlit tones. I expect it will be a while before the 17-carriage cortège arrives, following its circuitous route down The Mall, doglegging onto Westminster Bridge, along Borough Road and Borough High Street, across London Bridge into King William Street and through Cheapside into Cannon Street. The crowd is restless and expectant; faces are painted with patriotic smiles.

Twenty minutes down and I hear cheers erupting, eastwards along Cannon Street. Wish I was atop a horse to see the approaching spectacle. At last, I spy the first of Ma'ams eight cream horses, stately and resplendent in their ornate regalia, as they draw to a halt in front of the steps. I squash between two horses and stand on tippy-toes. There sits Ma'am in her gold carriage, dressed in her usual mourning black, partly obscured by her daughters-in-law, Princess Christian and Princess Alexandra, and her own white parasol. She waves sedately to the crowd – the sea of loyal subjects before her. It has been reported in the papers that she was averse to a Jubilee celebration, but had acquiesced to Colonial Secretary Joseph Chamberlain's suggestion that it double as a Festival of the British Empire. She looks happy enough now though, if that's what passes for a smile.

Five full minutes of cheering and clapping almost strike me deaf. Ma'am has not yet alighted from her carriage. I nudge the leg of the mounted soldier beside me. 'Is she not getting out?'

He peers down at me. 'Too decrepit,' he responds. 'The rheumatism would not allow her to scale the steps.'

Poor Ma'am. Age weakens and slows us all. Not so when she was younger and would slap my arm quicker than a falling guillotine if I laced her corset too tightly. Lost in reverie, I almost forget my mission. I scrutinise the crowd again. I peer around under the horse's neck to my left and see it. A pistol, wavering in unsteady hands, aimed directly at Ma'am. Without ado, I draw the rolling pin from my pocket, step under the horse's neck, and thwack it down on the gunman's wrists. The gun discharges. I swing around, fearful that I've failed to protect her.

Fortunately, Ma'am is intact, though she does *not* look amused. The princesses are cowering in their seats, hands on heads. All eyes are on me and the lad wailing at my feet. I can't help but laugh. He's shot himself in the foot.

He's quickly pounced upon by a half-dozen soldiers, who pin him to the ground. I look at the girl standing behind him; she's covering her mouth – and her large strawberry birthmark – with her hand. She's wild-eyed and rooted to the spot. She turns, tries to run, but is quickly nabbed by two spectators.

'An assassination attempt,' one of the soldiers says, stating the obvious.

'He's a thief as well,' I say. 'His name is Georgie Bent, and bent he is. And this one,' I eye the girl, 'Mary Havers, I believe, is in cahoots with him. Tell him to produce the Queen's brooch forthwith.'

'But I ain't got it,' Bent mumbles.

'I trust you haven't fenced it.'

'No, I never.'

'Then where is it?'

'A man cornered me last night. Knew I had it. I had to get rid of it. I took it back to the Royal Mews.'

'Why there, on earth?'

He doesn't answer, but I suspect I know. 'Ah, I see, to implicate somebody else. Divert the blame from your lover here.' The girl drops her eyes, so I know I'm on the money.

One of the soldiers eyes me suspiciously. 'Who are you madam, that you're privy to such knowledge?'

Gawd, I wanted no public acclamation, but I can't lie. 'I am landlady to Mr Sherlock Holmes.'

'Ah. Big shoes to fill. Is he present here?'

'No, sir. He's down Folkestone way.'

'Well, madam, you have done Her Majesty a great service. You can leave this pair to us and the constabulary now. We'll wring the truth from them.'

There's a touch on my arm. A soldier bends to whisper in my ear. 'Her Majesty requests an audience.'

Oh, good Lord. I cross the road to her carriage. She looks me up and down, beady-eyed as always, though not disapprovingly.

'We should like to meet our saviour,' she says.

I curtsy. 'Ma'am.'

She peers at me imperiously, then softens her gaze. 'Goodness me,' she says, 'Murgatroyd Mather. It's some years since you left Our service.'

I'm surprised she's recognised me. Not since I left her employ has anyone, save for my short-lived husband, Horace, called me by my first name. I'm tempted to address her as Drina, but that's a touch too familiar. 'Yes, Ma'am. Thirty-three to be precise. I am now Mrs Hudson, though widowed.'

'Ah yes. Mr Holmes has spoken of you, though he never apprised me of your assistance in his detective work.'

'Oh no, Ma'am. He doesn't know of it.'

Ma'am laughs, silently I might say, and winks...yes, winks. 'Let's see if we can keep a secret.'

'Yes, Ma'am. I do hope your treasure will be returned to you before the day is out.'

'We live in hope. But now, we must allow the ceremonies to continue.'

I curtsy again and start to back away, alongside the right, rear horse. And I see it. Glinting incongruously on a blue circle on the horse's ceremonial coat – right there for thousands to see, but not notice. The diamonds dazzle in the sunlight; the sapphire blue as a deep ocean. I unpin it carefully and approach Her Majesty's carriage again. Her head is turned towards the proceedings, but Princess Alexandra spies it in my hand and whispers to Ma'am. I pass it to her and her eyes widen in disbelief.

'It was right there, pinned to the horse's coat,' I tell her, just as surprised.

'Good heavens.' She kisses it, as lovingly as if it were Albert himself.

I'm pulled away by a soldier and meld back into the crowd. The Archbishop of Canterbury resumes his speech as I'm resuming my composure. The choir sings a Te Deum and then it's all over; the cortège departing to the Archbishop's cry of, 'Three cheers for the Queen.' Strains of God Save the Queen echo from Fleet Street as the procession wends its way back to the palace.

I'm soon caught up in the revelry. Sir Thomas Lipton has generously sponsored free food for 400,000 of London's poorest, along with free bottles of ale and pipe tobacco, though I don't fancy partaking of any of that largesse. I hear those Temperance Movement souls are vexed that the pubs will be open until 2.30 in the morning. I shall have been long in bed by then, but for now I'm happy to join in the festivities. I'm swept into a merry dance in the middle of the street by a frock-coated stranger and discarded as quickly as he nabs another partner. I swear my leg is bruised from the rolling pin banging against it. A handy weapon, it turned out to be.

Not a cab to be had. I contemplate taking the underground home, but suspect it will be too jolly crowded, so anticipate with dread a 90-minute walk home, which will undoubtedly test my mettle. I'll be pleased to kick off these jolly shoes, which weren't designed for three-mile strolls, and attend to the blisters on my heels. At least I've only to cook for myself tonight.

The *Pall Mall Gazette* and two telegrams, one for Sherl and one for me, await my arrival. I deposit his on the hall table and open mine.

We are grateful that one attended with her rolling pin today. A reward awaits. Drina.

Goodness gracious. From the Queen herself. Am I more surprised at the mention of a reward, or that she signed it Drina?

I nestle into my armchair with a hot cuppa, intent on perusing the *Gazette,* but I'm struggling to keep my eyes open; it's been such a tiring day.

I am snapped awake by the click of the door to my own apartment and am surprised to see Sherl and Dr Watson there. I tuck the paper down the side of the cushion.

'Mr Holmes, I wasn't expecting–'

'The case was a trifle. Solved overnight. No need for us to tarry longer. Tea, if you will.' He's in the hall and halfway up the stairs to 221B before I answer.

'Of course.' Evidently, he's unaware of the day's events; else he'd have mentioned it.

Sherl is already in his brocade dressing gown and slippers, sitting smugly in his armchair when I enter with the tea tray. I can't read his expression, though Watson looks much as one would if trying not to break wind. Not a word is spoken. I place the tray on the table and hand Sherl his cup.

'Come, sit, Mrs Hudson.' I confess I'm a little taken aback; his directive a first. 'Regale us with your impressions of the Jubilee celebrations.'

I'm almost struck dumb. He doesn't know. What to say? 'Oh, it was a wonderful day, Mr Holmes. Grander even than the 50th Jubilee; so much colour and excitement.'

'It rather sounds, Watson, that we missed a spectacle indeed.'

'It certainly does, Holmes.'

Sherl steeples his fingers in front of his mouth, as though hiding a smirk. 'Pray continue, Mrs Hudson.'

'Gosh, Mr Holmes, what more can I say?'

'Might I suggest that you start with how you came to be there armed with a rolling pin?'

I gasp. I open my mouth but words fail me. 'You thought you could keep your little escapade a secret?'

I'm still dumbstruck. 'I, I–'

'Can I not go away for two days without you assuming to take up my mantle? Allow me to read the headline in the *Gazette*. SHERLOCK HOLMES' LANDLADY SAVES THE QUEEN.'

'Oh, good Lord.'

'The cab driver filled us in on your exploits on the way from Waterloo. This article merely expands on that.'

'Oh, you scoundrel, Mr Holmes. You appeared oblivious when you arrived home.'

'Mrs Hudson, I am *never* oblivious.'

'Forgive me, sir.'

'What we *don't* know is how you came to be a part of this adventure – masquerading as a detective.'

I tell them the full story, from the moment the distressed young William Churcher crossed the threshold, until the moment Ma'am's carriage departed the cathedral. All the while, Sherl's expressions fluctuate from vexed to stern to humoured to astonished – and back again.

'Marvellous! And that explains my missing moustache.' Sherl's applause prompts Watson to follow suit.

'Extraordinary,' Watson says. 'You might need to be careful Holmes, that Mrs Hudson does not eclipse your reputation for crime solving.'

'Poppycock. Beginner's luck, I'm sure.'

I can't contain myself. 'It was such fun, though I found those trousers of yours somewhat scratchy doctor, and your hat, Mr Holmes, a little small for my head. Oh, and can you believe it, I received a telegram from the Queen. I gather she is planning a reward.'

Sherl stifles a grin and picks up the telegram from his side table. 'As it happens, I am also in receipt of a telegram from Her Majesty.' He pauses for what seems like forever. Rotten sod, drawing it out like this. 'I am to escort you to Buckingham Palace tomorrow.' My mouth falls open. 'Do be careful, Mrs Hudson. You would not want to be caught agape if the wind were to change.'

'Oh, Mr Holmes, you try my patience.' He's loving this, I can tell.

'It would appear that the Queen intends to endow you with her new Royal Victorian Order – the one she can personally bestow for services performed on her behalf.'

Now I'm truly speechless. I fear my mouth might form an "O" for life.

Sherl has a glint in his eye. 'It will remain to be seen Watson, whether we shall, in future, be compelled to address our landlady as "Dame Murgatroyd".'

VICTORY OF KYRNOS

'THE BOKANS WERE COMING THICK AND FAST. THE ONLY THING standing between them and Huxley, Deacon and me was...me. It wasn't our job to guard the cache but we had no choice. The depot guard had left already, leaving us to finish loading the zy-pod. Mylan had recalibrated my Rizer gun. Damn thing would only shoot straight and, as you know, that's as useful as firing marshmallows at the Trojan army. To counteract those bastard Bokans, with their goddamned breakdance moves, you need a weapon with a reliable arc trajectory. You know, aim at their front, hit 'em in the back. It's their only soft spot. But we only had the one; Huxley and Deacon were unarmed.'

Milla eyed me across the table with her unilens. I wished she'd put on her frontisplate. It was so distracting; that left bottom breast pointing at the floor and swaying like a divining rod. 'So what happened next?'

If I knew that, we wouldn't be standing here with Huxley and Deacon's inert bodies on the slab between us. 'Beats me. I opened fire and I know I hit at least seven of them. Enough purple serum flew into the air to show I'd downed a few anyway. But when I fired a second time, nothing much happened. They were still coming. When I turned to ask Huxley to hand me the radargogs, he was flat on his back. And Deacon. Those pinholes appeared all over them, yet as you can see, no blood. I couldn't do a damn thing.'

'Do the Bokans have new weapons? Something we haven't seen before?'

'Don't know. Can't figure how they missed me. Hell, I was the only line of defence; the only one firing at them. Yet they missed me and got them even though they were behind me.'

Milla unzipped Huxley's zetashirt. His torso was dotted like an old Braille text. 'Nothing for it but to open him up. Hand me that scalpel.'

I obliged but turned away. I didn't need to see my closest ally sliced and diced.

'Oh,' she said, 'you didn't know he was a Morpho?'

What? How could I have not known that minor detail? Seven years and I'd never seen him out of uniform. I still didn't want to look. But I had to. The grey blubber protruding from the incision was patent. That, and the missing navel. It explained a lot really. 'No. I didn't know.'

'Which means–'

'Deacon is too.' That didn't bother me so much. He'd never struck me as a paragon of humanity.

'How did you get away?'

'Afraid to say I took the coward's exit. I didn't stand a chance on my own, so I ran like a gazelle to the vanocraft and–'

'Vanished.'

'Yep. But I hovered overhead. Watched them skulk off with every darn scrap of thyonite.'

'Bugger.'

'I'll say. Which means they'll be able to refuel their VKs and come after us.'

'How long do you think we have?'

I mentally calculated the coordinates and the time required to liquefy the thyonite. 'Eighteen, twenty hours. Best guess.'

'Shit. We're going to have to get your Rizer sorted if that's all you've got. Hang on.' Milla drummed her digoids on the table. 'Show it to me.'

I unslung it and handed it to her. She drew the unilens from her forehead, tweaked it with her digoids and scanned the weapon. 'Uh oh.'

Didn't sound good. 'What?'

'See this here? It's back-shot.' She pointed to its arse end and retracted her unilens. 'Hate to tell you this Nike, but this is what killed them. It's been tampered with.'

So I'd killed my own confederates. 'Bloody hell. But how? *Mylan*. I'll kill the bastard.'

'Told you not to trust him.'

'But why would he sabotage us? What would he gain?'

'Good question. Let's go find out.' She minced to the door and tapped the code. It slid up, sucking the breath out of me. I should be used to the pressure change after so long but it got me every time. I followed her through, careful not to step on her quagswagging tail. It was a hike around to the armaments and munitions pod, one involving a sixty metre traverse of the great Kyrnos outdoors, which meant a ten minute stop for me to don my zetagear while Milla attached her breastplate. Should have taken a tubemeal. I was hungry enough to eat a valliddon.

It was blustery outside and the green dust quickly caked my mask. I flicked the automatic visor-wipe on. What was Mylan up to? Had he intended to get me killed? We passed through the three-way entry and I was relieved to pull off my helmet. We trundled around the maze of corridors towards Mylan's weapons repair workshop. It was strangely quiet. Not a sound aside from the skittering of the pesky orters along the wall. Bigger than tarantulas, these hairy motherfuckers. I knocked on his door. No answer. I pressed his thg code into my wristich and waited. No response. Where was the sod? Avoiding me? Just when I was busting for a confrontation. Bugger.

Milla stooped to the touchpad, pressed her unilens to it and the door snapped open.

'Never knew you could do that.'

'It's got a short-circuit feature.'

'So much for security.'

The workshop was a mess. Looked like someone had ransacked it with a VaeloRod. The floor was littered with broken Rizers, Flo-guns and unidentifiable shards of plastic and metal. Milla scanned the room and zoned in on a monitor which strangely was the only thing apparently working.

I sidled up beside her.

'I don't recognise this code. These symbols are foreign to me. Can't decipher them.'

'Looks Greek to me.' I wasn't saying that flippantly. It really did look like Greek characters. How did I know that?

'What's that?'

'Greek? It was one of our Earth languages. One of the oldest in fact. Not used of late by anyone other than scholars and those few remaining of Greek descendancy.' Like me. *So I'm Greek? How do I suddenly know that?*

'Peculiar. Can you read it?'

'Enough to know bad news when I see it.' Was it an incoming or outgoing message? I tapped the monitor. Outgoing. Recipient, Xenos Varatassi. Who the fuck was Xenos Varatassi? 'Ever heard of Xenos Varatassi?'

Milla looked blank. 'Is that a person?'

'Beats me. Greek name.'

'What does it say?'

'Closest translation is, "*Thyonite secured. Resistance neutralised. Bokans idol. Retrieval at 3900 hours, grid U34B*".' So, Mylan *was* a traitor. Stupid fool. Did he not know the penalty for treason? Banishment to Eephos was not something to aspire to. But the message raised more questions than it answered. What was the Bokans' idol? And was it the thyonite or Mylan—or both—being retrieved? And by whom? And since when did Mylan speak Greek?

Milla did a thing with her proboscis that made me think of elephants. Weird. Prior to today, I had no recollection of elephants, or gazelles or tarantulas for that matter. 'You don't think Mylan speaks Greek?'

'Stop reading my mind.'

'Sorry. Transparent.'

I checked my wristich. 'Looks like we've got to get to U34B within two hours.'

'We'll have to fire up the Helicon.'

'The only way. Only it better not get a dose of the hiccups this time.'

'You talk so funny.'

I snapped an image of the screen. Something about the message didn't click. 'Do you need a weapon? We could maybe salvage something here.' I grabbed another Rizer gun which appeared to be intact. Hopefully it would fire forwards, not backwards.

'Do you forget I have these?' Milla rolled up the loose plates on her top forearms revealing a veritable arsenal of wicked missiles.'

'Oh. You know how to use them?'

'Of course. Just never had to.'

Great. Going to battle with a novice Zircoid. We headed back down the corridor. Milla stopped dead. I smacked into the back of her. 'Did you hear that?'

'What?'

'In there.' She pointed to a storage depot door on the left. 'Moaning.'

'Better investigate.'

She did the same trick with her unilens and we were in. The room was about ten by fifteen metres and filled with rack upon rack of provisions. I scanned each aisle. Nothing. Until the last. There was Mylan, pinned to the wall with flitnails. Which was exactly where he deserved to be. Blood dripped through his intero-suit from each of the spike wounds; each nail as thin as an acupuncture needle, yet barbed to grab the wall like high tension bolts. I presumed his face bore the signs of pain, though, as always, it was obscured by his stupid mask.

'Nike. Thank God. I knew you'd come.'

'I suppose you want me to get you down.'

'Ah, ye-ah.'

'And why should I? After you bloody sabotaged my Rizer and fed me to the Bokans.'

'I what?'

'You know. Don't deny it.'

'I never.'

I don't trust you.

'Me either,' Milla said.

'You're a shit.' I said it in Greek. Waited for his reaction. Either he genuinely didn't understand or he had a flawless poker face. 'Who did this to you?' In English.

'Don't know who they were. Are you going to get me down?'

'Well, were they human, or Morphos, or Bokans or what?'

'I dunno. They came from behind, knocked me out. Next thing I find myself here. Please get me down. I've got an itch.'

'Where?'

He looked at his groin.

'Suffer in your jocks.'

Milla touched me on the elbow. 'We have to go.'

'Don't bloody leave me here.' Mylan was as frantic as an immovable object could be.

'Sorry, but until we've sorted out this mess, you're staying right where you are.'

'What if you don't come back?'

'Why would you think we wouldn't come back? Unless you already know where we're going.'

'I don't...know where you're going.'

'We're going to find Xenos Varatassi.'

'Who the fuck is Xenos Varatassi?'

'You should know. You sent him a message, not two hours ago.'

Mylan looked blank. Again, it could have been a ruse. 'No. I don't believe I did. I haven't even used the computran today. And I don't know anyone called Xenos whatwasit.' He sounded convincing. But if he didn't send the message, who did?

'We'll sort that later.' Milla was prodding me now.

'Okay, okay. Let's go. But we'll have to get back up from the others.'

'No time.'

Fifteen minutes later, we were in the cockpit of the Helicon. A tight squeeze, given how much space Milla's multifarious appendages occupied. I punched the coordinates into the pre-flight programmer, swivelled the joystick to launch position and pressed the "GO" button. Nothing happened. Not even a hiccup. 'Bastard machine.' I retraced the procedure. Nothing.

'Talk to it pretty.' Milla's tone was deadly serious.

Worth a try. 'Sweet, darling Helicon, please start.' I tried again and it whirred to life. Milla gave me a "told you so" look. We hit cruise altitude so abruptly, I was glad I hadn't partaken of a tubemeal after all. The good thing about the Helicon was that, once airborne, it didn't require a helmsman. I could sit back and enjoy the ride. Something about the sensation of the ride made me think of home. *Why?* I remembered nothing about Earth. But now, I was hovering in my Honda glide-o-copter over the wasteland that was Sydney. The waterless harbour. Life after the invasion. The only difference was the colour of the atmosphere around me and my choice of passenger. Liam. Slim, taut and incontrovertibly human, unlike the half-ton Kyrnossian Milla. I could picture him, naked and appetising beside me in bed. Liam, who gave up his life to get me aboard the shuttle and away from the apocalypse.

'He was good looking, your man.'

'Milla, will you knock it off? Just a memory.'

'You are lucky to have memories.'

'I haven't until today. But now, I have memories of a planet that is no longer blue and a man who is no longer...well, no longer.'

'My memory resets every Kyrnos week.'

'Do you mean you remember nothing from three days ago?'

'Nothing.'

No wonder she asked my name so often. 'But you have always told me not to trust Mylan. How can you constantly know that?'

'Naturally, I read his mind. He has scattered memories too. And he was not always called Mylan.'

'Milla, we all changed our names when we came here. So what does Mylan's mind tell you?'

'He has little memory of Earth. Naturally, I remember no more than that, aside from what I gleaned just before.'

'Which was?'

'He did not knowingly impair your Rizer. He does not know Xenos Varatassi. And he is in love with you.'

My head swivelled so quickly I cricked my neck. What to process first? 'He is in love with me?'

'Even a man can't hide that.'

'So it's unlikely he tried to get me killed. And I left the poor bastard nailed to the wall.'

Milla's proboscis twitched, which always meant uncertainty. 'He may have a higher allegiance.'

There's that, of course. 'Or he may not have sent that message.'

'Possible. But then who?'

Yes, who? The Helicon hiccupped, throwing us forward in our seats. The flashing red light indicated it had switched to stealth mode. It started its descent. 'Bloody thing gets me every time.' Milla rubbed the top of her head where it had hit the ceiling. I surveyed the landscape. The only thing that appeared to designate U34B was a slight mound and a couple of parked zy-pods. I looked further afield where a plume of green dust, maybe two kilometres off, indicated movement. I pulled on my radargogs. 'Bugger. Bokans approaching at ten o'clock.' That's when it hit me. What was wrong with the message. I tapped my wristich to bring it up. "ειδωλο"

– meaning "Idol". No way did Mylan send that message. He was too good a speller. A Greek translation wouldn't confuse the words. It should have said "άεργος" – meaning "Idle".

Milla focussed her unilens. 'Not too many though. Maybe a hundred.'

'Guess they're no longer idle.'

I zoomed in on the zy-pods. 'Just two or three defenders on the ground that I can see. Where do you suppose they're taking the thyonite?'

'The most valuable resource in the Universe? My guess is back to Earth.'

'Earth? But why? And how?'

'In that, do you suppose?' Milla pointed directly across my field of vision to the right.

I turned to look. A huge shuttle, not unlike the one in which I had travelled here, loomed large and low, and was lowering its landing gear. 'Holy cow. It's going to hit us.' I poked the manual override button and pushed the joystick forward. We catapulted heavenward like a Harrier Jump Jet on speed. *A Harrier? How did I know that?* The shuttle passed beneath us and landed. 'Shit. Couldn't see us.' I pressed the button again and the Helicon resumed its landing pattern. 'Right, let's go see what the fuck is going on.' I sounded more gung-ho than I was. This could be a really bad idea.

I slung a Rizer over each shoulder while Milla fiddled with her intrinsic weaponry. We covered the ground to the zy-pods in no time. One of the defenders swung around, stunned at our arrival out of nowhere, and aimed his Flo-gun at my face. I aimed my Rizer at his. I did not recognise him. Just another Morpho of indeterminate appearance.

'What are you doing here? And you, Miss Uglyfugs?'

'I could ask you the same thing. What are your intentions?'

He didn't answer. Kept his Flo-gun pointed at me. I whispered to Milla, 'What is he thinking?'

'He's thinking about...Xenos Varatassi,' she whispered.

Fucking Xenos Varatassi. 'Take me to Xenos Varatassi.'

The Morpho's eyes dilated. 'Who? How did...?

'We're mind readers.'

'He is just arriving now.' I turned to see six men approaching from the shuttle; the leader, a tall, muscular figure with a distinctive swagger. They were still 500 metres away. 'Stay right there.' The Morpho headed off towards them, joining the other two defenders who had gone ahead.

I lifted the cover on one of the zy-pods. Ran my fingers through the brown, grainy substance. Not the right consistency. 'If this is thyonite, I'll eat my hat.'

Milla probed a digoid into the stuff. 'You're right. Chemical and geological reading does not indicate thyonite.'

'So what's going on? Someone's trying to pull a swifty here.' I'd no sooner said it, than I felt something stick into my back. I swung around. The Flo-gun was now aimed at my chest. A fourth Morpho. Hadn't figured that.

His ultra-visor was down; his face unrecognisable. But his suit was pocked with pinholes. Deacon?

'Deacon. You arsehole. You're dead.'

'That was what I wanted you think.'

Stupid, stupid me. We didn't get to check his body. 'But how did you get here?' Then the penny dropped. 'It was you. *You* collected the Rizer from Mylan for me. *You* doctored it. *You* killed Huxley, or planned it that I would, and then what, pretended to be dead?'

He nodded. 'He would have foiled my plans. It should have killed you too. Your survival was not intended.'

'And your plan is...what? To send these humans back to Earth with worthless dirt?'

'Something like that. The Bokans have a greater need.'

'So you're in league with the Bokans. That's why they're advancing. They're almost here.'

'They have other plans for you humans.'

'Which is what?'

'You will see.'

And I did. The Bokans spun themselves into a whirlwind, surrounding the approaching visitors in a blur of dust. Milla reacted before I did. She was off like a kangaroo, bounding towards the fray, arming herself in transit with all manner of projectiles. Poetry in motion and far superior to my Rizers. Conscious that Deacon undoubtedly still had his Flo-gun zoned in on my back, I bolted after her. A Flo-gun might work against Bokans, but not against my zetagear, so I felt safe enough. By the time we reached the melee, three humans were down. I propped to aim my Rizer and opened fire on the Bokans on the fringe. Took out half a dozen with a single shot. Milla cast a net from her wrist arsenal like a Spiderman clone and caught a dozen; their globular bodies frying in the electric current. She repeated the manoeuvre, leaving another mass of puce slime that was once Bokans. The human visitors' rudimentary weapons were useless against their assailants. The three still on their feet had no option but to try to outrun them.

'Leave them to us,' I yelled. Their leader acknowledged with an "okay" gesture and they took off sideways, keeping their heads down. I fired again and punched the air with glee as another ten Bokans erupted. More fun than *Space Invaders.*

Milla fired a barrage of shit – razor strings, flitbombs and stun darts – and, just like that, the Bokans were history.

But our victory was short-lived. We turned to see the Morphos circling the visitors; their Flo-guns trained on their chests. *Bugger.* 'Can you take out the two on the left?' I whispered. 'Leave fucking Deacon to me. Aim for their knees though. I want them alive. They deserve a worse punishment than death.'

The words had barely left my mouth when two Morphos bit the dust clutching their knees. I liked a girl who didn't muck around. I took out the third with my Rizer, leaving only Deacon standing. We both had him in our sights. 'Drop your weapon, Deacon.'

Outgunned, he dropped it immediately. The lead human picked it up and aimed it at Deacon.

'Thank goodness for you two,' the man said as I stepped beside him. 'What's going on?'

'My best guess is that these rogues have abrogated their responsibility to defend us humans. They have sided with the Bokans to prevent you taking the thyonite. Those pods are filled with worthless dirt.'

'Where is Mylan? Is he behind this ambush?'

'I thought so, but now, I believe not. He's sort of indisposed though.' I spoke in Greek.

He answered in Greek, 'You have done well. And you.' He nodded to Milla, who looked blank. 'Allow me to introduce myself. I am–'

'Xenos Varatassi.'

'Yes.'

'So is the thyonite your only reason for coming here? What use is it on Earth?'

'We have learned that one grain of thyonite can recreate one hundred litres of water.'

'You're kidding me.'

'I would not kid you, Nicola.'

I was stunned. *That* was my name. 'You know my name.'

He pressed his hand gently on my shoulder. 'I should. I gave it to you.'

Huh? 'Dad?' He swept me up into a familiar hug. 'I don't believe it. I thought you were dead.'

'Sorry. I had to make you believe that or you would not have left.'

'You're damn right about that.'

'I didn't want you to see the Earth turn to shit.'

'Fair enough. So...are you staying here?'

'Only for as long as it takes my remaining colleagues, Stefan and George,' he said by way of introduction, 'to load the thyonite and for me to conduct an inquiry. We need to know whether the Morphos have malfunctioned.' My dad, always the lawyer.

'Well this ought to be proof of that. Deacon appears to be the brains behind this shemozzle.'

'We have reason to believe that the issue is systemic, that they have been manipulating the human cell here for some years.'

'How?'

'That's what we need to find out. But part of the reason that the 50 of you were chosen to evacuate Earth was to procreate and yet, as I am sure you are aware, there has been not one live birth in seven years.'

All those failed pregnancies. 'Yes, you're right. We'd all put it down to the atmosphere or whatever.'

Dad shook his head. 'They have been systematically wiping your memories of Earth and, we suspect, interfering with your reproductive cycles.'

'But that's weird, because just today, I have had snatches of memory from Earth.'

'That, my dear, is because we were in range and able to override your memo-chip.'

'Oh. I have a memo-chip?'

'They were designed only to erase bad memories, but it appears the Morphos have tweaked them.'

I eyed Deacon. He could not return my gaze. 'Is this true, Deacon?'

He stared at the ground. Didn't answer. That said it all.

'Well Dad, let me show you some Kyrnos hospitality. We'll go back to base in the Helicon and I'll shout you a gryphos.'

'We can do better than that. We've brought beer.'

'Beer? There's no fresh water on Earth, yet they're still making beer?'

'There's still Arctic ice, but it's fast receding.'

'So life's not all bad there.'

Dad turned to George. 'You guys follow in the shuttle. We'll find the thyonite later. Better take those three with you.' He pointed to the downed shuttle crew.

George nodded and motioned to Stefan to follow him.

'Right, got to get these pricks on board.' Dad and Milla helped me squash Deacon and the other Morphos into the Helicon's cargo hold and then Dad squeezed himself into the rear passenger seat.

We were back at base in no time. The shuttle docked behind us. Milla shambled over to the barrack pod to muster some muscle. I so wanted to grill Deacon but my first mission was to rescue Mylan and get him to Medi-Deck. Milla said she'd meet me there shortly.

Mylan was stroppy. 'Where the hell have you been? I feel like a pin cushion.'

'Sorry, just off saving the Universe.' I twigged. 'You know what a *pin cushion* is?'

'Why wouldn't I?'

'Pin cushions are an Earth thing. Do you remember that?'

'Yeah. I've been having weird recollections for hours.'

'I'll explain why on the way to Medi-Deck. This is going to hurt. I'll have to pull you out a bit to cut those flitnails.'

'I'm brave if you are.'

It was no mean feat, but the razor saw was thin enough to slide down between his back and the wall to cut through the pins. 'Can you walk?'

'I could dance a fandango, whatever that is.'

Milla was ready with her surgical kit when I guided Mylan to the examination table. 'Strip off,' she instructed. She was a fastidious surgeon, but not so hot on bedside manner.

Mylan looked reluctant.

'Come on. I'll help.' I unzipped his inter-suit. This was a first. I'd never seen him in the flesh. I pulled the suit down off his shoulders from behind. His flesh was creamy olive and toned like an athlete. I resisted the urge to run my fingers down his back. It reminded me of...

He turned and spoiled the moment. But only for as long as it took me to survey his buff torso and an appendix scar I knew I had seen before. That cute little curly thing I'd kissed a hundred times. 'Oh my God. Get that bloody mask off.'

'It's not a pretty sight.'

'I have a strong stomach.'

He peeled the prosthetic mask up from under his chin. His face was a mess of scar tissue, but underneath was the familiar square-set jaw and pronounced cheekbones. I laughed. Then I cried. Then I flung my arms around him. 'Liam!' He reeled backwards as though hit with a battering ram. He looked quizzical and shook his head. 'Liam, it's me, Nicola.' Still no recognition.

I remembered seeing the aliens' heat ray explode beside him as the shuttle door slammed and he fell to the ground. I had presumed he was dead. And then...I'd lost all memory of him. As he had of me.

Milla lowered him onto the table. 'Go find him. Your father.'

I nodded and bolted out the door. I found Dad in a cubicle by the communications room; Deacon chained to the chair opposite. 'Dad, you've gotta come and override Liam's memo-chip. He doesn't know me.'

Dad, now recognisable without his helmet on, smiled. 'Ah. Yes.'

'Seven frigging years and I never knew it was him. And...hang on. Liam *does* speak Greek. Does he remember that?' *Oh, shit no.* 'Dad, how long have you been communicating with him?'

'Since he arrived here, some weeks after you. That's part of the reason we've come. It was evident that our communications were being intercepted and we suspected the Morphos. Only today's reciprocal messages were in Greek. It was a test to ensure it was Liam. The Morphos wouldn't understand Greek.'

'So the bastard led you straight into an ambush. Telling you the Bokans were *idle* as he put it.'

'Yes, it would appear he set us up, but I can't fathom why.'

'No. It doesn't fit. Besides, he misspelled idle, which is not the Liam I know. Wait, maybe that was deliberate. Maybe he was warning you.'

Dad looked sceptical. Deacon fidgeted and looked away. I addressed him in Greek. 'Deacon, you look uncomfortable.'

He turned slowly. Locked his eyes on mine. 'I do not understand Greek. Mylan sent the message.'

'Yes, but you dictated it, didn't you? With a gun to his head?'

Deacon's annoyance was manifest in his strident voice. 'Yes, I did.'

Dad was annoyed now. 'But you are programmed to defend humans.'

'Depends who's doing the programming.'

'Meaning?'

'You have a traitor among you.'

'Among us where?'

'You should choose your crew more wisely, Xenos.'

'My crew?'

'Go ask Stefan why your mission was doomed to fail from the outset.'

Dad rolled his eyes backward as the realisation struck him. 'Stefan.' He looked at Deacon and then to me. 'Stefan was a last-minute replacement, Nicola. He came to us from Cosmos Lab, the Danish company that developed Morphos and our human memo-chips. He's their chief programmer.'

'So...' I said, 'something's still rotten in the State of Denmark, methinks. And he seemed such an affable bloke.'

Dad rose and pointed at Deacon. 'You stay right there. C'mon Nicola, "One may smile, and smile, and be a villain".' Typical Dad, always quoting Shakespeare.

As we headed to the barracks pod, something occurred to me. 'Danish company? So Denmark is still functional?'

'The remaining population is now resident above fifty degrees north and below fifty degrees south. The aliens can't cut it. Too cold for them.'

'Well I'll be. And I'd figured it'd be our germs that would knock 'em out.'

Dad sniggered. 'I can tell you, a Jipoid with a cold is a funny thing.'

As we entered the pod, it was evident the beer was a hit. Stefan and George were regaling the Kyrnos settlers about the goings-on on Earth. Dad grabbed the back of Stefan's collar and dragged him off his chair. 'As you were,' he said politely to the astonished group.

It was the closest I could come to a family reunion. Liam, Dad, Milla and me, sitting around sinking beers. It was no VB, but it was pretty darn good. Afterwards, Liam and I would tear up the sheets like the old days. Maybe make a baby now that our memo-chips had been replaced. Stefan and Deacon were consigned to solitary confinement, charged with murder, sabotage and treason. Killing a Morpho was classified as murder here, no matter who did it. Dad would give them the choice tomorrow. Banishment to Eephos, or return to Earth – destination Jipoid-occupied territory. Stefan, with the aid of his Morpho-clone, Deacon, had been manipulating us for years. The Kyrnos colony was planned to fail. Without population growth, it would die out within 15 years, given that our life expectancy was foreshortened by the inhospitable environment here. Dad had relayed a message to the Earth Council, and Cosmos Lab was being raided as we spoke. Cosmos was developing technologies to monopolise inter-planetary mining operations; to first harness and then synthesise thyonite so it would become Earth's sole supplier of fresh water.

Milla was getting merry. Beer was a new thing to her. 'Nike, I've been meaning to ask you, what's a gazelle?'

FOUR HUNDRED HECTARES OF NOTHING

Chloe Harper stared at the pulpy mess of what was once a recognisable face and frowned. The flesh appeared to have melted from the facial bones and the eyeballs were as hard and shrivelled as prune pits. Burnt. *What the hell had happened to this guy?* The cadaver's hair was matted with russet dirt. Strange that his hair was not singed like the rest of his face. His hands and fingernails were also caked with dirt, though his green Infinity Energy shirt was dirty only across the chest area. Chloe suspected that the man had died of asphyxiation – possibly both positional and inert gas asphyxiation – but where and how?

Certainly not in the car in which he was found, head slumped over the steering wheel, somewhere west of Chinchilla. The police were dumbfounded. It was clear the vehicle had run off the road and hit a tree, but that was evidently not the cause of death. So how had he got there? And where had the injuries and suffocation occurred?

'I think that our Mr Tancred here has been the victim of foul play.' Chloe looked across the table at Kieran, the young trainee who had just arrived and who now looked decidedly green around the gills. She had chosen well for his first autopsy. If he could stare this corpse in the pizza-like face and not vomit, he might be made of the right mettle for the job.

'I thought they said it was a car accident,' the tattooed 20-something commented. 'And how do you know his name? It's not on the sheet.'

'Right there.' She pointed to the dust-covered badge on the shirt pocket. 'Gregory Tancred. You need to be observant in this game.'

Kieran rolled his eyes. 'D'oh.'

'So what do you think? There's no sign of broken limbs, contusions, abrasions, blood loss – any of those things you might expect to see in a road accident. And yet we have this.' She pointed to the gruesome face.

'It's pretty gross.'

'Gross is an expression best left for when your mates chuck up at the pub. It's not a word I expect to hear at my post-mortem table. Now, how about something scientific? Educated.'

'Something exploded in his face, I reckon.'

'I think so too. But it was some weird sort of explosion. See this?'

Kieran craned his neck to watch her trace a circle above the victim's face.

'See how there's no injury to the top centimetre of his forehead, and it's less severe here back near his ears? And his hair isn't burnt.'

'Looks like he stuck his face in something round. Like a saucepan or, I dunno, a pipe of some sort.'

'Yes, that's what I thought too. Of course, given that he works for a gas company, it's probably a no-brainer that it's something to do with a gas pipe.'

'Bloody big gas pipe. That's gotta be, what, 100, 110-mil diameter.'

'Yes, I thought about four inches too.'

'There's nothing like that in a car. Which makes me think this didn't happen in his car.'

Chloe peered at him over the top of her glasses. 'I think we can rule that out.'

'So maybe it happened somewhere else and he was driving to get help. Or maybe it happened somewhere else and someone else was driving him and...'

'He was in the driver's seat. It was a company car. So I would normally be inclined to think the first scenario was the more likely, but he wouldn't have been able to see to drive. Not with these eyes.'

'But why do you presume somebody did him in?'

'Have a closer look at his forehead. You can actually see an impression, an indent clearly defining the edges of the circle.'

Kieran shrugged and pulled an I-don't-have-a-clue face.

'I'd say that whatever it was, was pressed into his face, or his face was pressed into it. Who would do something like that voluntarily?'

'Not me, that's for sure.'

'No, me neither. Which is what makes me think somebody else has forced his face into whatever the hell it was. Here, help me turn him over. I want to look for any traces that someone else was involved.' Chloe pulled her magnifier across and studied the back of the victim's head and hair. 'Pass me those tweezers please. Hmm. I don't think *that* belongs there.' She plucked a dark wiry hair from the mass of dirty fair curls and examined it closely under the magnifier. 'Not human. Looks horsey to me. I'll have to get the lab to check it, but it sure doesn't belong. And there's something else here.' She pulled a tiny white fibre from the victim's hair. 'Here get me a slide. Looks like it's got some sort of powder on it.' Kieran obliged and held the slide out so she could place the fibre on it.

'Now see, the other thing that makes me think someone else was involved is that his hair is matted with dirt at the back and yet the back of his shirt is clean, so he wasn't, at any time, lying on his back. But look at the heels of his shoes. Dirt caked in the back there.'

Kieran nodded but hoped Chloe would elaborate.

'I think that someone wearing muddy white gloves and recently in the vicinity of a horse has done this. And then they've dragged the body to the car and presumably driven him to where he was found.'

'Amazing. I should call you Sherlock.'

'Very funny. Hand me the scissors will you?' Chloe cut up the outside of the victim's shirt sleeve, across its shoulder and through the collar so that she could pull the shirt off. She inspected the garment's armpits. This was easier than trying to raise the man's arms, given that rigor mortis had a firm grip on his body.

'Looking for BO?'

'No. Looking for dirt. To see whether the same dirty hands have dragged him by the armpits. But it's clean. Hmm. I've got to say I expected to find the same dirt there. Which could mean...'

'Two people.'

'Precisely. One with dirty hands; one with clean hands.'

'Or one person with dirty gloves who then took them off. Or one person with dirty hands who washed them.'

Chloe nodded. 'All possible.' She rolled the body back and bent over to sniff the face.

'Ew, what are you doing?'

'Trying to identify any chemical or gas smell. Won't smell anything if it was nitrogen or methane because they're inert and have no smell. What they *do* do is starve the blood of oxygen so the person suffocates, often without even experiencing the hypercapnia alarm response. Which is what, Kieran?'

'Huh? Oh, hypercapnia is abnormally elevated levels of carbon dioxide in the blood and the usual response is to try to breathe more oxygen.'

'That's right. But I'm guessing this guy didn't have the opportunity to take any breaths of fresh air. What I can't be sure of is whether he suffocated before his face was burnt. Might know more when we open him up. If he was still alive when the gas ignited, his airways will be burnt too.'

Chloe took the sharpest knife and carved through the breast. She placed a large portion on a plate for Paul and a smaller serve for herself. She was positively drooling at the smell. Toowoomba Charcoal Chicken had the best roast chicken in town. She loaded the meat with gravy and plonked some roast potatoes and vegetables beside it. 'Sorry, but it's takeaway tonight. Didn't feel like cooking,' she called out to Paul, who was happily ensconced in his recliner watching TV.

'No drama. It smells great. Hey look at this. Did you hear about the guy they found out near Chinchilla this morning?'

'Huh,' Chloe snorted. 'Sure did. I have an intimate acquaintance with him. You can't wade through someone's intestines and hold their heart in your hand without feeling like you somehow know them personally.'

'Oh, you mean you...'

'Yep. Who else? It's not like the place is overrun with forensic pathologists.'

'The cops think he was dead before the car hit the tree.'

'He sure was. I'm pretty sure it was murder. I suspect somebody else drove him there and made it look like an accident. Apparently he was out inspecting gas wells over in the Goombi area. And judging by his face, and the fact that he died of asphyxiation – most probably from a whopping fiery dose of methane – he'd got a bit too close to one.'

'So have there been any reports of explosions? No mention on the news.'

'I don't know. Do you think they tell me anything? You know, I give *them* information – they don't reciprocate much. But methane won't explode of its own accord; there has to be an ignition source.'

'Bet he was one of those bastard gas company people who invade people's property and force them to agree to setting up test wells so they can frack the fuck out of the countryside.'

'What do you know about that? I didn't think you were interested in that sort of thing.'

'Saw something about it on *Sixty Minutes* a while back. Don't think you were home that night. These bastards make people's lives a living hell. Turn their properties into wasteland and then offer to buy them for some ridiculous price when they're no good for anything else. And the bloody government lets them do it. It's obscene.'

'I'll say. I don't really know much about it,' Chloe confessed.

'If you want to see what they're doing, these bloody gas companies like QGC, Origin and this guy's mob, Infinity, go Google the Condamine State Forest. It looks like a spiderweb of tracks with little square test wells all over the bloody place. And then they spread onto private property. Somebody's gotta stop these bastards before they fuck up the whole country. They've got no conscience. It's as bad as what they did to Mum and Dad.'

Chloe recalled the last time she had heard such vehemence in Paul's voice. His parents had never got over having their land compulsorily acquired by the Queensland Government for a freeway project – for a quarter of its worth. Paul was convinced this was why his father had committed suicide. Evidently this fracking business had pissed Paul off and yet he hadn't mentioned it until now. Or had he? Maybe he had and she hadn't been listening. She often switched off when he launched into one of his political tirades. He thought he could change the world by arguing with himself.

'So why don't you do something about it? You're good at causes. Why not take up this one and put your mouth where your sentiment is?' Chloe cajoled. 'Beats sitting around here looking at Google Earth and 70s reruns all day.' She tried not to sound too sarcastic. Paul was a talker – not a doer. And since being retrenched from Telstra, all he did was talk about what he was "going" to do.

'I might just do that, you know.'

'I'd like to find out more about this. First hand. What say we take a drive out to Chinchilla tomorrow?'

'It's two hours away.'

'So? Did you have other plans? You could take your fishing rod.'

Chinchilla was 165km north-west of Toowoomba along the Warrego Highway and the further they travelled, the drier and sparser the vegetation became. Not much to see – not much to do unless you were a sheep or cattle farmer or a melon grower. Chloe had been to this part of the Darling Downs only once, about 15 years ago. An unmemorable experience.

Things had changed since then. The place was burgeoning with a new housing development, the by-product of the construction of the Kogan Power Station and QGC's $1.7 billion coal seam gas developments. Good for employment prospects. Bad shit for the environment.

'What do you think you're going to find out coming here?' Paul asked as they approached the town.

'I'm not sure. Maybe somebody with a motive to kill Gregory Tancred.'

'That's the police's job.'

'True, but I want to ascertain how he died. Sometimes you have to see for yourself, especially before I send my report to the Coroner. The pub's probably the best place to get some local goss.'

The bartender placed a XXXX and a bitters lime and lemonade on the bar. 'This'll wet your whistles,' he said. 'So, are you passing through or staying a while? I can always spot a non-local.'

Good. A talker. 'Just here for the day; maybe overnight,' Chloe said as she swigged the beer. They bantered a while about the weather and the state of the economy before Chloe broached the subject. 'Wasn't it around here that guy was found in his car yesterday?'

'Yup. A few kays out of town; out on the Kogan-Condamine road.'

'Did you know him?'

'Vaguely. Unfortunately.'

'Why unfortunately?'

The bartender bent forward conspiratorially. 'Arsehole – with a capital A. Don't think anyone around here will be sorry to see the back of him.'

'Why so?' Paul asked.

'He was one of those gas company pricks who goes round forcing people to let them set up test wells on their property.'

Chloe glanced at Paul and acknowledged the I-told-you-so look on his face.

'Bastard has been harassing people from Greenswamp to Condamine with these fucking unreadable contracts and then once they get their foot in the gate, well it's all over red rover and they'll pump the gas out and fuck up the water supply and there's bugger all anyone can do about it.'

Chloe shook her head in disgust. 'So, if some altruistic-type souls like us wanted to take issue with this travesty, who should we talk to around here?'

'I say what?'

'If we wanted to do something about it,' Paul offered, 'who...'

'Oh. You could talk to Roger down at the Shell servo. He used to work for Infinity. Until he couldn't hack it anymore.'

Chloe handed the man her Visa card for the petrol and eyed the name on his badge. Roger Abbott. 'The guy up at the Commercial Hotel told us you worked for Infinity Energy.'

The man looked wary. Noncommittal. 'And you are?'

'I'm Chloe Harper and this is my husband, Paul.'

'You cops or something?'

'No. Not cops. I have an interest in the guy who died yesterday.'

'Greg? Didn't know him personally. Sorry.'

The guy appeared to be hedging. Like he wanted to talk, but didn't want to talk.

'Do you reckon somebody might have, um, bumped him off?'

Roger shrugged. 'Don't know. Wouldn't altogether surprise me though.'

'Why's that?' Chloe said.

'Let's just say he was eminently suited to the job.'

'Which was?'

'He was a land access officer.'

'What's that exactly?'

'His job was basically to bully people into letting fucking Infinity onto their properties to set up test wells.'

'Is that what you used to do?'

'Only for a month or so. Until I threatened to blow the whistle on their underhanded bloody tactics. You know, some arsehole at head office would badger us to badger these poor farmers; get them to sign contracts they couldn't even decipher and tell them we just wanted to set up an appraisal well. Next thing these poor people knew, there'd be roads dissecting their properties, they're getting locked out, and we're digging great fucking pipeline trenches and forcing them to sell when they had no intention of ever selling. Some of these properties had been in the family for generations. Now they're like barren bloody wastelands. It's criminal. Absolutely criminal.'

'That's awful,' was all Chloe could think of to say.

'Anyway, I couldn't hack it. It's not in my nature to be an arsehole and fuck up people's lives like that. So there's any number of people around here who might have wanted to smash Gregory Fucking Tandred's face in. You wanna drive over to Condamine and see what they're doing. Stop at a few farms along the way and see if anyone will talk to you. Actually, you should try the Stephenson's place out on Goombi-Fairymeadow Road. Name's on a red barrel by the gate. Old Bernie Stephenson topped himself a couple of months ago. He was that desperate. His daughter, Jess, has taken up his fight with Infinity. She was trying to get the local pollie to investigate. Of course he's done fuck-all. Too much vested interest. Probably has shares in QGC or Infinity.'

Chloe looked at Paul. 'I might do that. I could drop you somewhere for a spot of fishing if you like.'

'Wouldn't go fishing anywhere out there,' Roger interrupted, 'creeks are full of methane. Look like fucking Rotorua.'

'You're kidding.' Paul was incredulous.

'I kid you not.'

Paul stopped the car at the gate. 'Can't drive in. It's padlocked.'

'You coming with me? For moral support?'

Paul rolled his eyes. 'I guess so. Can't see the house though. It could be a five-mile hike.'

'Might be just over the rise there, hopefully.'

They climbed the gate and surveyed the denuded landscape. The paddocks looked threadbare and dusty, studded with struggling tussocks.

'Not much chop as farming land,' Paul observed. 'What the hell's that over there?' A newly graded gravel road struck arrow-straight off to the right, unlike the grassy driveway which meandered off to the left.

'Looks like a gas well to me. Or what I imagine a gas well would look like.'

They crested the rise. A rambling weatherboard farmhouse, surrounded by a hay shed and machinery sheds, a few fruit trees and a weedy house-garden, stood about 60 metres down the slope to the left. Over to the right, about 200 metres away, a wire fence encircled a conglomeration of pipes and valves on a gravel pad.

'Nice view,' Chloe said.

'Not. Look at the bloody great trench over there.' Paul pointed further to the right along the fence line. 'There's someone over there. Will we go see?'

Chloe nodded. As they approached the rim of the trench, which Chloe guesstimated to be about 30 metres wide and longer than the eye could see – a pristine pipeline lying along its length – she called out to the Akubra-hatted person standing at the edge, one hand on hip, the other holding onto a bay horse. Chloe assumed it was a man until the person swung around.

'Who the hell are you? You'd better not be from bloody Infinity.'

Even from a distance Chloe could see that the woman, aged she guessed in her late 30s, had been crying. She wiped her face on her right sleeve. Chloe noticed the plaster cast on her wrist.

'No. Not from Infinity. We wanted to talk to you about the guy who died near here yesterday.'

The woman's shoulders sagged. 'I figured someone would turn up some time. Are you cops?'

'No. But I *am* investigating his death. I'm a forensic pathologist.'

'That's a fancy thing to be out here.' The woman sniffed and wiped her nose again.

'I've come from Toowoomba. Not officially, you understand. I just wanted to get a clearer picture of what happened. Do you know anything about it, by any chance? You're Jess, I presume.'

The woman nodded. 'Only what I saw on the news last night.'

'But this man, Gregory Tancred, have you ever met him?'

Jess looked away and shrugged. 'Yeah, I've met him. He's a bastard and

I don't mind saying it. Everyone around here knows what's been going on. See that?' She pointed into the trench. 'I can thank Gregory Fucking Tancred for that.' She was teary again.

Chloe and Paul moved closer. Three Herefords lay at the bottom of the trench. Bloated in death. Chloe gasped. 'Can't you get them out?'

'Bit late for that now. That makes 37 we've lost in that fucking trench. They fall in and they can't get out again. It's supposed to have been covered in. And then there's those, of course. One, two three.' She pointed off into the paddocks.

Chloe could see them better from this vantage point. Not one, but three gas wells.

'And that's not all of them. There's eight all together. And see all those bloody roads they've raised up. They stop all the natural water flow on the land, which is why it's so bloody dry. Eight thousand head of cattle we used to run on here. Now we can't even feed a hundred.'

Chloe was appalled. This was deplorable. She could understand Jess's desperation.

'You say "we". Is it just you and your husband here?'

'Nah. I'm not married. It's the family property, but there's only Mum and my brother Mick now, since Dad...'

'Roger Abbott told us about your dad,' Chloe said.

'I was the one who found him. Down there in the ditch with a couple of cows and his shotgun. I couldn't believe it. I knew he was desperate, but I never thought he'd do that. Never. But, those gas guys, Greg in particular, hounded him, bullied him. They wouldn't leave him alone. Five friggin' years this has been going on and he...he couldn't take it anymore. They just wore him down. Our whole livelihood has gone down the tube. This place is worthless now and yet they won't buy it. So we're fucked both ways.'

Chloe shook her head. She didn't know what to say. She pointed to Jess's arm. 'What happened to your wrist?'

'Oh, fell off Romeo here.' She nudged the horse's neck. 'Look, I was about to head back to the house for some lunch. Can I offer you something?'

Chloe had heard about country hospitality but she didn't want to impose on the woman. It was clear she had enough on her hands. She was about to decline when Jess motioned.

'C'mon, I can at least make you a coffee.'

As they neared the home paddock, Chloe spotted something in the adjoining paddock. A pipe protruding about 30 centimetres from the ground – erupting like a miniature geyser. 'What's that?' she asked Jess.

'What? Oh, that's our bore.'

'Does it usually spew water like that? Can I have a look?'

Jess hesitated a moment – long enough to pique Chloe's suspicion. 'Yes, if you like. It's been like that since they set up the wells. You see, methane is held in the coal seams by the water pressure, but when they start fracking it allows the methane to free flow, um...'

'To the point of least resistance,' Chloe said.

'Yes, you could put it that way.'

As they got closer to the pipe, Chloe could see that the ground around it was churned up with footprints. She elbowed Paul in the chest to draw his attention to two narrow trails, about 30 centimetres apart, and motioned to him to skirt around them. She bent over for a closer look. The pipe, 100mm diameter, erupted water like a bubbling fountain. Slightly beyond the edges of the wet area she could see two furrows in the dirt, around 40 centimetres either side of the pipe. A bit over a metre and a half back from one side of it were two other deep indents in the dirt, roughly 30 centimetres apart. An image appeared to her. A man lying prone, digging his toes into the dirt and tearing at the ground with his palms. 'Gosh, you can actually see the gas vapour escaping as it bubbles.'

'Doesn't say much for our water quality does it?'

'Would that ignite?' Chloe asked, knowing the answer full well.

Jess shrugged. 'Not of its own accord, I don't think, but obviously it's flammable if you light it.'

'Have you got your lighter in your pocket, Paul?'

'You're not...?' He handed her his Bic. 'Be careful, will you?'

Chloe squatted, held the lighter at arm's length and flicked the roller. The vapour ignited, burned momentarily and dissipated. 'Interesting,' she said. She looked up at Jess, whose expression showed neither surprise nor fear. It was more a look of resignation. Or guilt. Chloe wasn't sure.

Jess led the way along the veranda to the back door and called out. 'Mum, Mick, we've got visitors.'

Chloe and Paul followed her into the kitchen. A man sat with his back to them at the dining table. A sixtyish-year-old woman sat on the opposite side staring vacantly out the window.

'Mum, I said, we've got company.'

The woman didn't move. Did not acknowledge their presence.

'Sorry, she's been like this for a while. Grieving Dad, you know.'

Chloe nodded understandingly. The woman looked hollow. Defeated.

The man turned around. He was thin, weedy and unshaven. The downward cast of his mouth suggested he'd long forgotten how to smile. He looked at Jess for an explanation.

'This is my brother, Mick. This is...oh, I don't know your names.'

'Chloe Harper, and my husband Paul. I'm a forensic pathologist and I'm looking into the death of Gregory Tancred.'

'Oh, yeah,' Mick said disinterestedly. 'Sorry, can't help you there.'

'No?'

Chloe turned to see what the clicking noise was behind her. Jess was trying to light the stove with a gas gun.

'Bloody thing won't light,' she said.

Mick got up and walked past them into the kitchen. 'Here, show me.' He flicked the gun several times and placed it back on the bench. 'Must be out of grunt. You'll have to use the matches.' He returned to the table and sat again, but on the opposite side so he could see them.

Chloe followed the mother's gaze out the window. The scene was no oil painting. A few scrabbly gums did little to disguise one of the gas wells which lurked silent and menacing in the distance. 'I guess you used to have a lovely view out there.'

Mick nodded. 'Used to. We used to have a lot of things.'

Chloe could sense the resignation in his voice. 'I'm sorry about your father.'

'Why should you be? You didn't know him.'

'I know, but... My husband here knows how you feel, don't you, Paul?'

'Yes mate. My dad did much the same thing and for much the same reason.'

Chloe felt such empathy for these people, as she had done with Paul's parents. Life was shitty and sometimes people had more than their fair share of shit. But that didn't justify murder. Not in her book. A part of her wanted to tamper with the evidence, lose the slide with the incriminating white strand and powder, give the police a bum steer and falsify her report to the Coroner. But she couldn't. What she could do, was try to encourage these people to confess. They'd have a much easier time of it in court if all the mitigating circumstances were brought to light. But how to broach the subject? *Sympathetically?*

'You know the police are going to come, don't you? Would it be easier for one of you to tell me what happened? I think I have a vague idea.' Chloe looked at Jess, who was staring at the kitchen bench. 'Jess, I'm pretty sure that somewhere along the line, you pushed Gregory's face into the bore pipe. I found a strand of gauze from your cast in his hair. And horse hair, which I suspect will match Romeo.'

'Did she tell you how she broke her wrist?' Mick shouted. 'Should I say how *he* broke her wrist?'

'But you said you fell...'

'Yeah, I did. After he grabbed me by the wrist and twisted it until it snapped. That was five weeks ago when he came for the third time in a week to try to get Mum to sign this contract. Show it to her, Mick.'

Mick pushed a document across the table. 'It's a CCA, a Conduct and Compensation Agreement. Sign it and you're truly fucked. It's supposed to protect the rights of landowners but it's not worth the paper it's printed on. Dad refused over and over to sign it. So that bastard Tancred figured that once Dad was out of the picture, Mum would be a soft touch. Fourteen times he came to harass us to sign it. It's never going to happen.'

'So yes, since you figured it out already,' Jess said, 'I did push his face into the pipe. I told him that if he wanted the bloody gas so much, he could have it. For dinner.'

'But you didn't do that on your own, did you?' Chloe said.

'No, she didn't,' Mick said. He sighed loudly. 'She was struggling with him and called me. By the time I got over there he was flailing like a beached dolphin but she was having trouble holding him down because of her wrist. So I helped.'

'So, *you* ignited the gas? What did you use, this?' Chloe picked up the gas gun. 'How many times? Judging by the damage to his face it was more than once.'

Mick stared at her, lips pursed. Then looked at Jess conspiratorially. He nodded. 'Yeah. Yeah I did.'

'Oh no you did not.'

Chloe's head snapped around. The old woman stared at her through watery blue eyes.

'Yes, I used the gas gun – several times. And I helped get him in the car.

Bernard Stephenson was my best friend. My lover. My business partner. My soulmate. The father of my children. We are *nothing* without him. We have *nothing* here. And Gregory Bloody Tancred was a *nothing* man. I felt *nothing* for him as I watched his vile face burn and I feel *nothing* for him now.'

Chloe had never felt so conflicted. She wanted to hug Mrs Stephenson, to let her know she understood, recalling how she'd had to convince Paul not to attempt similar retribution for *his* father's death, though she totally understood his impulse for revenge. Instead, she had to acknowledge her professional duty. She placed her hand on Mrs Stephenson's.

'I'm so sorry to have to do this, but you know I'm obliged to call the police.'

Mrs Stephenson, her fingers bracing her forehead, nodded almost imperceptibly.

'It's not bloody fair,' Paul said, as he steered the car past the police vehicles in the Stephensons' driveway. 'Those people aren't criminals; they're victims. They're going to be put through the mill.'

Chloe fought back tears. 'Trust me, I know where you're coming from, but hopefully, the courts will be lenient on them, given the circumstances, and with any luck, the publicity of the investigation and ensuing trial will spotlight what these bastards have done to them and so many others. It may even bring about legislative change to prevent it from happening in future.'

'Makes me think Dad should have taken this road instead of the one he took. At least he'd still be here.'

Chloe patted Paul's leg. 'I know darling. But life's shitty. You might think what he did was a cop out, but he'd fought hard and was too good a man to have done what the Stephensons did. He wouldn't have had the strength left to cope with what they'll have to face – a whole lot more shitty shit.'

MURDER BY THE BOOK

THE END. AN AUTHOR'S MOST SATISFYING TWO WORDS. I'M amazed that I've thrashed out the final 15,000 words of my novel in five days. But that was the purpose of the exercise. A week at a secluded writer's retreat with no distractions apart from evening socialising with the five other temporary residents. It's done, with two days to spare.

If it weren't bucketing rain, as it has been for three days, I'd venture outside; wander through the bush, pretend I'm at one with the great outdoors. Nup. Instead, I'll head downstairs to the library and engross myself in another author's work until dinner. "Library" is a generous description; more a bedroom with bookshelves lining two walls.

I cross the sitting room and open the library door, bang my face straight into it when it doesn't swing in as I expect. Something's jamming it. The opening is just big enough to get my head around and peer in. The left-hand bookcase has fallen face-down; its contents strewn across the floor. How the hell? Everyone's in their rooms, aren't they? Poltergeist maybe. No way we'll get this door open. Ah. oh. Now I see feet. Someone's under there, prone, the soles of two shoes sticking out. Men's, I'm guessing. Lindsay, or Jim? Holy hell.

I trot back through the sitting room and run up the stairs, calling out, 'Hey everyone. Help. There's a body in the library. Squashed.'

Doors fly open and Susanna, Genevieve, Robyn and Lindsay appear in the hallway. No Jim.

'Quick.' I beckon them downstairs. 'It must be Jim.'

I rush down ahead of them. 'Can't get in from this side. Can someone go outside and try through the French doors?'

Lindsay volunteers and heads off through the kitchen. The others take turns to peer through the narrow opening. They call Jim's name but there's no response.

'Better call an ambulance,' Genevieve says. She punches 000 into her phone and gives the operator the lowdown. 'Darn,' she says, covering the phone, 'ambulance and police won't get through because the road is cut; creek's flooded over the bridge.'

'Oh, my goodness,' Susanna says shrilly. 'What are we going to do? What if he's dead? Nobody's going to come. We're—'

'Calm down, Susanna. Do not despair, Susanna,' Robyn says in her usual lyrical fashion.

'I'm in,' Lindsay calls.

'I'm going round. You lot stay here,' says I, the self-appointed leader of the pack.

'Who put you in charge?' Genevieve asks.

I'm already at the kitchen door. I hotfoot it around the veranda. Lindsay's inside the library, arms akimbo.

'I discern that he has forgone this mortal world.'

Jesus Lindsay, quit with the literary shit. 'I take that to mean he's dead.'

I step into the room, suspecting Lindsay is right. Jim's right arm and Trump-haired head protrude from under the bookcase.

'Help me lift it,' Lindsay says.

'Wait a minute,' I say, pulling my phone from my pocket. 'Let me take some pictures first. Police and Forensic Pathologist will need to see what happened.' I click a few pictures from the limited angles. 'Okay, I'll try to get round the other side.' That involves scrambling over the mountain of books thrown from the bookcase's top shelves. I grab the moulding along the top shelf and tell Lindsay to lift. Not as easy as I'd thought, with a sea of books and a body to negotiate, but with much exertion, we right the bookcase. 'Don't touch anything,' I instruct. 'I'll take more pictures.'

Lindsay is squatting, checking Jim's pulse. He shakes his head.

I imagine that a loaded bookcase could squash the life out of someone, but something is odd here. How could this have happened? Did Jim accidentally pull it over? How? I study the now empty shelves. Slim fingermarks in the dust there on the far edge of the third shelf. Curious, given Jim's hands are like ham hocks.

Genevieve pokes her head around the door; she still can't open it because of the books piled in front. 'They're asking whether he's breathing.'

'No. He's dead. Can't the police get through?'

'They say no. Might be a couple of days.'

'Shit. What are we going to do with him?'

'Hang on. I'll ask.' She disappears. I catch vague snatches of her end of the conversation. 'Okay, they're saying that if it appears to be an accident, we should move him somewhere cool and lay him out in the same position.'

'The cool room,' I suggest. 'But we've got to get all these books off him first.' Most of them have flung open in the fall. Lindsay's already placing some back on the shelf. I do likewise from my end. Shakespeare, Austen, Brontë – all the classics and many by contemporary Australian authors. We've finally unearthed the body. I take a couple more pictures. 'Okay, you lot. You can come in now.'

Susanna looks ashen. 'I've never seen a dead body. He looks like he's just asleep.'

Robyn has her hand over her mouth. 'Oh deary me, we think he's dead, an awful thing, it should be said.'

'Honestly Robyn, poetry at a time like this?' I can't help admonishing her. 'C'mon, let's get him out to the cool room.' Lindsay opens the other side of the French doors and we all grab Jim's still-limp body and carry him through, like pallbearers. As we reach the outhouse, Lindsay momentarily lets go of Jim's shoulder to open the door. Without his support, Jim starts to roll and we can't stop the fall. He drops on his back at our feet. That's when I see it. The purple bruise on his throat. How did that happen?

'Hang on. Look at that. There's an injury on his neck that doesn't fit. Looks like his windpipe has been crushed.' I take a close-up picture of his throat.

'How would you know?' Genevieve says. 'Unless you're a doctor, or a forensics expert.'

'I do research a lot about injuries and crime.'

'Just because you *write* crime, doesn't make you Miss Marple.'

'Well you tell me how he has an injury there, when he was face down.'

Genevieve snorts.

We pick up Jim again and lay him face down inside on the concrete floor. We're all freezing out here so I suggest that we go back inside.

We sit on the couches by the fire, with tea or coffee in hands.

I study my co-retreaters in turn. We're an eclectic bunch. Nothing in common except our urges to inflict our thoughts on innocent readers.

Lindsay, a dour 40-something-mid-life-crisis-wannabee-author writing some serious introspective literary work with too many adjectives; the sort of book that would put me to sleep.

Susanna, the ditzy machine-gun-mouthed mother-of-four lost in a fantasy world of possums, potaroos and fairies.

Genevieve, the spectacled headmistress-like spinster, who writes romance like someone who's never had any.

Robyn, wafer-thin, innocence personified; a lookalike Pam Ayres, whose rhyming speech would have driven the pious John Wesley to drink.

'Let's try to work out what happened,' I say. 'First, does anyone know whether Jim went back to his room after lunch?'

Everyone shrugs.

'I think I was the last one to go up, so I presume he was already in his room,' Susanna says.

'Okay, has anyone been down here since lunchtime?'

Genevieve shakes her head.

'I came down for some tea about three,' Robyn says, unable to resist a rhyme.

'Did you see Jim? And was the library door open or closed?'

'I saw him not, the door was shut.'

'I had not been down until I heard you call, so caught up in my philosophising,' says Lindsay.

'What about you, Jacqui?' Genevieve says accusingly. 'What were you doing down here?'

'I've finished my manuscript and came down to find something to read.'

Susanna giggles. 'This reminds me of one of those murder mystery parties I went to a few years ago. It was–'

'Only, this is no game, Susanna.' I don't say, however, that it reminds *me* of an Agatha Christie denouement.

'It appears simple to me,' Lindsay says. 'He, too, came down for a book, perhaps stepped on a shelf to reach one high up, and the bookcase toppled on him.'

'Doesn't work for me, Lindsay. If it had happened that way, his body would have been lengthwise, not crosswise under the bookcase and he'd have been face-up.'

'Yes, you're right.'

'I gather the outside door was unlocked, Lindsay.'

'It was.'

'Has anyone been out through the library today?' More head shaking. 'Nobody sneaked out for a ciggy, or fresh air? I locked the French doors last night.' I eye them all carefully, for telltale signs that someone's hiding something. Genevieve, I note, is staring at the floor; the others look innocent enough.

I pause in my amateur interrogation to ponder. Someone else must have been in the library with him. Someone whose only way out, once the bookcase had toppled, was through the French doors. Nobody else has been here today, which means someone is lying. I study the photographs. That's it! The last one I took before we moved his body. The one showing the open book *beneath* Jim's shoulder. 'Hang on.' I fly off the couch and into the library. It's still there on the floor. Face-down, unlike all the others. A hardcover edition of *The Complete Sherlock Holmes.* Was Jim planning to read it? Doesn't seem his style. Or...is it a murder weapon? The spine is slightly dented. I leave it *in situ* as Forensics might need to examine it, though I snap another photo.

'Okay,' I say, as I re-enter the sitting room, 'did someone have a bone to pick with Jim?'

Four resounding noes.

'Why?' Lindsay asks. 'You're not suggesting this wasn't an accident, surely.'

'I suspect he was dead, or dying, *before* the bookcase fell on him. Which means–'

'Huh,' Genevieve sucks in a breath. 'You think one of us killed him?'

'We're the only ones here. So, one of us must know something.'

Robyn looks doubtful. 'What about Mrs J? Maybe she was here today.'

'Would you come out in this rain if you didn't have to, Robyn? She'll be here with dinner soon, so we'll ask her.'

Susanna sips her coffee. 'Can't say I liked him much. Freaky looking, you know, reminded me of Gollum. Sounded like him too, when he called me "my precious".'

'He did?'

'Creeped me out, but not like I'd wanted to kill him.'

'What about you, Genevieve?' I ask.

'I had nothing against him, though his anecdotes bored me witless. He didn't speak like a writer.'

Lindsay nods. 'I agree he had not a mastery of the language. I cannot fathom how he was deemed worthy of a fellowship here.'

'Not a reason to kill someone, though,' I say. 'Did anyone know Jim before we arrived on Monday?'

Again, four noes.

The kitchen door clicks. Mrs J arriving from next door with our dinners. I head into the kitchen and pull the trolley through the door as she shakes off her umbrella outside.

'Horrible out there,' she says. 'Wish this rain would let up. We're cut off, you know.'

'Yes, we know. We've had a drama here. I should have rung to let you know we only need five dinners.'

'Why? Has someone left?'

'No. Someone died.'

Her look of unfeigned shock indicates it's news to her. 'Oh, goodness. Who?'

'Jim.'

'What was it? Heart attack? Accident?'

'Bookcase fell on him. We're still trying to figure out how. Have you been over here earlier today?'

'No. Once a day's enough in this weather.'

'Why don't you join us for dinner? Eat his meal to save wasting it.'

'All right. Why not? Oh, where is he? Not sure I'm up for dining with a corpse in the house.'

'Out in the coolroom. I'll set the table.'

I collect the cutlery canteen and the tray of wine glasses and head into the dining room. The others are still sitting by the fire, speculating about how Jim died.

We sit to steaming hot pumpkin soup, crusty bread and a choice of red or white wine. For the first time this week, our discussion isn't centred on writing. I get the impression nobody is rueing Jim's demise, but then he *was* a virtual stranger to us all.

Or was he?

I think of the lunchtime conversation as we'd sat here in the same seats, volunteering information about our lives and our writing interests, while eating Mrs J's home-cooked quiche. Genevieve's blather about writing non-sexual romance, Lindsay's sermonising about his academic pursuits, Susanna's incessant mummy-knows-best talk, Jim's admission that he'd been a prison guard. *Where did he say? Somewhere in Victoria. Relevant? Probably not.* Me, divulging some of the creative ways I've killed off characters. And Robyn, talking in rhymes until she suddenly disappeared; left the table halfway through her quiche.

'I wonder,' says Susanna, 'whether he has family. Would the police notify them? Surely–'

Genevieve cuts her off. 'I'm sure they will, though all I could tell them was his name and that he came from Melbourne.'

'He didn't mention anything about his family, at least, not that I heard,' I say.

Genevieve dabs her mouth with a serviette. 'I got the impression he lived alone. Remember? He mentioned something last night about how Mrs J's meals were a welcome change from TV dinners.'

'My kids'd live on microwave macaroni if I let them,' Susanna says.

Genevieve grunts. 'Not much nutrition in that. You'd never find me eating a TV dinner.'

Susanna giggles. 'Bet you would if you had children.'

Genevieve glowers at her. 'If I'd had children, young lady, they'd have had meat and three vegetables every night.'

'Good for you.'

Mrs J clears the soup bowls and heads to the kitchen. She returns momentarily with the main courses. 'Hope you all like lasagne. Home-cooked of course.'

'Does anyone know what Jim was writing?' I ask.

'Autobiography, or memoir, I think,' Genevieve says.

'He mentioned at lunch that he was a prison guard. Did he tell any of you where?'

'Told me yesterday,' Genevieve says. 'Fairlea Women's Prison.'

'Well that could make for interesting reading. Maybe we should check out his room and his laptop. See what he's written.'

Robyn stares at her lasagne. Excuses herself and heads upstairs, hand over her mouth.

'Is she okay?' Susanna asks.

Mrs J looks crestfallen. 'Maybe she didn't like the lasagne.'

I recall her sudden lunchtime disappearance. 'Maybe she's not well. She disappeared at lunch too.'

'Looks anorexic to me,' Genevieve says. 'Maybe bulimic.'

I finish the last few mouthfuls of lasagne. 'I'll go check on her.' I head upstairs. The sounds of dry retching emanate from the communal bathroom. I knock on the door. 'Are you okay Robyn?'

'I'll be okay. Please go away.'

I figure that while I'm up here, I'll check out Jim's room and grab his laptop so we can check it later. I open his door and am taken aback by the sight. Bed unmade, side table littered with chocolate wrappers and empty beer cans, jocks hanging on the wardrobe handle, desk awash with papers and junk. A pile of near-illegible notes look scribbled by a madman. I leaf through them. Random, decidedly unflattering descriptions. *Jill wants it big time. Finally scored Rob's sweet little fanny. Worth the wait. John's a mongrel prick. Doesn't even know what he doesn't know.*

Who are these people? Characters, or family? I gather them up and unplug his laptop, then head into my room to grab mine.

'Wait till you see this stuff,' I say when I reach the bottom of the stairs. 'Oh, I'll leave it for later. Tiramisu beckons.'

I'm tempted to lick the plate. Best tiramisu ever. We farewell Mrs J and adjourn to the sitting room, resuming our earlier seats – aside from the one left vacant by Robyn – each with a page of Jim's notes in hand.

'He's a nutter. *Was* a nutter,' Susanna says. 'Listen to this one. Kath's a fat-arse, smelly turd – murdering bitch.'

'And this.' Lindsay says. 'No, it's beneath me to read it aloud.'

'Show me.' Genevieve snatches it. 'Caw. You're right.'

I'm all ears. 'What does it say?'

'Ahem. Cunnylingus in the laundry. Best place for a dirty girl.'

'Sicko. Do you reckon this is real, or ideas for his book?'

'I can't help wondering whether these women were prisoners under his charge,' I say.

'God forbid,' Genevieve says.

I open his laptop and click through the login page, thankful there's no password protection. I open his file manager; click My Documents. Open a Word document entitled *On Guard*. Look at the word count – 9540. Within the required word count to have applied for a fellowship. The opening line...

Being a prison guard was in my blood; passed to me through Dad's bedtime stories about his days supervising Jika Jika's wicked, hardened criminals.

Too eloquent, I reckon, to have come from Jim's hand. Doubt he'd know what a semicolon was for. I open his email account, scroll through the dozens of messages in his inbox. Aha. One, dated three weeks ago from Hilltop Writers Retreat.

Dear Mr Haley,

Further to earlier correspondence, we advise of a cancellation for the week starting June 7. Although we cannot offer accommodation as a Fellow, since your excerpt was not deemed of literary merit, this placement is open should you desire to pay to attend. Please advise as soon as possible, or the offer will be passed to the next in line.

'Very interesting,' I say. 'Jim wasn't here as a Fellow. He *paid* to be here.'

'How do you know?' Lindsay asks.

'Reading his emails. Hang on, I'll look for his reply.' I open his Sent emails. 'Here it is. Dear blah, blah...*June 7 suits perfectly. Will transfer payment today...*'

I return to his inbox. Several from someone named Margaret McCoy. I open the most recent; May 24th.

Jim, given that you have failed to pay my invoice for the first four chapters, I hereby advise that I will not write any more for you...

'Holy shit. He had a ghostwriter. That explains it.'

'A ghostwriter?' Susanna giggles.

She obviously doesn't know the term. 'Someone else has been writing his story for him,' I explain.

'Oh, haha, I thought you meant–'

'That means,' Genevieve interrupts, 'that he's plagiarised it to submit for a fellowship.'

'Sure seems like it. Hang on.' I scroll to Margaret's previous email – a demand for payment. The previous one, dated February 9, has an attachment, entitled *On Guard*. Sure enough, it has the same opening line. 'Yep. Here's her email with it attached.'

'Well, the more I learn about Jim, the less I mourn him,' Genevieve says.

'Hear, hear,' Lindsay says.

Genevieve sets her wine glass down and stands. 'Call of nature.' She heads for the stairs.

'Can you check on Robyn? She was up there throwing up.'

'Will do, Jacqui.'

What other secrets do you have, Mr Haley? I click on Jim's photo file and immediately wish I hadn't. *God.* Dozens and dozens of porn pics – some magazine-style, some amateurish. They're the worst. Young, mostly unconscious-looking women in gruesome poses; many blurry except for their genitalia. Some, half-clad in what looks like orange prison garb. I'm so appalled, I don't realise I'm almost suffocating myself with my hand.

'What's the matter, Jacqui?'

I barely hear Susanna's words. I shut the laptop's lid. 'Trust me, Susanna. You don't want to know. Suffice it to say, Jim is no loss to humanity.' *Wait till the cops see this.*

'She's in bed,' Genevieve announces from the foot of the stairs. 'Wants to be left alone.'

'Thereby be my cue,' Lindsay says, as he stands. 'To die, to sleep – to sleep, perchance to dream – ay, there's the rub, for in this sleep of death what dreams may come...'

Susanna pulls a face. 'Huh?'

'Shakespeare, Susanna,' I say.

'Hamlet, to be precise,' Lindsay adds. 'I bid you fine ladies *adieu*.'

'I'm off to bed too,' says Genevieve, 'though maybe with less drama.'

Susanna slugs her last mouthful of wine. 'Well, you're all boring. I might as well go too.'

Though now deserted, I'm not tired enough for bed. And though I've written some gruesome scenes in my time – shitty things my fictitious characters have done to others – nothing prepared me for Jim's confronting images. Truth really is meaner than fiction. But I feel no closer to figuring out who murdered him. If, in fact, it wasn't an accident. None of them look like they'd have it in them. Certainly, none of them have me fearing for my own life. Lindsay might bore you to death, too long with Susanna would annoy you to death, Genevieve could feasibly *talk* you to death and Robyn...wouldn't, couldn't hurt a butterfly, unless she rhymed it to death. And I'm sane enough to know that I'm no Jekyll and Hyde.

But I still reckon one of them was in there with him. Who? I head for the library and switch on the light. Aside from Sherlock Holmes still there on the floor, and a wet patch on the carpet where Jim evidently peed himself, nothing else seems out of place. I inspect the far side of the bookcase and pull off a short strand of black wool caught on the back edge. Not Lindsay's methinks, since he's been in a beige jumper all day. I shut my eyes to picture the women's attire. All, from memory, were wearing black jumpers.

Something's scratching at the door behind me. I turn to see Tigger, Hilltop's resident housecat, bedraggled and desperate to get inside. I leave him there and trot into the laundry to fetch a towel.

'No, you're not coming in like that,' I tell him, as I try to fend him off and get out the door. I place the towel over his back, give him a good rub and pick him up. A metre further down the veranda, which is thankfully dry this side, I see a patch of ooky-looking stuff. 'Oh, poor Tigger. Did you barf? What have you been eating?' I wrap him tight, head back inside and lock the door. I carry him into the kitchen and dry him off on the bench, enjoying his headbutts under my chin. 'Ooh, you make me miss my Barney. Want to come to bed with me?'

Pretty sure I've solved this little mystery – in true Sherlockian or Marple-style. Or should that be Jacqui Bishop style? But I hate to think of the outcome. An hour of reading Jim's horrid notes and inspecting his laptop – forcing myself to look more carefully at his pictures – before I'd sneaked out to the coolroom, rendered me sleepless until 3am. But now, in the cold light of morning, most of the pieces have fallen into place. A plausible scenario, anyway, though one I can't actually believe.

I push Tigger aside, fling off the quilt, step into my slippers, don my dressing gown and head for the shower. Thankfully, it's vacant. I hear the murmur of voices downstairs, which means the others have beaten me to breakfast. I shower quickly, dress and head down, tempted by the smell of croissants.

'Morning, all,' I say to Lindsay, Genevieve and Susanna who are already at the table, chatting away over their cereal. 'Where's Robyn?'

'Hasn't come down yet. Obviously sleeping in, like you,' Genevieve says.

'Yes, well I was awake half the night.' I pour some Cornflakes into a bowl and sit.

'Yeah, me too,' Susanna says.

I'm halfway through a toasted croissant when Robyn appears, pale and bleary-eyed; her hair loose and crinkly, rather than plaited as usual. I offer to pour her a coffee. She nods and sits beside Genevieve. Fiddles with a loose thread on her jumper cuff.

I try to engage her in conversation. 'Who's Justin, Robyn? Is he your partner?'

She looks at me quizzically. 'Huh?'

'I just noticed the tattoo on your wrist.'

'Oh. No, that's stupid. Wish I'd never had it done. You know, Justin Beiber.'

'Oh. Well, we all do silly things when we're young. Some we no doubt live to regret.'

Genevieve changes the subject. 'I don't think I'll be able to get my head into writing today, what with yesterday's goings-on.'

'Me either,' Susanna says.

Now, how to broach the subject?

'I gleaned some useful information on Jim's computer last night.'

Everyone stares at me.

Genevieve raises her eyebrows. 'You mean apart from him being a smutty-mouthed plagiarist?'

'Yes. Worse. His photo file, in particular, was enough to churn my stomach. Trashy porn pictures, but more worryingly a bunch of pics that I suspect *he* took, of some unfortunate girls.'

'Shit,' Susanna says, hand on mouth.

'Oh dear,' says Genevieve.

'I thought him to be of low morals,' Lindsay says.

Robyn makes no comment, nor eye contact.

'Now, I'm sorry to put you on the spot, but Robyn, we need to know what happened in the library yesterday.'

Everyone gasps and stares at her. Robyn sucks in a deep breath, turns pale as a ghost, and looks set to run away. She sobs and buries her face in her hands.

'You knew Jim before, didn't you?' I say it gently, not accusingly.

She nods vaguely. 'His name's not Jim Haley. It's James Holborn.'

'He was your prison guard, wasn't he?

'Mmm.'

'Okay. None of our business why you were in prison, but I think what he did to you is naturally relevant here. Didn't you realise who he was when we all arrived here?'

She shakes her head. 'He looked so different, like, he had no hair or beard then. How did you know?'

'You disappeared twice from the table yesterday – both times when we'd mentioned prison. Several other things too. Do you want to tell us what happened yesterday, or will I have a go?'

Genevieve claps her hands. 'Oh, let's hear your version first Jacqui. See whether you're as good a sleuth as you think.'

'Okay. Here goes. First, I suspect Jim has been stalking Robyn for a while. Second, it was no coincidence that he was here this week. Third, I suspect that once he realised you knew who he was, he had to do something about it.' Robyn is nodding. 'So, I believe you came down to the library and he followed you. You already had the Sherlock Holmes book in your hand when he entered. He threatened you and, in defence of yourself, you thwacked him in the throat with the book. He fell, and somehow, you had the strength to pull the bookcase over onto him. Am I right?'

'Pretty much.'

'Then, you could only get out through the outside door, which you couldn't then lock. You vomited on the veranda, collected yourself, and went back to your room.'

'That's about right. I'm not sure he was stalking me. Maybe he saw my name when they announced the list of Fellows. I prayed when I left Fairlea – I was only there for three months, 12 years ago for a stupid thing I did – that I'd never see him again. He made it hell. Forever bailing me up, but I always managed to get away,' her voice cracks, '...until the time I didn't.'

Genevieve pats Robyn's arm. 'Oh, you poor darling.'

'Shit,' Susanna blurts, 'I reckon I'd have wanted to kill him too.'

'And me,' I say.

Lindsay stares at me, his brows furrowed. 'I am intrigued at how you put all this together, Jacqui.'

'Before I went to bed last night, I checked out the library again, because I couldn't figure out why the Sherlock Holmes book was open, face-down, under Jim's body. Then I found this bit of black wool,' I hold it up, 'hooked on the bookcase. I'd already noticed finger marks on a shelf. Tigger was at the door, and I blamed him for the vomit. I went back to my room and read all Jim's notes again because one had stuck in my head. For Robyn's sake, I won't read it out, but it referred to someone he named Rob. Then, when I looked through his pictures, I found one which looked a whole lot like

Robyn, though younger. The plaits and tattoo gave you away, Robyn, and you had prison garb on. I found a recent selfie of Jim, bald and beardless, so I ducked out to the coolroom. Sure enough, that horrible hair of his is a toupee.'

'I must say, I am impressed Jacqui,' Lindsay says. 'I doubt I could have reasoned so methodically.'

I laugh. 'You don't write, or probably read, crime fiction either.'

'Not my realm of interest, I confess.'

'Now, I guess we have to decide, collectively, what we're going to tell the police when they eventually get here. I'm sure Robyn doesn't need the ordeal of being questioned, possibly charged.'

Robyn sobs. 'And no way I'm going back to jail.'

Lindsay looks sympathetic. 'I should say it was death by misadventure. What do you all think?'

'Huh?' Susanna says.

Genevieve nods. 'A terrible accident.'

'I know how to make it look more convincing.' I dash upstairs to Jim's room and grab the two porn magazines from beside his bed, holding them by the edges so I don't leave fingerprints. Back downstairs, I ask Lindsay to follow me into the library. 'Okay, can you lift me up? I'll make it look like they were on top, you know, leave a mark in the dust.' I then toss them at the opposite shelf and leave them as they fall. 'Okay, you're stronger than me. Can you stomp on that second-bottom shelf and bust it?'

'Happy to.'

'Now, to get our stories straight.'

'Yes, Miss Marple.'

I whisper to Lindsay. 'I do believe this little crime has cured her of her need to rhyme.'

He smiles. 'An observation methinks quite sublime.'

GONE FISHING

It's not like me to be so tartily dressed but I'm angling for a particular fish. I've already fended off several other gropers now lounging around the bar with spread legs and salacious looks. He's sitting at a table alone. A predatory shark. I've given him the eye twice. Think he's hooked. I finish my wine, sling my bag on my shoulder, adjust my ridiculously short skirt and head for the door. Halfway across the car park, I stop; long enough to hear the bar door click. I keep walking across the potholed bitumen to the riverbank path. I hear his footsteps crunching on the gravel; still far enough behind for me to maintain my pace. This isn't the right spot yet. I know the place. He'll wait until we're well out of earshot of the carpark and beyond the path lights.

He feeds on darkness. Odd, really. You'd think he'd want to see the fear in his victim's eyes. But evil and darkness go hand in hand.

His pace quickens. Mine doesn't. I *want* him to catch me. His hand's on my shoulder sooner than I expected. He pulls me up short. Another hand on my hip and I'm being tossed like a ragdoll into the grass off the path. I land on my back. He's immediately on top of me. Beer breath in my face. I don't scream. That'll confuse him. He'll take it as submission, permission. Willingness, even. I've dreamed about this so many times, I'm surprised my heart's beating double-time.

'You want it, don'tcha?'

'Yeah.' *Go along with him and he might leave my hands free. Not clobber me.*

He's astride me, fumbling with his belt. I rub my hand up his arm like I'm wanting it. I hear the zip. His weight lifts off me as he shrugs his pants down. His hands are up my skirt, grappling at my knickers. He rips them down my thighs. Puts his hand between my legs. He stops dead. 'What the fuck is that?'

I can't see his face, but I use his distraction to flick the knife open. I swing it in an arc over my body and feel it connect. I close my eyes to avoid the spurts of blood. It's hot as it squirts across my chest. *Good shot. Must have hit his jugular.* He's gurgling like a water fountain. Body goes limp and falls sideways. A few splutters and gasps, then silence. I wriggle out from under his legs and find my bag. Pull out my phone and switch on the inbuilt torch. I pull the tiny menstrual cup from my crotch, dip my fingers in and smear the goop on his shrivelled dick. *Innocuous little pee-pee.* Hard to believe it's done so much damage.

I pop the cup into a ziplock bag, slip off the high heels, pull my runners from my bag, put them on then head through the shrubbery and across the park to the back of the shops. Plonk the heels into the Salvos collection bin and head home, keeping out of sight whenever a car approaches.

The Coonara's burning steadily when I enter my bungalow. I strip and put my clothes and the wig into the firebox; watch them erupt. I shower, wash my hair, and, once dry, slip into my pyjamas. I head across the yard to the house. Mum's comatose on the couch, a glass still in her hand. *Good.* I hear the TV down the hall and presume Tash is still awake. She's in bed staring blankly at the screen. Wordlessly, she pulls back the doona and I snug in beside her.

'Your hair smells nice,' she says.

'Just washed it. What are you watching?'

'Don't know. Wasn't really.'

'What say, tomorrow night you come to the pub with me? Get out of the house.'

She shrinks away from me. 'Can't Em. You know I can't.'

'Sometime, you're going to have to brave it. You can't stay in here all your life.' I put my arm around her, run my fingers though her hair.

'He might be out there.'

'No, Tash. He won't.'

'How do you know?'

'I just know. You're safe now.'

The sergeant holds up the cordon tape so that Homicide detectives Brett Johnson and Jacqui Ryan can duck under to survey the body. Behind them, a policeman is questioning the woman jogger who found the body an hour earlier. Johnson introduces Ryan to Robinson, the forensics officer collecting samples from the body and its surrounds.

'Not a pretty sight,' Ryan says. 'Talk about an initiation.'

'Oh, for you? Yes,' Johnson says. 'First dead body is a thing to grapple with, but at least you didn't vomit like my first newbie partner.'

'Any ID yet?' she asks the sergeant.

'Oh yeah. Well known to us. Jason Anthony Heard. Rap sheet as long as your arm. Assault, sexual assault. Paroled last week after 18 months in jail for rape.'

'Eighteen months? And he's out already?'

'On appeal. I guess *his* lawyer was better than hers.'

'That sucks.'

'Big time.'

'So, what's the thinking here?' Johnson asks the sergeant.

'Probably someone with a bone to pick. Came up behind and sliced his throat. He bled out pretty quickly.' The body is on its side, foetal position, pants half down.

A photographer paces carefully, snapping shots from every angle.

'What's your impression, Ryan?' Johnson asks.

She studies the scene. 'Weird that there's blood spray over there and here, but not that 40 centimetre patch in the middle where the grass is flat, like–'

'Like someone was lying there.'

'Exactly. So, maybe, rather than someone coming from behind, someone was *under* him and lashed out to defend themself.'

'Spot on, I'd say. Well done. Always assume more than one possible scenario.'

'So, where's the other person?'

'Good question.'

'Can we roll him on his back now?' Johnson asks Robinson.

'Sure.'

Johnson crouches to inspect the corpse's neck wound. 'Slashed from left to right, so probably right-handed.'

Ryan's barely listening. She's more interested in the guy's bloody penis. She kneels and sniffs it; careful not to lose balance and faceplant in his crotch. Her first impression was correct. 'That's menstrual blood.'

Johnson stares at her. 'How can you tell?'

'Think I don't know the smell?'

'Fair enough. Robinson, take a sample, will you?'

Ryan sits back on her heels. 'Best guess is, he's penetrated the victim – who was obviously menstruating – and she's slashed out with whatever she could get her hands on; his knife maybe.'

'Sounds plausible.'

Johnson looks up. 'Any sign of a knife?' Robinson's already shaking his head. 'Better search the bushes.'

'Not to mention the river,' Ryan says.

'That'll be the second option. No point getting divers in yet.' Johnson's radio crackles. 'Yeah?'

'Barman says Heard was there last night, drinking alone. Thinks he left about 9.30.'

'Ask him if there was a girl, maybe on her own, who might have left at the same time.' Johnson waits.

'Yep. Says there was. Says he didn't know her. About 18 or 19, attractive, heavy makeup, black bob-style hair, wearing a miniskirt, dark shirt and high heels.'

'Thanks Steve. See what else you can find out. Find any customers who were there.'

'Will do.'

Johnson looks at Ryan. 'Usual MO for a sex offender. Scope a girl on her own and follow her.' He turns to one of the officers. 'Jerry, can you check the hospital and doctors' clinics; see if a young woman has presented with assault or rape injuries?'

'Why would a young girl walk alone along here in the dark?' Ryan asks.

'Maybe she had to.' Johnson points across the river. 'There's a footbridge about 100 metres down there; leads over to a new housing estate.'

I roll over and flick on the radio. Some shit about a footballer. More shit about the economy. Then...

"Homicide detectives are on the scene of a suspected murder at Riverlea. The body of a man, aged in his early 30s, was discovered early this morning. Police say the victim is known to them, but have not yet released his name."

Definitely dead then. How long's it going to take them to turn up here? I dress and head across to the house. Tash is sitting at the kitchen bench, a half-eaten bowl of cornflakes in front of her. I hate how hollow she looks. No light in her eyes. Hair matted. PJs hanging off her wasted frame. Wrists still bandaged.

I put bread in the toaster. 'Mum up?'

Tash shakes her head. 'Didn't go to bed. Still in there on the couch, snoring.'

I grunt. I've stopped commenting on Mum's drinking. She was so vibrant three years ago; a waste of space now. The toast pops. I spread on margarine and Vegemite and sit beside Tash. 'They're a bit past it; those PJs. How about we go to Kmart and get you some new ones?' I know she'll say no. Stepping out the front door gives her palpitations and sweats.

'Don't care.'

'You'll get over this one day, you know.'

'All right for you to say. He didn't pick you.'

'I know. But it could just as easily have been me.'

The contempt in her face cuts like a knife. 'And you just sat and watched.'

'No, Tash. I've told you before. I froze. I just,' I fight the tears, 'I didn't know what to do. I was so scared for us both. But you don't have to worry any more 'cos he's dead.'

'Dead?' Her eyes show the first spark I've seen in ages. 'How do you know?'

'On the radio.'

A door-to-door of the housing estate turns up nothing. No household with a teenager fitting the girl's description. Ryan and Johnson sit in the car eating KFC.

Still chewing a mouthful of chicken, Ryan asks, 'What do we know about his previous victims?'

'The CIU guys are checking that. All I know so far, is all four girls were 14 or 15.'

'Jesus. Virgins?'

'All but one. The one he was in jail for. Apparently, the appeal judge ruled that the prosecution hadn't proved that the girl wasn't a willing participant.'

'Bloody hell. Blame the victim.'

Johnson's radio buzzes. 'No shows at the hospital or clinics.'

'Thanks Steve.' He hangs up. 'Some poor girl's probably at home going it alone.'

'Probably scared to death. Reckon it's worth talking to his earlier victims? Maybe...what am I thinking? Maybe one of them set him up.'

'Possible.'

Julie Withers, Tiffany Myers, Taylah Welsh and Courtney Hyland were all glad to hear their attacker was dead, but all had been home with their families last night.

'Now what?' Ryan asks Johnson as they depart Courtney's house.

'Blood test might give us some answers, but that's only going to work if the girl's on the DNA criminal databank, which is highly unlikely.'

'I reckon she's local, though. Can't they cross reference the sample with hospital records here?'

'Not the done thing. But...I'll ring forensics.'

Five days have gone by and still no sign of the cops. Things obviously take longer than on *CSI*. No witnesses have come forward. Cops have no clue who killed him. I *want* them to know who. *And* why.

We're sitting here eating TV dinners. Mum's on her third Bundy. Tash is absently twirling macaroni around the plastic dish with her fork. Same scenario, different night.

There's a knock at the front door. I get up and open it. The man and woman show me their credentials and introduce themselves. Their names go in one ear and out the other.

'Are you Natasha Fraser?' he asks.

'No, I'm Emma. Tash's my sister.'

'Can we speak to her please?'

'Yeah. Come in.'

'Tash, these people are from Homicide. They want to talk to you.'

'Me? Why?' Then it dawns on her. 'Is this about that prick, Heard?'

'Yes,' he says. 'We'd like to ask where you were last Friday night.'

'Here.'

'You didn't leave the house?'

Mum grunts. 'Hasn't left the house for three years.'

They both look stunned. 'May we ask why?' he says.

'Since that bastard raped me.'

He looks shocked. 'There's nothing on the police files. Did you not report it?'

Tash glares at Mum, whose face is buried in her glass, then looks at the detectives and shakes her head.

'Why?' he asks.

'Ask her.' Tash points at Mum.

Mum's seething. Looks like she's ready to explode. 'Told you this'd come back to slap us in the face. Little tart.'

My blood boils. 'Mum! How could you? She didn't do *anything.*'

'Yeah, and neither did you,' she spits.

'Whoa.' The woman detective raises her hand. 'Let's all calm down. Emma, do I take it correctly that you were there when your sister was assaulted?'

'Yes. And Mum's right I didn't *do* anything.' I can't stop the tears. 'I saw it all. What that bastard did to her. But what could I do? I was so scared. I hid until I was sure he was gone.''What happened then?' she asks.

'She was half unconscious. I carried her home. Told mum *everything.*'

'And you didn't call the police, Mrs Fraser?'

'No,' Tash says. 'She told me I was *asking* for it and that the cops'd say the same. More like she didn't want to be embarrassed. Y'know, what would her *friends* think?'

'Instead,' I say, 'look what it's done to us. Mum's an alco, Tash's an agoraphobic, too afraid to...*live,* and I've got to deal with them both. We all cheered when he went to jail for raping that other girl and then we find out two weeks ago that he's out again already.'

He looks at us individually. 'Guess you were happy to hear he was dead, then.'

'You bet.'

'Hang on a minute,' Mum says, 'if you didn't know about Tash, how come you're here?'

He leans forward, looks at Tash. 'Forensics took some samples at the scene. Menstrual fluid. It was a 99 percent match to a blood sample taken from you at the hospital a fortnight ago.'

Tash looks astonished. 'Can't have been. A – I wasn't there. B – I haven't had a period for yonks.'

He turns his gaze on me. 'DNA tells us it's just as likely to have come from a full sibling.'

I look at him, deadpan. 'No kidding.'

Mum looks horrified. Her mouth's open but nothing's coming out.

The woman detective's got her hand on her mouth. 'You were there.'

He looks gobsmacked.

'Yep.'

'Did he rape you?'

'Ten seconds longer and he would have.'

Tash gasps.

'But you were armed?'

'And ready.'

'You mean you deliberately led him there?' he asks.

I explain what happened. Every detail. 'One week out and he does it again. You guys can't keep these bastards in jail. So, I killed him to give Tash her life back, and to show those fucking lawyers that this is what women have to do to protect ourselves. I'm quite prepared to spend 18 months in jail. I sure don't deserve longer than him.'

I should have known it wouldn't be 18 months. My crime was, as the judge said, premeditated, but my counsel successfully had the charge reduced from murder to involuntary manslaughter. I was, after all, defending myself. The judge, thankfully, took into account the mitigating circumstances; the fact I wanted to be caught, that I cooperated with police, that Heard was killed while committing a crime, and that I pleaded guilty. Ten years, with a minimum of eight, which leaves maybe six more given the time I've already served.

What will I do with the time? Keep my head down and continue my law studies, that's what. Okay, so with a criminal conviction I won't be able to practice law, but it will be a handy adjunct to being a social worker and helping others like Tash. Tash, by the way, is making small steps back to normality and braves visiting me each month.

So, was it worth me slitting the bastard's throat to stop him doing it again?

You bet it was.

RED ROBIN

THEY CALL ME RED ROBIN. NOT BECAUSE MY HAIR IS NATURALLY red. Nor is my name Robin. But I don't mind the sobriquet. To have earned it at the tender age of 19 is quite something, I think. And given that my name is Scarlet – Scarlet Deverall – they're not so far off the mark.

Whoever dreamed it up had a vivid imagination, given that the witness accounts were so vague. One minute brunette, the next blonde, another, mousy. It's bemusing that none had mentioned my diminutive stature; perhaps one doesn't notice such things when one has a gun in one's face.

I am tiny, but what I lack in height, I make up for in gumption. It helps my cause immeasurably that I am, invariably, described as the bold young lad with the falsetto voice. Who would suspect that this intrepid, gun-toting bandit is a demure young woman with a flair for embroidery and a score to settle?

The scrubby gum trees around us provide a perfect ambuscade. A different spot from last time. I put my finger to my lips to hush Ebon and Indigo's babble. It's their jolly jabbering that'll get us all caught one day. But I know I can rely on their pluck when it's needed. The *Great Leviathan*, on its regular run from Ballaarat to Geelong, is due to round the bend any minute. It's the most luxurious Cobb & Co coach ever built and bestows the ultimate in luxury for its 48 or so well-heeled passengers. I can hear the snorting of the horses and feel the ground tremble almost before I hear the thunder of their hooves. It's a magnificent sight; the team of 12 greys with periwinkle rosettes on their ear buckles, resplendent in their polished harness and mountings. It's a shame to startle them.

Our pistols, two apiece, are already loaded with powder and lead balls when I give the boys the nod to pull their black kerchiefs – now ornately embroidered with red robins, since I have adopted the name – up over their noses. No time for second thoughts. As fore-planned, they dash onto the road and stand abreast, pistols aloft, 80 yards ahead of the approaching *Leviathan*. I remain, crouching low, guns holstered, shanghai loaded with a two-inch stone. I take aim, pull back on the leather pocket and wait until the driver's head is in range.

Don't get me wrong, I bear no ill-will against Ned Devine – already dubbed the "emperor of coachmen" – but it is the driver I must indispose, if only temporarily. Thus, I lower my sights. Already he is pulling back on the reins and calling to the four postilion riders to do likewise. It takes some distance to pull up such a behemoth; not unlike stopping a sailing ship.

The moment is propitious and I let fly my missile. A glancing blow to Devine's shoulder suffices to cause him to let go the reins. I see the passengers atop the carriage all leaning forward as though they might stem the vehicle's momentum.

Ebon and Indigo stand their ground as I emerge from my cover, pistols aimed, and join them. The mighty coach shudders to a standstill, close enough for us to see the trepidation in the horses' eyes. I am tempted to call out stand and deliver but regard the instruction as prosaic, when I prefer originality.

I see no fear in the eyes of the rooftop passengers, which takes me aback. They clap and call out, 'Red Robin. It's the fearless Red Robin.' To say I'm chuffed is an understatement, but I hold no score for such conceit. Besides, I haven't the time. I have a destiny to fulfil.

I muster the gruffest voice I can. 'I have no quarrel with you fine folk, excepting for one. But given that you have so generously stopped at our behest, I might encourage you to extend that generosity and hand over a trinket each.'

To my surprise, some of the women atop the carriage are already unpinning brooches or pulling rings off fingers. It is as though it is a privilege to donate to us, such is our heightening notoriety. But it is among the interior passengers – those prosperous enough to afford the higher fare – that I expect to disinter our nemesis. Surely this time our scrutiny of the man in question will find him aboard. I fully expect these passengers will be less inclined to relieve themselves of jewellery or valuables; the rich being almost invariably less charitable.

I move to the side of the towering red carriage, guns still steady. I am barely taller than its front wheel and the windows are high above my head. Too high to see anyone save those peering from their window seats. I gesture to Ebon to fetch the barrel we deposited by the roadside earlier for just such a contingency and he helps me climb up. I do not see our quarry amongst the 30 or so travellers. Too many bonnet rims and feathers on the females' heads to obscure my view.

'Rufus Babcock. Show yourself.' I realise that my voice can scarce be heard over the hubbub inside the carriage.

'Oh, he's so tall,' a young woman closest to the door says, 'and so handsome'. She casts me a wink as she pulls the silver and ruby earrings from her lobes and drops them into the voluntarily filled cloth bag. Pity I shan't be able to wear them. She appears almost overcome with fervour. I confer a reciprocal wink – to perpetuate the masculine guise, you understand. I open the door and she loops the bag cord over my pistol and left hand so it drops to my elbow, just as a second bag is tossed from above into Indigo's hands. 'Just wait till I tell Emmie and Anna that I met Red Robin. They'll be so jealous.' I nod at her and feign a blown kiss at which she puts her hand to her heart and batts her eyelashes. I repeat my earlier instruction to draw out Babcock, but the crowd falls temporarily mute.

'He is not aboard,' a woman calls from the third row back. I crane my neck to distinguish her, and tuck back an errant strand of hair that falls from beneath my hat. It is Bessie Babcock herself. She leans forward, her lilac bonnet, brim full of satin birds, shielding the face of the passenger beside her. But I know it is him. The Falstaffian figure with the flaming beard.

'I see you Rufus Babcock. You cannot hide behind your wife's aviary of a hat.'

Babcock leans forward, as best as his paunch will allow. His rheumy eyes hold my gaze. Those same rheumy eyes that I saw through the keyhole on that night that brought me to this day and the retribution I seek. 'And what business do you have with me, young man?'

I wonder whether that gumption I mentioned earlier has escaped me for, unexpectedly, I cannot reply. No words come. I realise, foolishly, that attempting to exact vengeance amid a multitude of onlookers necessitates disclosing the basis of such vengeance and may therefore reveal my identity. Yet what harm would come of that? This villain deserves to be hung out to dry. But I cannot possibly compel Babcock to demount the carriage, without those 20 in front of him first clearing the way. My hesitation eats seconds. I feel a prod on my calf and turn to see Indigo's quizzical eyes.

'What are you doing?' he whispers.

'Not today. Too problemat–' My voice is drowned out by an explosion from above.

I look up to see Willy Hanley with a smoking pistol in hand. Willy Bloody Hanley. I should have figured Babcock's henchmen would be aboard. Beside him, Tom O'Laherty is filling his pistol with powder. I look down at Indigo, there on the ground clutching his left hand to his bloody right shoulder. I'm mortified. I had not bargained on my brother being harmed, despite his unerring bravado.

I jump from the barrel and motion to Ebon to run. He flees into the bush as I help Indigo to his feet. 'Come on. Get to the horses.' As we stand, I hear the whip crack and a 'c'mon' from the mouth of Ned Devine. The carriage starts to roll and as I look back, I see dozens of waving hands at the windows.

Indigo sucks in a deep breath and tries hard not to wince, as I poke about in the wound, determined to clean it of gunpowder and fragments of his shirt that may have gone into it. Fortunately, the shot only clipped the fleshy part of his shoulder, and appears not as serious as I first thought. My expertise in embroidery and petit point has not stretched to stitching skin before, but for a 17-year-old, Indigo is being brave in the doing, though he looks a tomfool with the spoon between his teeth. 'Just another stitch or two and then I will find something as a bandage.'

'Don't ever want to be shot again. Not sure that being a bushranger is all it's cracked up to be.'

'Oh, where's your sense of adventure? But, and I say this to you both, we will soon be restored to our rightful place and our days of transgression will be over.'

Ebon looks downcast. 'But it is such fun. Well, maybe not for Indigo today.'

'Fun it might be, Ebon – and I acknowledge that we make a formidable team – but today was a close call, and I will have no brother of mine settle for a criminal future.'

'What are we to do,' Indigo asks, 'about Babcock?'

'We'll figure a better plan. Something more private and personal. Now, show me the booty and pass me that knife. I can cut a bag open and use it for a bandage.'

Ebon opens the bags that have been sitting on the table in Mrs McGillivray's parlour since we returned to the boarding house. He spills the contents onto the table. We're all rendered speechless. Such a haul we hadn't expected. Three tiny gold nuggets, necklaces, earrings, brooches of all imaginable colours, a cameo, a gold pocket watch and a polished silver hip flask replete with whiskey. I tear the bag into strips and bandage Indigo's shoulder. 'Now, go and pop a clean shirt on to hide the dressing.'

'I'll have this,' says Ebon, laying claim to the flask.

'Phooey,' I smack his hand, 'you're not even old enough to drink.'

'I say, if I'm old enough to rob a stagecoach, I am old enough to drink.'

I can't disagree with that. 'And you, Indigo, what do you choose?'

'The watch, absolutely.' He snatches it up.

'Just check that it is not engraved, or you might come undone.'

He checks it over; front, back and inside the covers, and shakes his head. 'What will you choose, Scarlet?'

I study the items carefully. No point choosing something too easily recognised. I select the largest of the nuggets and an exquisite lapis lazuli brooch and pop them in my beaded purse.

'Hey,' Indigo says, 'how come you get two things?'

'The brooch isn't for me. Now hush.'

'Pity we can't keep it all,' Ebon says.

'You know the rules, Ebon. Now go fetch the box.'

Ebon stands, but I put my fingers to my lips as I hear the telltale rattle of the outer door. 'Quickly, hide it. She's back.' Indigo swipes the loot into his lap with his forearm and covers it with a serviette.

'Ah, children,' Mrs Gillivray chortles, as she enters the room in her usual flurriedly manner. 'You haven't made yourselves tea? I'll put the kettle on.'

Glad am I that I took the time to change from my self-tailored trousers and jacket into my violet day dress, though the former is so much more comfortable than the constraints of corset and lace.

'And what have you cherubs been up to today?'

My face is all innocence. 'Ebon and Indigo have groomed the horses and mucked out the stable and I have been attending to my latest embroidery.'

'Wonderful. You've spent a productive day then. I can't abide unproductive children. Oh, word is just in that the stagecoach has been robbed. A rider, just back from Geelong, says it was the Red Robin Gang again. I say, that young man and his cohorts are veritable Robin Hoods. Word is that they give most of their plunder to the less fortunate. And so polite, I hear.'

I raise my eyebrows. 'Is that so? I hear he is very brave.'

'Brave indeed. It was none other than the *Great Leviathan.* Fancy anyone having the mettle to tackle such a giant.'

'It truly defies reason.'

We wait until Mrs McGillivray has tidied the parlour and retired to bed, with her usual parting words – "Don't stay up too late" – and set our agenda for tomorrow.

'First thing,' I say, 'is we ride to the mine and hand over the box to Li Chin.' Indigo and Ebon nod approval. The Chinese miners at Mount Egerton have a tough time of it and Li Chin is always grateful for our offerings. He dispenses the trinkets to those most in need, among them some of the desperate natives, so they can afford to eat and clothe themselves. He invariably offers us a tasty meal as a reward.

'And then?' Indigo asks.

'And then we have some business at the bank.'

'The bank?' Ebon says.

Indigo is equally puzzled. 'Which bank?'

'Babcock's of course.'

'But he won't be there. He'll be in Geelong by then.'

'As the proverb says, while the cat's away...'

'Ah. So are we to rob it?'

'Why not? Get back something of what he has taken from us.'

Ebon rubs his hands together. 'A topping idea. But will you manage, Indigo, with your injured arm?'

'I'll be all right. Feels better already.'

We're sitting atop our mounts opposite Babcock's bank in Mt Egerton, surveying the comings and goings of customers. Some might revel in the thrill of being held up, but we don't want too large a crowd. We learned that lesson yesterday. It's dusty and smelly and the boys are fidgety and impatient. We wait until we're relatively certain all male customers have exited the premises and I give the go-ahead. We pull up our kerchiefs and cover the short distance with alacrity.

Once inside, we draw our pistols. The lone teller is wide-eyed, flabbergasted, hands already in the air without me even giving the instruction. Two women are backed against the wall, hands on mouths but evincing surprise more than panic. They whisper to each other. 'It's the Red Robin Gang!'

'Hand over the money and nobody gets hurt.' My voice sounds thin, fragile. I must practise more.

The teller grabs a bag and begins to stuff it with sovereigns and half-sovereigns from the drawer. I keep my eyes on him closely but am distracted by a gasp from one of the women. She's staring at the teller, her mouth agape. Indigo's eyes widen and he raises his pistol.

'Let go the weapon,' he shouts.

I turn my gaze back to the teller, his pistol still in hand. 'Drop it, or I'll shoot.' He's taking too long, so I pull the trigger. The ball disappears through the timber ceiling. He drops his pistol on the floor and raises his hands again.

'Sorry. I must at least appear to be protecting Mr Babcock's interests. I don't mean you no harm.'

'Well come along,' I say, 'just hand over the bag and we'll be off.' I turn to the customers. 'Just so you know, this is Babcock's money we're stealing, not yours.'

'Hallelujah to that,' one of the women says, 'there's no end to the man's greed and villainy. He's been stealing from us for years. I say it's about time somebody showed him how it feels to be robbed.'

We depart to the sound of clapping hands.

We give the horses a day's break before riding at dawn for Ballaarat. Ebon and Indigo have some suspicion about my plans but I tell them it is for a good cause. They are excited at the prospect of seeing Grandmamma again, but I haven't apprised them of my ulterior motive. That will come first, before I resign myself to reverting to plain old Scarlet, the meek and dutiful granddaughter. The weather is fine, which makes the three-hour ride a touch less arduous. We stop several times to give the horses a break and to stretch our saddle-weary legs and buttocks.

It is some time since we have ventured back to Ballaarat. Grandmamma, of course, thinks our departure from her homely clutches several months ago was a case of adolescent gold-fever, not some scheming mission to regain our birthrights. I have no cause to have her think otherwise. She still mourns the brutal and untimely loss of her daughter, our mother. But like everyone, other than Ebon, Indigo and me, she knows not who to blame. I am glad that the boys did not bear witness to the bloody events that fateful night. It was a scurry to draw them from their beds, get them silently clothed and out to the horses before Babcock had an inkling of our presence. At least today's ride has not been as dark and furious as that hasty flight from Creswick Park to Grandmamma's.

It was but a year ago, when I felt the twins were old enough to understand, that I imparted the horror of our parents' fate. They were immediate in their oath of revenge. Perhaps more vehement than me; such is the nature of boys. But I have had to rein in their youthful ebullience and invest them with cool-mindedness lest they go off half-cocked.

We are trotting along the broad boulevard of Sturt Street, admiring the tree-lined centre gardens, when Indigo spots it first. He points, his face a profile of disgust. 'He's renamed the store. Bastard. Look at that. Babcock's Haberdashery.'

The name is so mocking and obtrusive. Mamma and Papa would die their deaths again to see this outrage. It was their sweat and blood that built the business from a mere market stall to the grandest emporium in town. I have the whim to visit it, in the vain hope of being reacquainted with Florence, should she still be there. I secretly hope she is not; that common sense would not see her prevail under Babcock's perfidious regime.

'I have a change of plan, boys. We will adjourn to Lester's Hotel for some sustenance and so that I might change my clothes. You two will stay at the hotel while I reconnoitre the store and find out what's what.'

'But we want to come too,' the twins say in unison.

'You cannot. You have no other disguises for my later plan.'

'Which is what?'

'I will tell you later.'

Indigo is disgruntled. 'Can't keep up with you, sis.'

Satisfied with a belly full of mutton, potatoes and beer, I emerge from Lester's as my charming and sophisticated self, complete with bonnet and gloves. I saunter along the street and enter what *was* Deverall's Haberdashery. Not much has changed, except that the milliner's mannequins appear laden with dust and the full mannequins are decidedly woebegone. The merchandise does not sparkle as it did under Mamma's keen eye. A surly floor walker inspects my every move, yet offers no assistance. Looks like he wouldn't know a button from a bow or a hat from hosiery. Customers are as scarce as a red note on a pianoforte keyboard.

'It is very quiet,' I comment.

The man nods. 'Has been for a while.'

'And why is that? The street is positively bustling outside.'

He shrugs.

'Is Mr Babcock in, by any chance?'

'Seldom. See him but once a fortnight when he comes for the takings.'

'What about Florence? Is she still here?'

'Nup. Gone to Bailey's.'

'To Bailey's you say?' Bailey's is Ballaarat's *other* haberdashery. 'Why would she leave? She loved it here.'

'Aye, as did Wilhelmina and Dorrie, but they have gone too. Can't say I blame them.'

'Was there some problem?'

'I shouldn't say, madam, but it seems they were not too enamoured of Mr Babcock.'

'Oh. And when do you expect to see him again? I have some business with him.'

'Comes of a Thursday afternoon, every other week, so he'd be due this week. Should I tell him of your enquiry?'

'No sir, that won't be necessary.'

While still appropriately attired, I summon the boys from their table and we take up the reins again for the short ride to Grandmamma's cottage by Lake Wendouree. She is delighted at our unexpected visit and ushers us inside with open arms. 'How long are you staying?'

'Just a few days,' I reply.

'I will have to get baking then.'

We regale her with a fabricated version of life on the diggings and assure her that we have the best of care under Mrs McGillivray's roof.

'And here's me been thinking you'd been out under canvas or lost down a mine.'

I open my purse and pass her the brooch. The brilliant blue stones match her eyes.

'For me? Why's it's lovely, but you shouldn't be spending your hard-earned money on me.' She pins it to the bodice of her peach-coloured dress.

'It's a mere trifle, Grandmamma, and it suits you perfectly. Oh, we saw, coming through town, that Babcock has his name on our store.'

'Ugh. What I wouldn't do to that sod if I could get my hands on him. Half of Ballaarat is afeared of him; the other half wants to shoot him, and I'd be happy to load the gun. Out there at Creswick Park like the lord of the manor, living the high life in my own daughter's house, no less.'

I smile at her wit. She doesn't know the half of Babcock's skulduggery; that he forged Papa's signature on the property and store deeds the day before he murdered them in cold blood. Nor does she know what her mild-mannered grandchildren have in store for him. 'Yes. He is certainly bolder than a hyena at a carcass feast. But what can one do? He has the whole town in the palms of his grubby hands.'

'That's to say nothing of his standover tactics at the Mount Egerton mine,' Indigo says. 'He's a bastard through and through.'

Grandmamma raises her finger. 'Mind your language, young man, though I can't say I don't concur with your epithet.'

We have three days to wait for Babcock's return, so we spend the morning helping Grandmamma with some chores before heading for a swim in the lake. All the time, my mind ticks with plots to take my revenge on Babcock. We dip and frolic in the water, the sun warm on our backs, then fall about on the shore in exhaustion. The boys also must be scheming. 'How do you think we should best deal with Babcock?' Indigo asks.

Ebon sits up. 'I say we get a barrel of black powder from Li Chin and blow up the bank. With him in it, of course.'

'Not a bad idea, Ebon, but remember, our deeds are most probably in his safe.'

'Then we blow up the *Leviathan* on the return run.'

'We cannot take out innocent people, not to mention those handsome horses. No, I am thinking something more personal; a direct approach. Aha, I have it. Today, we hold up the haberdashery, tomorrow his hardware store, on Wednesday, the tobacconist. If my presumption is correct, I believe his staff will be only too willing to hand over his take.'

'A champion idea,' Indigo says.

'Then, come Friday, we return to Mount Egerton, and without the camouflage of our bandit attire, we conscript the aid of the constabulary and confront him at the bank on Monday. Compel him to hand over the deeds and reveal him as the murderous rogue he is.'

'We're all for it,' Ebon says as Indigo nods.

'But we must not get caught in the meantime, else we'll be the ones in gaol.'

We're galloping back to Mount Egerton, our saddlebags heavier. We laugh at the Wanted notices placed all around Ballaarat before our departure, and the hastily produced sketches – none of which bear any resemblance to any of us. It seems that all our amenable victims were inexplicably divergent in their descriptions. Most of them happily acquiesced to our demands, given the rewards we offered in return for such consideration. The Ballaarat constabulary, it seems, were most confounded that the Red Robin Gang should be so inscrutable and elusive.

Upon our arrival, we see that the townsfolk are already apprised of our exploits, courtesy of the latest edition of the *Courier*. The mood about the village is buoyant as they gather around the store and cheer at the notice in the window. *All hail the Red Robin Gang.* We can't help grinning at each other.

Mrs McGillivray is pleased to see us and is full of gossip. 'Seems to me those traders were more than happy to hand over Babcock's money – if you read between the lines, that is. Did you chance to see them? The dashing Red Robin Gang?'

Indigo and Ebon look set to burst. I speak before they're tempted to let the cat out of the bag. 'No, it seems we missed them by moments on more than one occasion. But they are the talk of Ballaarat.'

'I would love to have seen Babcock's face when he heard the news. You know he was also aboard the *Leviathan* when it was robbed.'

'So we heard. Such audacity.'

I'm dressed in my new turquoise dress and bonnet, bought at Marshall's, Ballaarat's most exclusive boutique, while Ebon and Indigo look most debonair in their smart new day suits. As we enter the bank, we're flanked by Constables Hessop and Daly, who seem only too eager to grant Babcock his comeuppance. They were not at all surprised to hear our story of his murderous skulduggery. They asked only why it had taken us so long to come forward.

'I was a mere child of 14, and my brothers just 12, on that terrible night. What could we do?' I had explained.

For someone who has undergone a week of trauma, Babcock looks surprisingly calm, smug even. He sees through me to the constables and raises his hand in greeting. 'I hope you're bearers of good news. That you have nabbed those nefarious scoundrels.'

'On the contrary,' Hessop says, 'it is you with whom we take issue. Your grief of late comes as no perturbation to us, in fact I might say, and I am sure my colleague will agree, we applaud it.'

'What? What's that you say?' Babcock is rising from his chair, red-faced. 'But is it not obvious I have been the target of these wilful attacks on my business interests and, indeed, my own person?'

'Come now, Babcock, it is but a small quittance for the torment and grief you have inflicted on others. Is that not so?' His last comment is directed to me.

'Indeed.'

Babcock finally focuses on me and the boys. 'And who might you be?'

'I am Scarlet Deverall, daughter of Lewis and Elizabeth Deverall, and these are my brothers, Ebon and Indigo. Need I say more?'

Babcock loses some of his bluster. 'And what should that mean to me? Why, you're just a child.'

'No, I was just a child when you slaughtered our parents five years ago.'

'Me? I never–'

'I saw you, through the keyhole. I saw you run my father through with a poker like some crazed musketeer. I saw my mother already–' I can barely contain my tears, '–bludgeoned on the floor, and you wiping her blood from your beard, the marble bust from our mantelpiece still in your hand'.

Ebon and Indigo gasp simultaneously.

Babcock looks wildly at Hessop and Daly. 'She's lying. Never trust a woman. They're all liars.'

Hessop raises his hand to silence Babcock. 'And I suppose Florence Bournemouth and Wilhelmina Pearce also lied when they told of your lewd advances and your short pay. And that Li Chin lied when he spoke of your constant short-changing.'

'Never trust a Chinaman, either. They're the worst of all liars.'

'Face it, Babcock, you're through. We, the constabulary, have long suspected you for murdering the Deveralls, but until now have had no witness accounts to prove it. The fact that Miss Deverall has accurately described the manner of her parents' deaths, as only an eyewitness could have, and the fact that within a week you had taken possession of their property, lends great weight to your guilt. We can muster any number of victims who will testify to your chicanery, thievery and aggression, not to mention forgery. With all that under your collar, I can see they will need a large noose indeed.'

'It is quite something,' I say to Florence, as we unfurl a bolt of newly-shipped crimson brocade, 'to be back here after all these years.'

'It is so good to have you back, and so good of you to restore my position. They have not the same class at Bailey's. Still, it is not the same without your dear mother.'

'I know. There is so much I still need to learn. But Grandmamma is a willing teacher.' She is there, now, at the front window fluffing the hats and laying out the latest stock from England.

'You have been so generous Scarlet. Millie at the tobacconists tells me she was quite overcome with your recompense.'

'I felt obliged to right some wrongs. The fact it was with Babcock's own money made it all the more sweet.'

'Fancy you, being the infamous Red Robin. You're a colourful trio, you three.'

'Shh, you must never mention it, in case the others hear, and I take it you are referring to our names.'

She hastily covers her mouth, but her eyes twinkle in the confidence of our secret. Straight as a die she is. I know she will never tell. She changes the subject. 'What are the boys up to?'

'Oh, they love it out there. All that lovely pasture in which to chase sheep around, ride their horses, swim in the river, entrance the neighbour's daughters. They're happy as a pair of sandboys. What say you come to

Creswick Park for the weekend? See them for yourself. I know they would be most pleased to see you. We shall have such fun. We shall ride and swim and picnic and party – just like the old days. Although now that I am old enough, we will drink too. We will toast our newfound fortune.'

'Oh yes please.' Florence waits a moment until Wilhelmina and Dorrie are out of earshot and whispers to me. 'Perhaps you will show me your Red Robin outfit. Do you think you will ever don it again?'

'Only if another Babcock comes along.'

WILD JASMINE

THE KNIFE WAS BLUNT AS BUGGERY – GIVEN THAT HER WHETSTONE had vanished – but that didn't mean it couldn't inflict some serious damage. She slipped it up the sleeve of her flannelette nightie; the tight cuff held it in place. The bastards would never suspect that a wiry granny with three daughters, a wayward son and their umpteen progeny might be packing a weapon.

Besides, they didn't know her history.

It was a nightly ritual: slipping the knife into place when her eyelids started to wilt, no matter how good the book; making sure her glasses were handy; checking that all five stars remained in the box; turning off the bedside lamp; and succumbing to the oppressive darkness.

It wasn't that she was obsessive. Nor was she afraid. It was just that she'd have been a good boy scout.

No, it wouldn't pay to mess with Jaz Hyland.

The neighbourhood's septuagenarians were being terrorised in their beds by balaclava-clad burglars, who evidently thought that a bunch of lone oldies were easy prey. Especially a bunch of oldies spread far apart on five-acre blocks in an edge-of-town hobby farm enclave where no-one would hear their screams.

Winnie McTaggart had been beaten rainbow-coloured in the wee small hours – all for a pearl necklace and a purse with fifteen dollars housekeeping. She'd earned a week in hospital and was too scared to come home again. She'd been bundled off to a nursing home.

Frank Harwood's stint in Vietnam had been too long ago for his combat skills to come into play. He was deaf and near-blind and never heard his 3am attackers. Their baseball bats left him shattered and broken. Then his heart gave out. His gold Rolex and spoon collection would have barely raised thirty dollars at a pawn shop.

Mary Sanderson had tried to defend herself and suffered broken wrists, concussion and a purple eye. Her Cairn terrier's back was broken. The spoils? A dodgy microwave, a temperamental TV and her cards purse with all of five dollars in coins. She too, had decided a nursing home might be a safer option. The For Sale sign was already up.

And what had the police done?

Eight-tenths of bugger all. The crimes were too sporadic to warrant surveillance on the street and the victims too incoherent to give them useful perpetrator IDs. So they'd filed reports and hoped the mini crime spree was over.

Of course, they'd knocked on Jaz's door, the day after Mary's attack, to ask whether she'd seen or heard anything. She'd shuffled ahead of them into the lounge and cupped her hand to her ear to encourage them to speak louder. It was a useful ploy in such situations. He was burly, with a misogynistic mouth, while she was inoffensively subordinate and tacit; no doubt *because* of his misogynistic mouth. His attitude and rank were a dead giveaway; the town's highest ranking officer, Senior Sergeant Warren Frick, known widely as Frick the Prick. They'd assured her they'd watch out for her and the other not-yet-victims in the street.

"Make sure your doors are locked, don't leave valuables in plain sight, keep a phone beside your bed," they'd said.

Blah blah. What good was locking your doors if the bastards have no qualms about smashing a window?

They'd offered to check out her house; make sure everything was secure, but she'd waved them out the door like a pair of blowflies.

No way was she letting them check under her bed. Or in the chest freezer.

If the truth be known, she hadn't missed her neighbours at all. She was done with their complaining about her backyard menagerie. The dogs, cats, chooks, ducks and guinea fowl were one thing, but they'd collectively bridled at the emu, roos and excavating wombat. But it was the fox cubs she'd nursed, fed and released after their mother became a roadkill victim that snapped the amicable rubber band. Not to mention the dingo that lurked in the reserve behind and patrolled their back fence lines in search of dinner.

Things were quieter now that Frank wasn't hurling abuse over the fence. Just because he'd served in Vietnam didn't mean he wasn't a bastard. She'd seen him out there taking potshots at the dingo, Zeus, over the fence. His property would come up for auction soon – as a deceased estate; a conveniently cheap way to invest in real estate. The dam on his property would serve her adopted flock nicely.

Actually, it had been pretty quiet for a while – since Richard had gone. She hadn't missed him either. Not one bit. She'd got rid of his recliner, so the lifebuoy-sized depression in the seat no longer reminded her of his utter impotence. A TV-watching turnip whose only animation was to bark orders like a salivating hyena.

Fortunately, nobody else had missed him either, given that he hadn't ventured outside for years, save for Friday nights when he'd come home pissed and penniless from the pokies at the pub. Goodness knew who he poked in some public place on the way home. He'd loll in the door stinking of beer and spoof and try to pass it off as a night out with the boys.

Never had a clue that she was there lurking. Keeping tabs on him. So she hadn't bothered reporting his missingness. If she didn't care, who else would?

What was she thinking all those years ago? But then, he'd been different in Paris. Isn't everyone? They'd met on the Pont Neuf: he scouting for available arse; she scouting for a suitable vantage point. He'd been a welcome post-assignment distraction. And pretty hot in the sack to boot. It should have remained a mere holiday romance. After ten years he'd started to look like a boot, or maybe a worn out moccasin. After 30 years his leather had collapsed entirely. Why was it that people changed when real life kicked in? He didn't *need* to work, because of her handsome income, so he just didn't. Nothing about him worked.

Another night passed without incident, aside from the momentary intrusion of car headlights through her bedroom window. Jaz, dressed in jeggings and a sloppy Wonder Woman T-shirt, stepped over the creaky floorboard at the bedroom door and strode to the kitchen for the breakfast feeding regime. A duck egg mixed with each tray of vegie and meat scraps ensured her brood got plentiful protein; a good use for them since she wasn't into baking sponge cakes. A whistle at the back door summoned the pets and native interlopers. They gathered in an unruly gaggle, almost tripping her as she laid out the trays. *Was that an extra roo? No keeping up with them.* Gargoyle, Pepper and Minty shimmied around her legs in figure eights, smooching up her calves in anticipation, while Fred, Roger and snappy little Horace barked and wagged tails. 'No scraps for you lot. Come on, inside for some steak.' She bent from the hips and flattened her palms on the concrete, before scooping up Pepper and Minty and holding them by their scruffs above her head. They purred at the morning ritual. After satisfying their appetites, she retrieved the last plastic-wrapped meaty bone from the freezer and jogged to the back fence.

She'd named the dingo Zeus, for his thunderous bark and his transcendent dogliness. It had taken many months of coaxing for him to trust her, but now she had him feeding from her hand and inviting a pat to the head. She hadn't lost one duck or chook to him since she'd tempted him with her freezer-borne offerings. And he'd commandeered Fred's old kennel. Today though, he had a mate. Jaz spotted her behind the junk pile over the fence. She was reticent; looking set to turn tail and run. Jaz edged along the fence to get a glimpse from the side. The dingo's belly was swollen. 'Ah Zeus, we're about to have pups. I'd better stock up on meat. Sorry, this one's a bit small.' He took the bone and eyed her as though he understood fully.

She diverted from the path to the shed and unrolled the mat. Twenty hand-clap press-ups, 20 knee bends and 10 minutes of aerobic weight-training later, she was ready for coffee. Then she remembered she'd run out. Bugger, that meant a trip into town.

Heading down the hall with her helmet under her arm, she saw the dark shadows through the glass front door at the same moment the bell rang. She dashed back into the bedroom, tossed the helmet on the bed and encased herself in her floral dressing gown. When she opened the door, a swathe of black clothing confronted her.

'Oh, hello,' she said to the taller of the police officers, 'what's up?' She cupped her hand to her ear.

He introduced himself as Senior Constable Stewart and his colleague as Constable Bryant. 'Sorry to say, Mrs Hyland, that there's been another aggravated burglary in the street.' He spoke loudly and slowly, as though she were stupid as well as hard of hearing.

'Oh golly gosh. Who now? It wasn't Jeanette was it?' A no-brainer really, given she was the last remaining resident of Woodbine Court aside from herself.

Stewart nodded and dropped his gaze.

'Is she all right?' Of all her neighbours, Jeanette Wilson was the only tolerable one, provided she didn't outstay her welcome.

'I'm afraid not. It was a brutal attack. Her cleaner found her just after 9am.'

'Goodness me. I thought this was all over. Might have helped if you lot had patrolled more regularly after Mary and the others.'

'Sorry, but we were convinced the burglaries had run their course here. There's been another spate of them out the other side of town keeping us busy.'

'Similar MO?' Jaz bit her tongue. Wished she hadn't said that.

He furrowed his brow at her police-speak. 'MO? Ah, yes.'

'I watch a lot of those US cop shows. Probably a load of bunkum, but I like a good crime thriller.'

Stewart dismissed her remark, evidently trying to avoid unnecessary dialogue. 'We're just wondering whether you saw or heard anything suspicious last night.'

'No, I didn't hear anything, though I did see headlights around 2.30-ish.'

'Did they wake you?' Bryant asked.

'No. I was still awake. Reading, you know. I'm right into Michael Robotham at the moment. A gripping read, his latest. Didn't think anything of it, despite, I suppose, it being unusual around here that time of night.'

'Your husband, would he have seen or heard anything? Is he here?'

'No, he's...not here anymore. Took off some time ago. Got the wanderlust, you know. Well, the wandering hands and lust. He wandered over anyone with perky breasts and a sassy attitude.' She paused as the constable spluttered. 'Last I heard he was in Byron Bay or up thataways somewhere with some rhubarb-haired, loud-mouthed tart named Rhonda, or Rhona or Robyn. Something starting with "R" anyway.'

'How long has he been gone?' Stewart asked.

Jaz shrugged. 'Two, maybe three months.'

'And you haven't heard from him?'

'Nup.'

'Have you filed a missing person's report?'

'Why? I'm not looking for him.'

'Oh, fair enough. In light of last night's episode, we strongly recommend that you go and stay somewhere else until we have these perpetrators in custody. Do you have other family? Children? Somewhere you could go for a while?'

'I can't leave here. Who'd feed all the animals? Besides, my children are far-flung. One in Amsterdam, one in China somewhere–'

'We're very concerned for your safety, Mrs Hyland. Perhaps we could arrange for someone to stay here for protection.'

Not bloody likely. Jaz drummed her fingers on her mouth. 'Please, call me Jasmine. Mrs Hyland sounds so...official. I could stay with my friend, Beryl. Just at night. It's not like they're going to come here in broad daylight, is it?'

'That might be a suitable arrangement.'

'I'll do that then,' she lied.

She had to wait nearly three hours until all the emergency services vehicles had departed the street before she donned her helmet, straddled her Kawasaki and sped off into town. Aside from coffee, she needed new batteries for her torch and a new whetstone to sharpen her gear. Upon her return, she noticed the auction sign on Frank's fence. Just 10 days away. Sooner than she'd expected.

She poured herself a stiff brew and headed for the laptop. She deleted seven spam emails and then opened one from Layla. They were intermittent while Layla was on assignment, so maybe this heralded a return. It did.

Flying in from Rome Friday. Be there Saturday. Layla XX.

She'd been gone for six weeks and, crazy as it was, given her dedication to her job, Jaz always worried about her daughter, though it wasn't necessary given how well she'd trained her.

Jaz replied. *Wonderful. We've got work to do. See you Saturday. XX*

Before retiring to bed, Jaz rolled out the plastic sheet in the bedroom doorway. After two hours of engrossing reading, she repeated her nightly ritual – her knife freshly honed – and had not long nodded off when she heard the creak. Someone was right outside the door. A shaft of light threaded through the keyhole. Silently, she donned her goggles, turned the switch to night vision, removed the contents from the box and waited. The door opened slowly. A hand groped for the light switch. Jaz flung two shuriken in quick succession. One pinned the hand to the architrave, the other hit his neck. He dropped his baseball bat and spat the torch from his mouth.

'Ow. Shit.'

'Sh. Be quiet,' the accomplice whispered.

The door opened a tad more, just enough for her to get a fix on the second assailant. He copped a ninja star in the thigh and another in his chest.

'Fuck. What was that? Hurts like fucking hell.' He was bent double, not knowing which injury to attend to first.

'Dunno. Must be a booby trap or some shit.'

While the two were busy fathoming their wounds, Jaz grasped the katana under the bed, flung off the quilt and launched herself into a somersault toward them.

'Shit what's that?'

'Don't know. I can't see shit.'

'Fuu-uck,' the first attacker wailed as the blade slashed his Achilles tendon. He dropped to the floor beside her, screaming in agony.

'Fuck this. I'm outta here. Fuckin poltergeists or something,' the other guy said as he backed out the door.

Jaz grabbed another favourite weapon from the robe hook, stepped over her first victim and followed the other into the pitch-dark hallway. Pitch dark for him, anyway. She could see the green haze of his body. She didn't want too much more blood in the hallway. Too damn messy to clean up.

He hadn't got far and he got no further. He swung his bat but she caught the end mid-arc. A decisive blow to the head with the nunchaku felled him on the spot.

Jaz switched on the light and removed her goggles. Number two was out to it for the time being but number one was still moaning and cursing

– sobbing too – while holding his foot. She bent over and pulled off his balaclava. He looked like he'd face-planted into a Margherita pizza, his skin so scarred from acne. Jaz grabbed his baseball bat. He instinctively raised his hands to shield his face.

'No, don't hit me. I'm sorry. I'm sorry.'

'Good grief. How old are you? Still a bloody teenager.'

'What the fuck? You're, like, ancient.'

'Ancient and deadly, young man. They don't call me the Ninja Granny for nothing.' Jaz sat on the bed, tapping the bat on her left palm, and glared at him. 'So, you thought a bunch of defenceless oldies were a sure bet, didn't you?'

'I, I didn't think.'

'That's right. You didn't think.'

'You've got to help me. I could bleed to death here.'

'Yes, you will. I can say that with certainty. You've got five minutes – maybe 10.'

'Well, do something.'

'Like what? Call an ambulance so you can explain why the two of you were here at stupid fucking o'clock? Call the police? Just how many aggravated burglary and murder charges will they get you on? At least five that I know of. That's life imprisonment, young man. Several life sentences in fact. Did you stop to think about that?'

'No, I never. Shit this hurts. And I feel sick.'

'No surprise. That's the hypovolemic shock kicking in. Starts when you've lost 20 percent of your blood, so your heart hasn't got enough blood to pump around your body. You'll feel really sick before you exsanguinate.'

'Ex-what?'

'The last new word you'll learn. Ex-sang-uin-ate. Bleed out.'

'Fuck.'

'Same thing, really.'

'What about Robbo? Is he dead?'

'Not yet. I've yet to deal with him.'

'Bloody hell.'

'You can say that again.'

'They never warned me about you.'

'They? Who? Did someone put you up this?'

'Yeah. Said it would be easy. All the others were.'

'Who?'

'Don't know. Robbo sorted it. Ask him.'

'I will if he regains consciousness.'

'Are you just going to let us both die?

'Uh huh. So, no harm in telling me.'

'Think it was a woman...some...he...at the...pub.' His words were becoming slurred.

'You don't know her name?'

Pizza face shook his head.

'Hmm.' Jaz smiled and nodded to herself.

Five minutes later, pizza face was as good as gone. Jaz checked his pockets and pulled out his wallet. 'Ah, so you're at least old enough to have a driver's licence. Gabriel Antonio Vella. Gabriel Vella of the local Vella mob. Well, ain't your daddy Tony gonna wonder what happened to his little Mafioso boy. Silly boy. Should have stuck to fruit picking instead of picking on vulnerable people.'

The Vellas were well known in the district for their orchards and vegetable cultivation, but that wasn't their prime stock-in-trade; more a front for the local underbelly they cultivated. Their tap roots germinated far and wide. According to the local rumour mill, their influence spread at least as far as a certain sexist senior sergeant and perhaps others besides. Despite the local awareness of Tony Vella's criminal activities, he'd never been convicted. He was a master of the alibi. Witnesses mysteriously recanted testimonies or became the victims of inexplicable accidents.

Robbo moaned.

'And then there's you.' Jaz grabbed the katana, took a couple of steps into the hall and crouched beside Robbo. 'What have you got to say for yourself?' He wasn't quite with it yet, so she rummaged through his pockets and found the car keys. She inspected them carefully. 'Mm. Lexus. A bit flash for a pair of no-good teenagers. Hope it's got a big boot.'

'Huuh.' The boy roused and rubbed his head.

'Oh good, you're back with us. Robbo, I believe.'

'What's going on?' It was evident he couldn't focus yet.

'Well, you and your young partner in crime picked the wrong old lady to mess with. That's what's going on. Now, tell me about this mystery woman who put you up to this. Is she one of that arsehole Vella's consorts?'

'Huh? How did–?'

'Your buddy squealed. Amazing what someone will tell you with their dying breaths.'

'What? Gabe's–?'

'Yep. Dead as a Dodo.'

'Fuck!'

'Funny, but that's what he said, too. Now, this woman?'

'I don't know. Never seen her before. Got talkin' to her at the pub a while back and she offered me big bucks to roll over the street. Make it look like burglaries.'

'What did she look like?'

'Blonde, dark glasses, maybe in her 30s but hard to tell. Not sure if it was her real hair. That's it.'

'And she paid you?'

'Yeah. Coupla grand. After the first two. So I figured I was on a winner. Look, I could bleed to death here.'

'I'm counting on it.'

'What? Aren't you gonna help me?'

'Now you tell me, young man. What were you planning to do to me, if I weren't a martial weapons expert?'

'Just rough you up a bit.'

'And what if that had led to my death, like two of the others?'

'Yeah, well we didn't mean that. It was Gabe. He went a bit far.'

'That's an understatement. Also convenient that he's dead and can't dispute your allegation.'

'I didn't hurt no-one and I won't hurt you. I won't say nothing if you let me go.'

Yeah, sure. 'You're not in a position to hurt me. And if I were to let you go, how would you explain your injuries?'

'Dunno. Make somethin' up, like I cut meself or somethin'.'

'And what about Gabriel's sudden disappearance?'

Robbo shrugged. 'I don't know nothing about it.'

'All right. I'll give you the benefit of the doubt.' She stepped over him. 'Follow me to the kitchen and we'll get you fixed up.'

She didn't look back at him, but she knew he wouldn't lie down so easily. He grunted as he got to his feet. She saw the shadow of his raised arms in the glass of the watercolour on the wall. Her timing was precise.

She reversed her grip on the katana and swung it backwards between her elbow and hip, piercing him through the gut as he lunged. She spun around and withdrew the blade as he cupped his hands over the gruesome incision and fell to the floor.

'Silly, silly boy. Now look at the mess you've made.' Thank goodness for the plastic runner she'd recently laid over the red-patterned Axminster, though red carpet ideally disguised the occasional blood spillage. Despite that, she was in for a long night of cleaning. But the car was the first order of urgency.

Dressed in her all-black stealth gear, gloves and balaclava, she wheeled her bicycle out of the carport and 50 metres down the street to where the Lexus sat innocent, pristine and almost certainly stolen. She loaded the bike into the boot and took off towards town. She stopped the car in Orchard Street, removed the bike and propped it against a fence, then drove to the corner of Talbot Avenue and killed the headlights before turning in and pulling up in front of Number Eight. How would Frick explain that a stolen vehicle turned up right in front of his own house?

She felt surprisingly invigorated after the ride home and was pleased that she'd not seen another living soul all the way there and back. But she had work to do, requiring sharp implements, brute strength and a truck-load of heavy-duty freezer bags.

Layla arrived at 11am looking surprisingly buff and relaxed despite jet lag and the three-hour drive from Melbourne. She lugged in more paraphernalia than a 34-year-old woman should seriously need for a weekend stay.

'What's all this?' Jaz asked.

'Got some great new gear. The latest from Italy. Wait till I show you.'

Jaz rubbed her hands together in anticipation. 'So how did the assignment go?'

'Piece of cake. It's handy when two targets align themselves in such a way that you can take both out with one shot.'

'Bravo. Saves ammo too. Who were they?'

'Two of the Calabro brothers. Couldn't get the third. He'd taken off to Lucerne, but his time will come.'

'Good pay?'

'You bet. $500,000 apiece.'

‘Whacko.’

‘That was on top of my other assignment in Venice. C4 and gondolas don’t mix. A nice little earner that one too. Took out three at once, with no collateral damage. So what’s been going on here? Do you plan to tell me about the blood all over the table?’

‘Oh, that. Had a late night. Haven’t finished cleaning up yet. Nabbed a couple of would-be burglars. They’d already taken out the rest of the street. Poor old souls.’

‘Don’t waste crocodile tears on me, Mum. After what they all did to you; stymieing your plans and making your life miserable. It’s a blessing.’

‘Do you plan to tell me about how that blessing came about?’

‘Me? Mum, have some faith.’

‘They’re all gone. Two dead, two packed off to nursing homes.’

‘So before long you’ll own the whole court and you can have the sanctuary you always planned.’

‘Yep. You can choose whichever house you want. If you’re ever home long enough. Tanya, Brit and David can fight over the other three. Great holiday homes for them and the kids.’

‘Excellent. I always rather fancied Jeanette’s house, though I’ve no doubt it’ll need a major update.’

‘Yes, I’m sure net curtains, pink walls and garden gnomes aren’t your thing.’

‘Any grief from the local constabulary?’

‘Completely clueless. Parked these two dickheads’ stolen car on Frick’s nature strip. Just watch him try to explain that.’

‘Mum, is there no end to your audacity?’

‘Show me what you’ve got.’

Layla unzipped her backpack and pulled out what looked like a snazzy pair of binoculars. ‘The latest in thermal fusion night vision, the L3 AN/PSQ-36. Made by Warrior Sensor Systems and preferred option of the Italian Ministry of Defence.’ She handed them to Jaz.

‘What, no box?’

‘Sorry. You don’t get a box when you snatch them off someone’s head. Saved me 45 grand.’

‘Whoopee. Can’t resist a bargain. What’s the thing sticking out of the bag?’

‘Oh, this?’ She pulled the impressive weapon from the pack and handed it to Jaz. 'This, mother dear, is the Heckler & Koch 7.62mm semiautomatic sniper rifle, modified for the US Army to replace the G28.'

'Whacko. Do I need to ask how you came by this?'

'Let's just say I'm a better sniper than this guy was.'

'You never cease to surprise me.'

'Honestly Mum. There's so much work there. I knocked back two jobs 'cos I was itching to come home for a while. You should come next time.'

'Think I'm getting a bit past it.'

'Oh bullshit, Mum. I could sure use your help. And you haven't been to Italy for yonks.'

'True. And I do so love Italians. Well, some of them. I might just think about that.'

'Great. Oh, and another thing. I had these specially made for you.' She handed her mother an ornate cigar-sized box.

'I do love presents.' Jaz was almost blinded by the shiny silver shuriken as she opened the lid. 'Wow. They look mean. Good timing too. My old set are – shall we say – a little shop-soiled.'

'By the way, where's Dad?'

'Gone.'

'Really?'

'Really.'

'Well, good riddance, I say.'

'My thoughts precisely.'

'So, where's he gone?'

'Hah. All over the place. Layla, sorry that I've never told you this, but I'm not altogether certain he *was* your father.'

'You're kidding. Well that would explain a lot. I always thought there was something...not right about him. So who–'

'I'd put my money on André. Remember I told you about him?'

'André the detective?'

'Well he sure wasn't André the Giant. I seriously thought he was onto me. Turned out he was just *turned on by* me.'

'Oh, you old hussy.'

'Hey, I wasn't old then. Not much older than you.'

Layla laughed. 'Come on, I'll help clean up this–' Layla was interrupted by the doorbell.

'Darn, who's that? Stay there.'

Jaz made her way down the hall, stopping to toss the baseball bat into the bedroom. 'I'm coming,' she called out.

Darn. Cops again. 'Hello officers.'

'Morning Jasmine. You remember us?' Stewart asked.

'Yes, of course. I hope you're here to tell me you've caught those mongrels.'

'No. Just a routine visit to ensure you're okay.'

'Oh, I'm fine. Couldn't be better.' Jaz opened the screen door and stepped out onto the patio. 'Sorry, my daughter's not long arrived. A bit jet lagged, so she's having a snooze in the bedroom there.'

'We'll keep our voices down then. Everything was okay when you arrived home this morning, I take it? No break-in during the night?'

Jaz momentarily forgot about her promise of the day before. 'Nothing untoward here.'

'Very good. It's just that we've had our eye on a couple of possible suspects, but they've been reported missing. Didn't come home last night.'

'Probably busy hiding their loot somewhere.'

Stewart chuckled. 'You're probably right. We'll leave you to it then. Don't hesitate to call us if you find yourself needing help.'

As the officers headed down the front steps, Jaz heard Stewart whisper to Bryant, 'Poor old dear. You'd think she'd be terrified.'

Layla was wiping the kitchen table to a spotless gleam. 'Honestly mum, you made a mess.'

'I'll have to tackle the hall carpet next, but after we've checked to see whether there's pups yet.'

'Pups?'

'Zeus has a girlfriend.'

Layla rubbed her hands together. 'Oh, let's go see. No, hang on. Tell me about the job first. Will the new rifle do it?'

'You bet. Maybe you can show me how to take out Vella and Frick the Prick with one bullet.'

'Still trying to clean up the neighbourhood?'

'That, and I do love a meaty criminal investigation. They'll naturally have no shortage of underworld suspects. Almost as good as fiction. Now come on, we're on a dingo safari. But hang on, I'll grab some fresh meat first.' Jaz retrieved a newly-packed bone from the freezer before they headed out the back door.

'Mum, it's a bloody zoo out here.'

'Yes, isn't it wonderful? And I've only just started.'

'What's that? Over there in the jasmine? Is that a possum?'

'Oh, he's new. Unusual to be out in the daytime. Must be after the nectar.'

'It's getting a bit wild. The jasmine, I mean.'

'Rampant, I'd say.'

'Sounds like somebody I know.'

THE HARDER THEY FALL

His face is an overboiled turnip. I hate turnips almost as much as I hate him. His nose, a pocked strawberry; his eyes, insipid marbles under bloated lids and caterpillar eyebrows. Mr Potato Head in a tailored suit, basically. He sits there smarmy and full of shit. I'd love to do him as a caricature, features exaggerated like a Weg cartoon. Not sure how well that would go down with the judges, but then, there've been some shockers. Portraits straight out of a fifth-grade art class that would make a Picasso look good. Eyes in all the wrong places.

He's gracing my studio for two hours for his first sitting. Fitted me in at 7am, before work. Too early for me. That, according to his Lurch doppelganger minder, is his only available time. You know, busy busy. Important man. Legend in his own lunchbox. Pay homage please. He can't sit still. Jigging up and down like a ventriloquist's dummy and about as clever.

'Been painting long?'

'A while.'

'You going to do me like him?' He's eying Bob Hawke on the wall.

'Got something a bit different in mind.'

'He's a bit fuzzy. Not realistic.'

'Always was. If you want realistic, take a photo.'

'Never liked the man.'

'Wouldn't expect you to. Politically.'

'Been a Liberal all my life. Way to go.'

'No politics thanks.'

'Don't talk much, do you?' His gaze drifts to my cleavage, down to my bare knees, telegraphing his thoughts. Doesn't look me in the eyes. Probably can't deal with my rainbow-striped hair and nose rings.

'Concentrating. Hold that pose. Mouth closed.' *Please*.

Lurch's phone rings. Should have told him to switch it off. A couple of 'uh huhs' and he says, 'Sorry, we'll have to cut this short. Minister has an important matter to attend to.'

What? A leaky bladder? 'Oh. Tuesday afternoon then?'

Two desultory nods and they're gone. I exhale for the first time in an hour. I study my outline. Ears need to be bigger; eyes smaller and closer together. He might have aged twenty years since our last encounter but Jock Edmonson is still ugly.

I message Tiff. **LB* – code for Elvis has left the building. She replies >. *Following*. Ball's in her court now.

Back to work. Can't decide on a background colour. Initial thought was purple, but that indicates royalty, nobility. Doesn't fit. Also signifies power and ambition, which does. Yellow's a thought. Associated with optimism, energy, friendship, but more appropriately, betrayal, illness and danger. Hmm. Might look too cheerful. Puce might be the go. Just because it sounds crappy.

I make a cuppa and set to mixing some acrylics. Easier to mix and dries quicker than oils. Oils are a bit passé these days. I'm no Rembrandt. A dollop of violet and a double of burnt sienna. I apply heavy number-12 brush strokes around and above the shoulder outline, random directions, fade it out more around the ears. Add some Naples Yellow around the hairline. Don't want his mousey comb-over to disappear into it. Love my new studio, conveniently perched above my apartment, but complete with external stairs. Perfect, weak south-facing light through the window.

Get to thinking about him. Tempted to paint dollar signs on his forehead. Lacklustre teacher, turned pollie, elevated to Minister for Education and Youth upon the hasty departure of his predecessor owing to some funding rort. The irony of it. Minister for *Youth*. Artfully dodged the odd scandal himself. There was talk of some rough and tumble with a parliamentary intern. Pretty young thing. Aspirations squashed in disgrace.

She'd had a couple of drinks apparently. Maybe led him on. Accusations swept under the Lower House's green carpet with all the other hot air and detritus. A host of sins buried under there.

Coffee goes cold. Zap it and pick at a muffin. Wait for radio news. Third report: *Breaking news. Police are investigating an attack on Federal Education and Youth Minister, Jock Edmonson's North Ryde electorate office. Our sources advise that a brick was thrown through the front window of the office but that nobody has been injured. It is not known whether this is random vandalism or a targeted attack on the minister. Mr Edmonson, the Member for Bennelong, has just arrived at the scene, but has, as yet, declined to comment.* Blah blah.

I raise my mug and drink a toast to Tiff. Go girl. No doubt she's there among the rubberneckers.

'Followed him to his home in Lane Cove. Monstrous, tacky mansion overlooking the river. Security gates, cameras, the lot.' Tiff swirls her paper-cup cappuccino. Takes a sip.

'Tricky.'

We watch the ferries chuff into Circular Quay from First Fleet Park; the vague, milling tourists staring at phones, oblivious to their surroundings. The sun retreats behind a whiff of cirrus.

'Not an option. I've got another idea,' Tiff says.

'Do tell.'

'We'll conscript Lisa for it. She's the one with the irresistible bod. She's meeting us for lunch at Yuki's.'

'Yum. Gallery busy?'

Tiff crumples her paper cup. 'Not too bad. Finally sold that free-form yesterday. Not one of my best. Glad to see the back of it. There's three grand in my pocket.'

'Great.'

'Oh, and your Jimmy Barnes is sold. Woman claiming to be his number one fan has it on lay-by. You'd better give me another one.'

'Excellent.' There's two grand in *my* pocket.

'John Farnham, please, pretty please. God, you're so lucky to have met him.'

'Okay. Arm fully twisted.'

I'd walked into Tiff's fine art gallery two years ago, a bunch of canvases in tow. A cold call. We'd both had that déjà vu moment, like we'd met before. We twigged simultaneously. A year apart at St Anne's all those years ago. Turned out we had a lot more in common than we knew then. We'd praised, at length, Jane Fry, our inspirational art teacher. Jane Fry, who'd disappeared in 1991. Found a week later in Ku-ring-gai Chase, raped, strangled, left for dead. Cold case. Our friendship is now built on shared experience and mutual respect for our artistic talents. Tiff's sculptures are astonishing, and she's now *my* number one fan.

A ten-minute stroll to Yuki's. Our favourite table. View of the quay obscured by a cruise liner. A bottle of wine arrives a minute ahead of Lisa. As usual, a picture of sophistication in a powder-blue two-piece suit and implausible stilettos. Hair up, make-up, chin up, the works.

'Have to make it a quickie,' she says. 'Got a meeting at 1.15.'

We fill her in on the morning's events and she gives Tiff a friendly arm punch. She has her own news. I charge our glasses.

'I've finally found Barry.'

A trio of 'yays' and a toast.

'Where?' I ask.

'Retired to Coff's Harbour. Vice-president of the Rotary Club, member of the golf club, and, wait for it, volunteer at the Police Citizens Youth Club.'

I raise my glass in a mock gesture of praise. 'A true, upstanding citizen.'

Tiff agrees. 'Looks like a spin up the coast in our near future.'

'Yep,' Lisa says. 'Now we can start planning.'

'Who's the bigger fish?' Tiff asks. 'Edmonson or Barry?'

Linden Barry. Formerly Senior Sergeant Linden Barry. On the make. On the take. On the run.

'Hard call,' I say, 'though Edmonson's the more limited time frame.'

Lisa scans the menu. Decides on her usual. 'When's your entry got to be in?'

'End of April.'

'What's that? Five weeks?'

'Yep, but the finalists and Packing Room Prize aren't announced until May 27th. Winner announced fourth of June.'

'What if yours isn't selected?'

'Bugger. Plan B maybe. Though it still might be selected for the Salon des Refusés.'

'What's that? I'm no arty-farty, you know.'

'Sometimes the gallery displays entries that aren't selected for the Archibald. It's sort of like a consolation thing, but at least the public gets to see them.'

Tiff pats my forearm, looks at Lisa. 'But she's going to win this year. Last year, Packing Room Prize, this year, Archibald Prize.'

'I'll drink to that. A big difference between a $100,000 prize and a $1,000 prize.'

'Imagine the kudos. You'll have every big-note and his dog swarming at you. Wanting their own Jac Tyler original.'

'Haha. Dream on.'

Lisa drums her fingers on the table. 'I reckon we've got time for Barry then. Doesn't matter the order.'

I mull it for a moment and nod. 'Okay. Reconnaissance trip this weekend. I'll drive. Take the campervan and we'll wing it.'

We bypass Newcastle. Stop at a service centre on the Pacific Highway for greasy hamburgers and chips. Eat them in the van. Head off. Tiff in the passenger seat, Lisa at the banquette behind with her laptop. Coff's Harbour E.T.A. nine forty-five. Lisa's done some more homework. Barry's now batching. A nasty divorce, wife back in Sydney. Out of the picture. His favourite haunts, the golf club, fishing club, bowls club. An all-round sportsman.

'Anyone up for some fishing?' Lisa says.

'Nup,' Tiff says. 'Whale watching maybe. Anything beats The Big Banana.'

'Bang goes tomorrow's breakfast idea.'

We hit Coff's at 10. Do a drive-by of Barry's house. Run-down weatherboard in a nothing garden. No lights on. Maybe not home. Garage door closed, so hard to tell. Debate whether to surveil the joint or wait until morning. We're all pooped, so morning it is. We head to the caravan park, one block away, have a nightcap, and hit the sack.

Toast and coffee for breakfast. Into the lycra and looking the part of fitness fanatics. All eyes as we approach Barry's house. Nothing doing, but so handy there's a park with picnic table almost opposite. Sandwiches and thermoses in our backpacks, like good little Girl Scouts. Bide our time, discuss modus operandi and get it down pat, provided, that is, that he hits the golf course. If not, we'll have to figure Plan B. We'd decided on the way up to combine our reconnaissance with the mission, rather than doing the job in two trips. No-brainer, really. Why wait?

A long morning, bouts of sitting interspersed with the odd quick jog to avoid suspicion.

Eleven forty-five and Lisa freezes. Eyes directed across the road as the garage roller door lifts. 'That's him. Bastard hasn't changed. Saggier maybe.'

An Isuzu ute pulls out towing a golf cart on a trailer.

'Lazy bugger,' I say. 'Golf course is over his back fence. Yet he drives and uses a cart.'

'Yeah,' says Tiff, 'so much for the "golf is a good walk spoiled" idiom.'

We wait until he's well clear and then do a stroll-jog down Reid Drive, into Thompsons Road and into the golf course, contemplating a breezy lunch on the deck of the Lakes Café.

We enter five minutes after Barry. He's already at the bar, beer in hand, having a chinwag with two equally paunchy dudes. Such a jolly fellow. We choose a table outside, check out the menu. I go back in, order two sav blancs, a piccolo, a Fairway fishburger, a Birdie burger and a BLT without the bacon, as the only option for Tiff the vegetarian.

We take turns to eye Barry surreptitiously. Onto his second beer.

'I suppose he pees in the rough by the third hole after two beers,' I say.

Lisa snorts. 'I know I'd have to.'

'I'm guessing,' says Tiff, 'that he doesn't tee off until one. Any point in us hanging around all afternoon?'

'Probably not. He'll no doubt imbibe a few more after his round.'

Afternoon doing the touristy things. We wander the botanic gardens, check out the museum, watch the Pacific crash ashore for a while, find a suitable deserted track by the beach for later use. Return to the golf club, in the van, at five. Park opposite his car. A good view across the carpark from the rear banquette.

'Here he comes,' Lisa says. 'Makes we want to puke.'

I watch him drive his cart onto the trailer. 'Good, he's alone. You're up, Tiff.'

Tiff undoes the top two buttons of her shirt, ties it in a knot under her boobs, exposing her midriff, and heads for the van door.

'Remember, abort if anyone else appears,' I say.

She nods, sucks in a breath, exits the van and heads across the carpark. Lisa and I are all ears.

'Hi,' we hear Tiff say breezily. 'Don't suppose you know anything about campervans. I've just picked it up and can't figure out how to turn the battery on.'

'See what I can do, lovey.'

He follows her like a faithful dog towards us.

'Okay, assume crash positions,' I say to Lisa.

She hides in the toilet cubicle, I pull the tripwire across from the cabinet to the back of the passenger seat at the top of the step and resume my seat at the rear banquette. A few seconds, and the door opens.

'You first,' Tiff says politely.

His bulk fills the two-step stairwell, eyes peer around, focus on me.

'Oh looky, you didn't tell me you had a friend.'

The snare works a treat; he trips on the wire and now he's spreadeagled, face-down on the front banquette, arms flailing. Tiff quickly shuts the door, grabs the tape from the counter and starts binding his legs together. Lisa springs out and the two of them grab his arms so I can tape them together. Lisa's ready with tape for his protesting gob. We manoeuvre him into an upright position on the seat. Tiff reinserts the table and edges into the dining seat beside Lisa.

I peer out the side window. 'All clear.' I squeeze between the front seats and into the driver's seat, start her up and we're gone. Not a soul in sight.

'Guess you're more used to being on the opposite side of an interrogation,' Lisa says.

Grunts.

'Well,' says Tiff, slapping her hands together, 'are you in for some special treatment.'

Weeks later and the 4th June at last. My phone hasn't stopped ringing. Facebook page full of congratulatory messages, 162 so far. I've done it. Hasn't sunk in yet. Other things on my mind. It's now or never. But hey, don't mind if I do give myself a pat on the back and contemplate what to do with a hundred grand.

Pitiful sight. Concrete floor, bare brick walls. Edmonson – bloated, bare-chested, arms raised, hands captive in jury-rigged manacles. Chin on chest.

Out to it. Three scuffed kangaroo chairs in a semicircle. Three crusaders sitting astride them like Boudicas on horseback. Watching. Waiting.

'How much did you give him?' I ask.

'Just two, but he was already half sozzled,' Lisa says. 'Alcohol increases the effect.'

'Should have brought a pack of cards.'

'Some wine, more like it,' Tiff says.

'Who knew it'd be so easy, thanks to the irresistible Lisa.'

Lisa is still sporting a red wig and tiny dress. 'Piece of cake. Wish I'd brought a jacket though. Freezing in this skimpy thing.'

'Ha,' I snort. 'And he thought he was in for the ride of his life.'

Lisa shivers at the thought. 'Uh, oh. Think he's coming round.'

His head lolls back. Eyes flicker open, unfocused. Dry tongue lolls around his bottom lip chasing dried saliva strings. He tries to move. Can't. 'What the fuck?' Looks up. Can't fathom the chains. Gaze fixes on Lisa. 'What's this? What the fuck?'

'Thought we'd have a little party darling. You can be my sex slave.'

'Huh?'

'I've brought a couple of friends. Thought you'd like that.'

'Do you know who I am?'

'Yeah,' Lisa nods, 'you're a pervert paedophile.'

He shakes his head. 'No. Not me. You've got the wrong person. I'm a federal government minister.'

'Yeah,' I say, 'big, important man...who rapes children. Girls, boys, whoever takes your fancy.'

His head rolls drunkenly sideways. Eyes lock on Tiff and then me. Recognition kicks in. 'I know you. You're that artist.'

'So you *did* look at my face.' I look at Tiff and Lisa. 'And I thought he only looked at my tits and knees.'

'What's this all about?'

'This is about a second-rate biology teacher. Maybe you remember him. St. Anne's, 1997 to 2002.'

The penny drops. Gaze lowers to his crotch. 'Oh.'

'You might remember Jac Tyler better as Jacqueline Hill. Fifteen-year-old. Fucked against the wall in the gymnasium toilets.'

'I...I...didn't mean it.'

'How the fuck do you not mean to rape someone?' I wave my hand sideways, to draw his attention to Tiff. 'And you might remember Tiffany Bouch. A similar, unintentional rape on the floor of the biology lab.'

He sucks in a breath, realising it's pointless to deny our accusations. 'Wha...What are you planning to do to me?' He can't look at any of us. 'Are you going to kill me?'

'Hmm,' I say, 'I'd sure like to. Slowly, painfully. What do you think, Tiff?'

'Nah. Too easy.'

He shudders.

'What do we do with a bastard who robs children of their childhood? How many were there? How many more virgins did you rape or bastardise?'

'It was just you two, I swear. Couldn't help it. So provocative in those uniforms.'

'Oh?' I say, 'you don't remember my little brother Andy? Andy Hill.' This turnip looks positively blanched now. He opens his mouth but nothing comes out. 'Killed himself last year, you know. No. You wouldn't know. Stepped in front of the peak-hour train at Ashfield.'

'Nothing to do with me.'

'No? Happened an hour after you were exalted as Youth Minister. Maybe you'd like me to read you the suicide note he left me.' I pull it from my pocket. Unfold it for the ninety-sixth time. He closes his eyes. Doesn't want to hear it. '*Dear Jac*...a paragraph about how sorry he is to do this to me...*You've got to get the bastard. Fucking ruined my life. Yours too, I know. I should have protected you. I did nothing, and I can't live with that. Kill him, torture him, disgrace him. Whatever you want. Cut off his dick for me so he can never stick it where it doesn't belong again. Just do it.*

Tiff shuffles her chair closer to him. 'Pissed your pants, eh?' She looks at me and Lisa in turn. 'Better get them off for him. Can't have him broiling in his own pee.'

I give the nod. Pull the hunting knife from my bag, watch it glint in the light of the bare, dangling globe. He tries to shrink into the bricks. Tiff has his belt undone. Lisa helps drag his pants and jocks down as he writhes. I tap the knife on my hand and approach him. Kneel down.

'No, no. I'm sorry. Don't do it.'

I cut the tape binding his ankles together. We pull off his sodden duds.

I edge forward. Put my thumb and finger together. Flick his penis. 'Aw. What a sorry little willy. Shrivelled little sausage.' I look up at Tiff and Lisa. 'Amazing, the male anatomy. How something so pathetic can cause so much havoc.'

'What are you? A bunch of lezzos?'

Tiff tuts. 'Typical male fuckwit, misogynist response.'

I pinch his penis tip, pull it up, with the expression of a mother dealing with a soiled nappy. Wave the knife in a slicing motion.

'No, no.'

'Yeah, you're right. No.' I look at Tiff and Lisa. 'Let's adjourn. Give him some time to reflect.'

'Good idea,' Tiff says, 'kill for a coffee'.

I was at it early. Getting the studio sorted for a new subject next week. The PM himself. Can you believe it? Can't stand the man, but then, show me any likeable politician and I'll go hee. Radio's on. Nothing yet. Nobody's missed him yet. Eyed him through the garage peep-hole downstairs before I came up. Still there looking satisfyingly miserable. Give him another day to sweat. More time for media speculation.

Finally, 11am bulletin.

Police fear for the safety of Federal Education and Youth Minister, Jock Edmonson, who hasn't been seen since he left Marcie's Nightclub in Chatswood at about 12.30 this morning. Witnesses say he was last seen in the company of a red-haired woman, who left the premises shortly before him. Edmonson was said to have been in an intoxicated state. He did not return home and his disappearance was reported to police by his wife, Helene, at around 10 this morning. His Mercedes remains outside the nightclub and his mobile phone is believed to have been found nearby. His disappearance coincides with the announcement two days ago that a portrait of him, by Sydney artist, Jac Tyler, has won the 2021 Archibald Prize.

Ooh, got a mention. My phone pings. Tiff. *Just heard. CU dinner.* I reply with a thumbs up.

TV and radio reports all day. *Where is Jock Edmonson?* Reference to earlier attack on electorate office. Much conjecture about his whereabouts. Conspiracy theories. Great stuff. Clear they haven't got a clue. I dress for dinner. Comfortable, rather than flash, and head out the door. Ready for

Thai, a few drinks and round two in the Edmonson affair. Sneak peek through the peephole before I go. Whimpering like a baby. As it should be.

Well-fed and wined, we're all plonked on my uber-long couch watching something none of us is following on Netflix.

'Not the vaguest idea what this is about,' Lisa says.

'Makes two of us,' I say.

'Three.' Tiff checks her watch. 'Reckon it's time?'

'Yep.'

I slip a purple Sharpie into my pocket as we head out the back kitchen door and around to the rear garage door. 'I unlock the padlock, switch on the light. It's pretty dim, but not for someone who's been in total darkness for 24 hours. He blinks to adjust his eyes. His knees pulled up to his chest. Not a pretty sight; his saggy marbles dangling.

'We're ba-ack,' I say tunefully. 'Did you miss us?'

Sure, he's gagged, so he can't say much. Mmm is about his limit. We all resume our interrogation seats.

'Maybe we should take his gag off,' I suggest.

Tiff obliges. Steps forward and rips the tape from his mouth.

'Sh, now.' I silence him. 'Not a word unless it's an answer to our questions. This isn't parliament where you can holler like a school brat whenever you see fit.'

'What are you going–'

'Ah! What did I just say? Your chances of surviving this place will be better if you tell us what we want to know.'

He grimaces. Nods, almost imperceptibly.

'What happened to Jane Fry?'

'Who?'

'You know damn well who. Art teacher extraordinaire. Raped, strangled. Ring a bell?'

'No idea.'

'Tiff and I reckon that she sprung you *in flagrante delicto* with a student, didn't she? So you had to deal with her.'

'Rubbish.'

'Mmm.' I stand slowly, saunter to the pegboard over the workbench. Select the multi-grips. 'Ever wondered what it feels like to have the life squeezed out of your testicles?' I crouch beside him. Look at Tiff and Lisa. 'Reckon it'd hurt, don't you?'

'I reckon,' Lisa says.

'Don't know. Try it,' Tiff says. 'Or you could just cut them off with those blunt secateurs.'

'There's a thought. Nah, don't want blood on the concrete. Bitch to get off, you know.'

I hammer the multi-grips into my palm. Lower them under his legs. Press the cold steel against his thighs.

'Shit.'

'Haven't done anything yet, you big pussy.'

'You wouldn't.'

'No?' It's awkward, because I'm low on the floor, but I sandwich his sack in the grips. Squeeze a bit.

'Yow.'

Squeeze a bit more. Watch the veins pop up on his forehead. 'Aw. Does it hurt?'

Face screwed up. Teeth bared.

'Do you want me to stop?' I squeeze harder.

'Yes, yes. Please.'

'You didn't stop when *I* screamed stop, did you? Just rammed yourself right in there, didn't you?'

'Sorry, sorry.'

'Too late for that. Now, what about Jane Fry?'

'All right, all right. Yes, she saw me. Threatened to call the police.'

'So, what, you subdued her? Dragged her to your car? Took her to some lonely spot in the bush, had your way with her and then *did* away with her?'

He nods in defeat. Shoulders sag. 'Something like that.'

'And nobody ever suspected you because you were an honest, upright Anglican teacher.'

He shrugs.

'And now you're the Minister for Education and Youth. In charge of a system that enables child abuse, run by a government of mostly entitled he-men who at best condone it, at worst foster it.'

'You bloody women. Always griping about–'

'Ah!' I run my finger across my throat to shut him up.

'So what are you going to do? Torture me? Kill me?'

'No. Total humiliation, leading to your inevitable sacking from parliament and what?...30 years in prison for murder will suffice.'

Tiff claps her hands mockingly. 'And imagine what your wife and daughters will think.'

'Okay,' I say, 'let's do this'. I pull his legs down flat, start writing on the gaffer tape around his ankles.

Lisa undoes the manacles, barely gives him a chance to relieve his arm and shoulder muscles, before she and Tiff tape his hands behind his back. We roll him onto a tarp and pull him out the garage door into the pitch dark and Lisa's waiting delivery van.

The alarm goes off five minutes before the 7.30am radio news. I'm all ears at the headline report.

Federal Education and Youth Minister, Jock Edmonson, has been found alive this morning following his apparent kidnapping 30 hours ago. A woman walking her dog found Edmonson – who was believed to have been naked, with bound ankles and wrists – in parkland near Edmonson's Lane Cove home, and immediately called police. Initial reports indicate that Edmonson has been unable to tell police how he came to be there. Paramedics were on the scene but it is believed Edmonson was not injured. He is now in police custody for questioning. The circumstances of Edmonson's discovery are strikingly similar to those of former Sydney police officer, Linden Barry, who was found naked and similarly bound on the first tee at Coff's Harbour Golf Course, five weeks ago. Police have since charged Barry with a series of sexual assaults on children, committed over the past 30 years. Further reports as they come to hand.

Yes! I punch the air. Text thumbs ups to Tiff and Lisa and receive immediately responses. No doubting we'll all be glued to the radio and TV today until our planned celebration tonight; pizza and champagne at Tiff's.

After a day of piss-farting around the studio, mind not on the job, I pull into Tiff's driveway behind an unfamiliar Suzuki hatchback. I'm hoping this isn't some interloper who'll prevent us celebrating. Tiff greets me at the door, leads me into her kitchen and introduces me to Anita, the dark-haired 30-something woman sitting at the table.

'I hope you don't mind,' Tiff says, 'but Anita's in the loop.'

'What? You haven't told–'

'I have. Anita's a kindred spirit, Jac. She was raped and damn-near strangled by our hockey coach 13 years ago.'

'Oh gosh, Anita, I'm so sorry. So, what happened to him? Did you report it?'

'Sure did. Bastard got off on a technicality. His defence convinced the jury that I was, you know, willing. I've been a fricking basket case ever since.'

'Jeez, that shits me. Is he still around?'

'Yep. And still coaching at Glebe.'

Anita is halfway through telling us the sordid details, when Lisa arrives with the pizzas. Over marinara, capricciosa and margheritas, we glean as much info about Dean "Hockey" Milford as we can, until the ABC News comes on at seven.

In breaking news, Education and Health Minister, Jock Edmonson, has been charged with the cold-case murder of 31-year-old schoolteacher, Jane Louise Fry. A message written by his kidnappers on the tape binding Mr Edmonson's legs together – the import of which, police have not revealed – led to Edmonson's confession.

We're so busy 'yay-ing', we miss the next bit, but it's clear Edmonson's political career and life-as-he-knew-it is over. It's also clear that Jocko hasn't said a word about us for fear of the barrage of accusations that would ensue. Police are looking into the connections between Edmonson and Barry. Boy, what a barrel of snakes that'll open. Guess they're already discovering that they're merely a pair of bastards who've abused their power and shared a predilection for abusing children. Best thing is, with any luck, we'll never have to go through the mill of telling our own horror stories.

We clink glasses and I toast our success. 'Here's to you, Andy Hill and Jane Fry, and all the other tragic victims.'

Anita puts her glass down. 'Just as a matter of interest, what did you write on the tape?'

'*I am a paedophile rapist. I murdered Jane Fry. 23/10/91*. All that needed to be said.'

WHAT'S A GIRL TO DO?

I STARED AT HIM ACROSS THE TABLE AND WONDERED HOW, OR when, it was that he'd become such a useless, slimy fuckwit. He was completely bombed on ice and beer. He hadn't had the legs under him to get himself to bed when we'd arrived home at what, three o'clock, after the night from hell. Instead, he'd flopped onto the kitchen chair, barfed his Big Mac into his beard, taken a few more swigs of VB to rinse his mouth, snorted some ice and then just sort of slid a bit; legs spread, head lolling onto his chest. Stupor – or was that just stupid – written on his face.

Choice.

So, I'd been sitting here for two hours, give or take, while he slouched there snoring like there was no tomorrow – the guttural sounds intermittently interspersed with random farts. Some little piffers, others more volcanic in magnitude. He'd always been a snorer but it'd got worse since he'd given up on any notion of fitness. At night, it was like sharing a bed with some second-rate garage grunge band. And he should have chosen a better tattoo artist, not some amateur with the penmanship of a seven-year-old, 'cos the image of me on his left arm has morphed into a sort of demonic-looking green blob. Hardly flattering – especially to me. Nope, he wasn't a pleasant sight. And all the worse drunk and spaced-out than during his ever-diminishing moments of pseudo-sobriety.

I shook my head and sighed. I sighed louder, hoping it might elicit some response from him. I yawned a full flip-top-head, jaw-locking yawn complete with sound effects. Nothing. I was tired and starving and my feet were killing me. It may have been only a few hours since we'd scoffed our Macca's in the car, more as a means to avoid our pursuers than for its culinary satisfaction, which for me was, as usual short-lived, but God I was hungry. I walked the few paces to the fridge and pulled the door open. Typical. Bugger all. What I would do for a sirloin steak, blue, with baked potatoes and julienne vegetables. Even at 6am the thought made me salivate.

There'd been a time when I could look forward to that when my personal chef had been in his heyday. He'd enjoyed taking the time to cook a good meal, even if we did end up sitting on the couch in front of the TV to eat it, rather than at the table. Even after he'd done the day shift cooking for all the regulars at the Italian Club, I could still be assured of an excellent meal for dinner. He'd flounce around in the kitchen, usually with a red wine in one hand, and regale me with his day's events, while he worked up a stir fry or maybe a new pasta surprise. He was always in a good mood. But lately, since he'd met that bastard Guido and his cohorts, we seemed to be subsisting on pizza, Macca's and Weetbix. Okay for a while, but day in day out. Hell no! I mean a girl's got to think about how she looks and what this shit does to her skin, figure and hair. Thank God that occasionally, if he was out, I'd get a meal next door with Jack and Vronnie. Alright for him, he didn't seem to care about anything anymore. Except his piss and coke, or ice or smack or whatever the hell he was into at the time. He didn't give a shit about food now, or how he looked, or what he did, or how his breath smelled.

Or me.

Weird too, 'cos everything had started to go haywire around the time he'd come home with the humungous new flat-screen TV. Said he'd won it in a raffle but for some reason I didn't believe that. He was too stingy to ever want to pay even fifty cents for a scrap of paper with gazillion to one odds. Nope. I always suspected it was hot – I mean it didn't even come in a box and it never had a remote control. That was the day after he'd come home with the snazzy exercise bike, claiming he was going to turn himself into a new man. I think the plan was that the combination of the two – a big TV to watch while you're working out on the bike – was going to help him shed the kilos. Never happened. Too damn tedious for him to get off the bike to change the channel on the TV – and besides, riding the damn thing just made him perspire. I suspect he also found it difficult to hold on with a beer can in one hand and a fag in the other.

So his 'new me' scenario lasted about an hour. And was promptly followed by a beer-pizza-ice binge. The first of many. I reckon that was six or seven months ago. Now he was in a perpetually bad mood and nothing anybody did or said could shake him out of it. As I said, he just didn't give a shit about anything anymore.

He certainly hadn't given a shit about anything last night when he'd decided to pay an unscheduled visit to Guido and Gazza's den of iniquity to seek some sort of misguided moral satisfaction. I'm really not sure what the hell it was all about, but hey, you don't go visit a mate with a 12-inch stiletto down your boot unless you're thinking things might go banana-shaped – by which I mean seriously bent. As far as I knew, it was an innocent visit like usual. Y'know, a few beers, a few snorts, a few hands of poker. A whole lot of talk about crap - the sort of diatribe that comes out of fully grown derro-guys mouths when they've had a few too many, or a bit too much – or maybe not enough of the other thing.

We'd rocked up in the Calais as usual, but, I dunno – something didn't feel right from the moment we arrived. When we entered the less-than-flash, inexplicably gardenless (considering the name), yet eminently popular (at least with Melbourne's wannabe Mafiosa subculture) Guido's Giardino Taverna, the tension in the room was palpable. Everybody gave us the eye when we walked in and I felt really uncomfortable. Like someone had run a taser down my back. I'm pretty sure he did too and he seemed to be jabbering more than usual. Anyway, everyone seemed to cool down after a while and they finally sat down for a game. I just sat in the corner and minded my own business like I usually did. Looked out the window from time to time, watched the TV or the guys playing pool. Ate a few chips from the bowl on the table. Bored as batshit, I was. It was a pity that Shelley wasn't there. At least I'd have had someone to talk to, since the guys just ignored me as usual. They never used to when I was younger. God, they were all over me then. I'd do a sort of progressive lap dance from one to the next and they'd sweet-talk the eyelashes off me.

I don't know how long we'd been there; I must have zoned out, but suddenly the goings-on at the poker table had my undivided attention. Fucked if I know what started it, but before I could say anything, it was on for young and old. Guido was on his feet yabbering and pointing very pointedly at Don, Gazza was heading out from behind the bar tapping a beer bottle into the palm of his hand in a decidedly ominous gesture and Don was slipping his hand down the outside of his leg towards his aforementioned boot. No! Shit no! I shook my head and blubbered some vague warning. He wasn't listening to me, of course. Nothing new there.

'You think you can come in here and fuck with me, huh?' Guido said with a come-on gesture. 'Think you can go it alone and cut out the middle man, hey?'

'Ya full of shit, Guido,' Don replied. 'You think that just because you run this low-down dirty dive you can dictate everything in the neighbourhood...'

'Yeah. I can and don't you fucking forget it. And need I remind you how much pleasurable time you've spent in this – as you call it – low-down dirty dive. Since when did you become so high and bloody mighty? Huh? Huh? Huh?' Guido's demeanour became increasingly intimidating with each 'huh'. 'Get out of here and take that stupid bitch with you.' He pointed at me. My blood started to boil. It was one thing for Don to call me a stupid bitch but no way was I going to tolerate it from this dumb fuck. I took a couple of steps forward and pulled my meanest, bitchiest face. It was all I could do. If he was gonna call me a bitch, then I'd *be* a bitch. But I couldn't think of one intelligent or even sarcastic thing to say.

'You stay back, Gemma, I'll handle this,' Don said to me. I really thought it was time to hightail it out of there, but he had other plans. Stupid bastard thought he could fight his way out. Like some sleight-of-hand magician, he was suddenly armed with the stiletto and he started waving it at Guido menacingly, flipping it from hand to hand.

I don't know what was with the other two guys at the table, but they were backing away at this point, obviously not wanting to get in the middle of things. I felt like I was in a Wild West saloon bar. I half expected to see John Wayne walk in the door. Things were getting pretty hairy. That fingers-down-a-blackboard sensation ran down my neck. I really wanted to do something to defuse the situation, create a diversion or something, but I was stuck to the spot. As immovable as a pot-bound plant.

Then he did it. I couldn't believe it. An uppercut thrust and before I knew it, Guido was bent over double, a fountain of blood spurting from his guts. Probably some actual guts too, now I come to think of it. He was waving one arm in the air, like that was going to help, and the other hand disappeared into the folds of flesh and checked shirt. I hardly need to elaborate on the expletives that gushed from his mouth, but they were the last things Guido said.

I didn't hear all of it. Not after Don had turned to me and yelled, 'Run, Gemma, run. Get the fuck out of here!'

I wasn't about to argue and I don't even recall who got to the door first; nor do I remember crossing the car park. Before I knew it, we were in the car, Don driving and me cowering in the back seat. As we screamed out of the driveway and down the street towards Sydney Road, I looked out the back window. I could see three, maybe four guys straddling their bikes and revving them up.

'C'mon, c'mon, they're right behind us and gaining,' I blathered.

Don turned and shoved my head down. 'Get ya head down, ya stupid bitch,' he barked at me. I wish he'd believe me when I tell him I'm not stupid, but he never listens. He made a left turn into Sydney Road and gunned the motor. None of the pursuers had rounded the corner yet. Suddenly, he hung a leftie and then a sharp right and I saw the McDonald's sign loom overhead. Great. We were in a life and death situation being chased by four very pissed off Italians and he was thinking about his stomach. He headed into the drive-through – out of sight of Sydney Road. Maybe that's not so dumb, I thought. After a moment or two, I heard the bikes roar past and keep going.

We shared a sigh of relief.

'That was fucking close,' Don said.

'You can say that again.'

'Geez, that was fucking close. I think we'll just grab some burgers, sit here and eat 'em and then head home all casual-like. Whaddya think?'

'Sounds like a good idea to me.'

So much for that plan. By this stage, it was about 11.30pm and I was imagining that we'd be back home snugged in bed in about 15 minutes. I hadn't bargained on Don's innate stupidity. Things were about to go truly scrotiform.

The fact that he'd never actually killed himself with the dumb-arse things he'd done made me wonder whether he had a guardian angel working overtime on his case. There was the time he thought he'd give himself a wax treatment on his chest – with contact adhesive. That was about three days in hospital and two weeks recovery time. Then there was the time he'd sat on the loo, sprayed Glen 20 between his legs and lit one of his farts. Boom! Dumb prick couldn't sit down for a month after that. Burned the skin on his hand too.

Oh, and then there was the time he tried to tell the cops that the car we were caught speeding in, which he'd stolen from some scrapper in Mill Park a few days earlier, was actually his mum's. When they weren't convinced, he said he'd borrowed it for a few days; oh and he didn't realise it was unregistered *and* unroadworthy. The more he said, the worse it got. That cost him big-time, but he'd been a whole lot more careful since then.

So yeah, he's not the brightest planet in the solar system, my Don. You might well wonder why I stay with the prick. I guess because I've got nowhere else to go. Y'know – better the devil you know and all that shit. But I can't help but love him in some perverted way. He does give me a roof over my head – even if it's a new one every few months or so – and I know he tries, or at least he tries to try. Can't help wishing he'd try harder on the cooking front though, 'cos I can't cook for shit.

Anyway, we were just biding our time in the car park at Macca's when Don the Genius decided the coast was clear. He eased the Calais out of the car park, turned left into the side street and snuck up to Sydney Road. He turned the corner and drove maybe 300 metres and the car started spluttering.

'Oh shit!' He banged his hands on the steering wheel. 'Outta fuckin' petrol.'

'Oh my God. You fuckin' idiot.' I shook my head in disdain.

He scowled at me. 'That's enough out of you, okay.' He sat for a moment and then biffed his forehead with the palm of his hand. 'Got some in the boot – for the lawnmower.' He popped the boot release and got out of the car. Then I heard him cursing under his breath. It was then that I saw the blue flashing lights.

The police car pulled in behind us. Brilliant. It wasn't like he could jump back in the car and foot it – with no petrol. After an age of the two policemen looking up at Don and back down at something in their vehicle, they finally got out and spoke to him.

'Would you get back in the car please, sir?' Don obeyed. I stayed in the back seat and kept my mouth shut. The officer nodded to me as he leant toward Don's window. 'Can I see your licence, please?' Thank God he had it on him – that might've taken some explaining, otherwise.

'But I'm not driving constable – I wasn't even in the car.'

'We saw you driving, sir. So what are you doing parked here at this time of night, sir?'

'Er, ah, well actually – I've run out of petrol. I was just getting some from the boot when you pulled up.' He pulled his licence from his wallet and handed it to the constable, who examined both sides of it.

'Are you still residing at this address, sir?' the constable asked.

'Ah yeah, ah, no, ah I dunno.'

As I said. Genius.

'You're not sure? Where you live?'

'Yeah, course I know where I live – I just don't know what it says on that.'

'So, what is your current address, sir?'

'Mortimer Street, 46 Mortimer Street, Coburg.'

'You need to get this updated then, sir. Now, have you had any alcohol tonight?'

'Aah. Yeah. A bit.'

'A bit. Would you care to elaborate?'

'Naah. What?'

'What precisely have you had to drink?'

'Geez. I dunno. I sorta lost track. Just a coupla beers, I think.'

Good grief.

'Hmm. And have you, sir, partaken of any drugs tonight?'

'Nah. Not as I recall.'

Gawd, I could tell he was slurring his words; surely the police officer could too.

'Please blow into this, sir.' The officer poked a plastic tube at Don's face. 'Please blow until I tell you to stop.'

Don obliged. He was being remarkably meek, I thought. I just hoped the officer wasn't going to press the drugs issue. I'd definitely seen him snorting something back at Guido's bar.

'Mr Kempsey, I have to advise you that you have blown zero point oh four, which is, as I'm sure you're aware, just under the legal blood alcohol limit. How long since your last drink?'

'Mmm. I dunno, an hour maybe. But I've had a Big Mac and a thickshake in the meantime. That should've sobered me up a bit.'

The officer shook his head. I was sure he'd heard it all before.

'I have serious doubts about your capacity to drive this vehicle safely, sir. I think it would be highly advisable for you both to walk home from here. Just leave the car and walk. It's only a couple of kilometres. My colleague and I are going to stay here for a while until you're on your way. And don't get any big ideas about doubling back for the car because, A: we're patrolling up and down here for the next few hours; and B: we know where you live.' The officer smiled as though he'd made a funny joke and Don was his best buddy.

'Oh, bloody wonderful. Like I need exercise at this bloody time of night.'

Geez Don, don't get belligerent, I said under my breath. Looked like we were in for a hike. So, we walked home – not straight along Sydney Road as the crow flies, but in a meandering series of loops up side streets and down back alleys, since Don in his infinite wisdom didn't want to risk being spotted by Guido's goons. I reckon we walked five kays, not two as the policeman had said, which explained why my feet were now so goddam sore. I hadn't walked that far for ages, especially not in the middle of a fucking freezing June night.

So here we were. Me keeping vigil, while he snored...and farted...and stank. I think I must've been getting tired because I swear to God I kept hearing things. I got up and peered out the kitchen window. Nothing. Didn't lessen the heebie jeebies, though. I paced back to the table.

And then it hit me.

I think I felt the sting before I actually heard the bang. What the f...? I was just registering the pain that was shooting through my shoulder when I saw Don stir. The noise must have roused him. A split second later another ear-piercing bang echoed around the kitchen.

I looked at him again in what seemed like slow motion. He still had the same daft expression on his face – but his brains were plastered all over the wall behind him like a macabre graffiti tag. Yuck. Oh, vomit. It was surreal.

I didn't know what to do. I looked back at the window. I think I glimpsed a shadow but I wasn't really sure. I panicked and maybe ran around in a circle – or several – before I realised the gravity of the situation.

Don was dead. Absolutely no doubt about that. I didn't need to feel his pulse or see whether he was breathing. He had no brain left to send the "breathe" signal to his lungs. I couldn't ring the cops, since the home phone had been cut off ages ago and for me, trying to use Don's mobile would be like an ancient Babylonian being handed a computer in place of his abacus. Technology's just not my thing. Besides, I didn't really want to touch him now. Not with all that blood all over the place. I was losing enough of my own as it was. So what the fuck was I supposed to do?

Get the bastard that snuffed him, that's what.

Good, it was still dark outside. I reckoned I still had about an hour before sunrise to retrace my steps to Guido's and confront the arsehole or collective arseholes who did this. They wouldn't figure on that. Probably thought their first shot had taken me out too. So I'd have the element of surprise.

I decided, just as Don had last night, to stay off the main drag and hedge around a few side streets, even if it took longer to get there. Keep a low profile and not look too obvious. A girl out walking on her own at this hour of the morning could look either stupid or suspicious. I didn't want to attract any attention from anybody. They wouldn't be expecting me, so if I were lucky, I might catch them napping.

After what seemed like forever, I arrived back in the car park of Guido's Giardino. I knew Guido and at least two of his goons lived out back of the Taverna in a sort of falling down lean-to. Hardly salubrious digs for the self-appointed Don of the Coburg underworld – but I think it was only a temporary thing since his wife had kicked him out of their two-storey, white-balustraded, brick and concrete monstrosity.

All was in darkness as I stepped quietly past the front door of the Taverna and headed down to the back. So far, so good. I was pretty sure nobody had seen me. It only dawned on me then that it was odd the place wasn't crawling with cops. What with Guido being dead and all. Curious. Maybe he wasn't dead after all and had been whisked off to hospital in an ambulance. Maybe nobody had even rung the cops. Maybe everyone, apart from Don's and my shooter, had decided to just go to bed and think about it in the morning. Odd. Definitely odd.

Anyway, I snuck along past the Taverna's windows and around the back corner of the building where I could see the lean-to. No lights were on. Good, that meant nobody was up, unless they were good at seeing in the dark. My heart was beating faster and faster and my shoulder was throbbing big time, although it seemed to have stopped bleeding. I hoped that was a good sign. I sidled past a window but couldn't make out anything inside; it was still too dark. I crept further along towards a ramp that evidently led to the lean-to's door.

Suddenly a light came on over my head and a shrieking siren went off.

Shit! I hadn't figured on the place being alarmed. So much for the element of surprise. I could hear voices – two of them.

'Who's that?'

'Dunno. Who the fuck'd come here at this freakin' hour of the morning?'

'Go see who it is. Hey, and here, take your gun.'

Holy shit.

'Careful though, it might be the cops,' the guy whispered.

The door swung open and, as I cowered behind a bush just off the edge of the ramp trying to make like a shadow, one of the two goons from last night's card game appeared at the door. I gulped and hoped to hell it wasn't audible. He waved a handgun menacingly, although he obviously couldn't see anything.

'Who's there? You'd better show yourself and make it snappy.'

What to do? Should I come out and show myself, stay put, or make a run for it? I was starting to think this was a really bad idea. Any bravado I'd had in the heat of the moment had evaporated.

My foot was starting to go to sleep because of the awkward way I was crouching. I had to move a bit. As I did, a small branch of my shielding bush snapped. Bugger. My cover was blown.

'I know you're there, so you might as well come out and maybe, just maybe I'll be nice to you.'

I didn't believe him for a minute, but it was obvious he was going to find me so I really had no choice. I sheepishly emerged from my hiding spot and stepped onto the path.

'You?'

I could see he was surprised.

'What the fuck are you doing here, Gemma? I thought I'd taken care of you before I plastered that lowlife Don's brains all over the wall. Hey, Tony, come and see who's here. It's that dumb bitch, Gemma.'

Oh that was it. Now I was really mad. I didn't even think about my next move, it was like a spontaneous retaliation for all the times he, and everyone else, had called me a dumb bitch. He wasn't actually pointing the gun at me, so I lunged at him, obviously catching him off guard. He hadn't expected that. As he fell backwards, the gun went flying out of his hand into the garden. I knew, however, that it hadn't bought me much time.

And I was right. The next moment, Tony appeared in the doorway, also brandishing a gun, and looked down at the other guy who was getting to his feet.

'Shoot the bitch, Tony, I've gotta find my gun.'

Shit! I was pretty sure I couldn't tackle two of them at once, so I decided to run, as fast as I bloody could. Fortunately, I still had the cover of darkness, as I felt the turbulence of a bullet whizzing past my ear, at exactly the same moment I heard the bang. Phew. Missed. But I could sense Tony gaining on me as I sprinted across the car park towards Sydney Road. He was right behind me when I heard another shot. Suddenly, he dropped. Flat on his face. I slowed up a tad and turned around.

'You fuckin' idiot, Vince. You've shot me! Aaaa.' He moaned and gurgled. Then silence. Except for Vince's footsteps which were getting closer.

'Oh shit!' Vince exclaimed as he dropped to his knees beside Tony. 'Shit, what have I done?'

I'd stopped running by now and stood watching as Vince bobbed his head onto Tony's back and lifted it again, sobbing.

'Don't you worry, my mate, I'll get her. I'll get the bitch.'

Uh oh. Time to run again. I sprinted towards Sydney Road and then ducked around the edge of the building on the corner, a dry cleaners, I think it was. I ran into the entry alcove of the next shop, a bakery with tantalising smells emanating from the door, and waited.

I could hear Vince's panting before his footsteps. As soon as he got near enough I lunged at him. I'm pretty tall when I stand up straight and this guy was a weaner – a real short-arse. I took him completely by surprise and smashed him backwards onto the footpath. What I hadn't figured on was the No Standing sign he smashed his neck into on the way down.

Well he sure wasn't standing any more. But then neither was I. I think I'd used up every iota of adrenalin in my body during the pursuit. I sagged onto the footpath. I don't remember a thing after that, except the vague sounds of voices and a siren.

My shoulder was killing me, but it was obviously bandaged or strapped so tight I couldn't roll over. I also felt sluggish, like I'd been doped up on something. I could hear lots of irritating noises. People shuffling around, weird beeping sounds, somebody snoring. And it was so bright I could barely open my eyes. Finally I managed to roll away from the wall so I could see into the room. Hospital; I was in hospital. But how...?

Oh yeah, now I remembered. I was going to have to get used to life without Don. What was I going to do?

'Oh look, she's awake,' somebody said. Before I knew it, three people – a doctor and two nurses, I guessed, were staring at me like I was an amoeba under a microscope.

'How are you doing, Gemma? What a night you've had, eh,' one of them said.

'Tell me about it,' I sighed.

'But everything's going to be all right. The police are investigating everything so it should all come out in the wash,' the woman in the blue jacket said. 'It's so lucky that you were microchipped, girl. The good news is your owner's mum is on her way to see you. The police contacted her right after they found his body.'

Oh, good, I really like Don's mum. My tail started wagging entirely of its own accord.

'By the way, Gemma,' the blue-shirted lady said, 'the police are talking about a bravery award for you, for tracking down your owner's killer.'

Bugger that. I didn't do it for *him.* I mean, the bastard shot *me* first.

ABOUT THE AUTHOR

Fin J. Ross has morphed through several careers, from journalist, to woodworker, to boarding cattery owner and cat breeder, to creative writing tutor. She now spends her quasi retirement creating mosaic artworks and teaching the art in her Paynesville studio.

She has two novels, *AKA Fudgepuddle* and *Billings Better Bookstore and Brasserie* (Clan Destine Press); is co-author of three true crime anthologies, *Killer in the Family, Murder in the Family* and *Toxic*; is co-compiler of a cryptic crosswords book, *Nifty Fifty*; and has four novels lying in wait.

Since 2011, she has won several Scarlet Stiletto category awards and commenndations, culminating in her First Prize win in 2022.

Aside from writing, her passions include cats, tennis and lawn bowls.

ACKNOWLEDGEMENTS

Thank you to Sisters in Crime Australia for fostering and promoting women's crime fiction and for providing the framework, with its annual Scarlet Stiletto Awards, to inspire me to concoct all manner of devious methods to bump off obnoxious adversaries.

Thanks to my editing whiz, Narrelle Harris, for her wonderful insights.

Thank you also to Lindy Cameron for believing in me...all my life.

FIN'S PRIZE-WINNING STORIES

The following stories in Fin's collection won category prizes or special commendations in the annual Scarlet Stiletto Crime & Mystery Short Story Competition run by Sisters in Crime Australia:

Tuesday Jocks – 2022 1st Prize and trophy

Murder by the Book – 2020 Special Commendation

Deadly Ernestine – 2018 2nd Prize, Body in Library Prize
and the Forensic Linguistics Prize

Victory of Kyrnos – 2018 Cross Genre Prize

Four Hundred Hectares of Nothing – 2016 Environment Prize

Echo Wren – 2015 Environment Prize

The VOTOS Solution – 2014 Body in Library runner-up

What's a Girl to Do? – 2014 Third Prize